RIVER OF INK
MORTAL

RIVER OF INK
MORTAL

HELEN DENNIS

Illustrated by
BONNIE KATE WOLF

Hodder
Children's
Books

ISBN: 978 1 444 92048 2

Typeset in Adobe Garamond by Avon DataSet Ltd, Bidford-on-Avon, Warwickshire

Printed and bound in Great Britain by Clays Ltd, St Ives Plc

Hodder Children's Books
An imprint of Hachette Children's Group
Part of Hodder & Stoughton
Carmelite House
50 Victoria Embankment
London EC4Y 0DZ

An Hachette UK Company
www.hachette.co.uk

For Mum and Dad.
Thank you for everything.

'We all have our time machines, don't we? Those that take us back are memories . . . And those that carry us forward, are dreams.'

– H.G. Wells

DAY 192

7th September

There was a mirror propped in the corner of the Paris underground hideout they called the Court of Miracles. Jed could see himself as he worked at the desk. He wasn't sure what the reflection showed. A boy who could live for ever? A man who had control of time? Jed was both of these things. Yet neither. Right now, all he could be certain of was that he was in need of a miracle.

The desk he worked at was stacked high with books. Littering the floor at his feet were crumpled sheets of paper; rejected notes and discarded diagrams. A clock ticked. And a lamp threw light across him. But Jed felt as if he was working in the dark.

There was a glass of water on the edge of the table. He was too tired to drink. The water rippled in pulsing swirls as a metro train rattled through the tunnels overhead, ploughing towards its destination.

He blinked his eyes. They scratched with tiredness.

Ink dripped from his pen on to the scribbled notes in front of him. The blot soaked into the paper so that it totally consumed the words he'd written in a river of ink.

He took the ruined notes and screwed them up. Then he tossed the page away.

Suddenly a pain like nothing he'd ever felt before shot through his wrist. It was as if the nerves in his arms were being scraped over a cheese grater. His fingers shook and, as he pulled his arm tight against his chest to steady the convulsion, he knocked a stack of books over, sending them thudding to the floor.

He clenched his jaw, bit his lip and reached down for the books. But his hand caught against the drinking glass. Water splashed on to his skin, burning like acid.

Something was very wrong.

He'd felt uneasy before. Lightheaded, exhausted. There'd been times back in London, and then Prague, when he'd been overwhelmed by memories and fear. But this was different. This was new.

He recoiled and his shoulder caught against the clock. It fell, exploding on the uneven ground, a mess of escaping cogs and springs, its hands ripped clean away from the face, arrows now pointing in opposite directions.

Jed leapt up from the desk, desperate to stop whatever was happening to him. He pushed the chair back with his legs and it scraped across the flagstones.

'Jed?' Kassia was sitting on a makeshift bed in the corner of the room. 'Are you OK?'

He didn't answer her. He had no idea what he would say. How could he explain how he felt? Pressure was building in his chest. He was biting down so hard on his lip that a droplet of blood began to drip towards his chin.

He circled the chair he'd been sitting on as it rocked with the movement of being shoved so violently. He clenched his fingers around the back of the chair and a single splinter from the uneven wood wormed into his finger.

Kassia stood up too. 'Jed?'

He lifted the chair, holding it out like some sort of shield. He took a deep breath and then he let out a sound like an injured animal, swinging the chair around as he moved, as if he could fight back whatever was surging inside him and making every part of him hurt. The chair arced against the books that teetered on the desk. They scattered as if they'd been fired from a gun. The chair kept cutting through the air, as if there'd been no resistance from the books in its way. Jed did not let go. And the howl grew louder.

'Jed! Please! What's the matter?'

But he had no words to make sense of this. He just needed to push the feeling away.

Jed staggered, the swing of the chair propelling him forward. His arm shook. His sense of balance was out of kilter. The light from the lamp was upturned now, directed only at the ceiling. The chair broke as it thudded against the wall, snapping like kindling wood.

But this was not enough to drive out the pain and the panic. Jed kicked the desk. It skidded across the floor.

His arm trembled. The convulsion swelled.

So Jed flung himself at the mirror and tugged it away from the wall. The polished glass slab rocked backwards and forwards, taunting him. Then it toppled, the glass shattering on his shoulders.

He sank to his knees, pulling his shaking arm in tight to his body and then pressing his other hand down on the ground. A shard of mirrored glass cut into his palm, searing open a scar that had taken months to heal. Blood mixed with water and ink amongst the debris. And Jed closed his eyes completely and let the darkness in.

* * *

4

Kassia knelt beside him. 'Jed! What is it?'

The light from the lamp made his eyes look like they were burning red. 'I don't want to die,' he spluttered. His hands were thrashing against the clutter of books and manuscripts. 'Giseppi gave me all these! But nothing makes sense.'

Giseppi had brought them hope. This stranger who they'd met on the train as they'd raced away from Prague, and his beautiful friend, Amelie, had got them safely to Paris. Giseppi had shown them a place to stay in the underground of the city. He'd given them food. He'd given them safety. But he'd failed to give them answers. The books on alchemy he'd brought for them had offered nothing new, only yet more mysteries and never-ending questions. Kassia tried to grab Jed's arms to stop them from moving but he lurched away, refusing to look at her. 'We *will* find answers,' she stuttered.

'When?' He clamped his fingers to his head, driving furrows through his red hair, smearing blood from the cut in his palm across his forehead. 'I don't know what to do, Kass.'

She reached forward again but was too scared to touch him. She felt maybe he would break into pieces in front of her. 'You need to let us help you more,' she said.

'I don't deserve your help.'

'Jed, you can't keep doing this,' she pleaded. 'Jacob fell from Notre Dame. It wasn't your fault.'

'That's not what you thought at first.'

His words made her shiver and lean back on her heels.

For the first time he looked directly at her, his hands sliding down his face. 'I'm so sorry.'

Now she looked away.

He rested his hands in his lap, palms upturned. 'I had the answer, Kassia. The recipe for eternal life. And I destroyed it.'

She stared into his empty palms. Blood trickling from the gaping wound in his life-line. It snaked round his wrist. 'You couldn't let Jacob have it,' she whispered.

'Couldn't I? Maybe wanting the recipe just for me was wrong.' Blood dripped from his hand on to the floor. 'I'm so scared.'

'I know.' She wanted to say that she was too. But she didn't. Instead she reached out one final time. 'Here. Let me see.'

He lifted his arm. A bead of blood splashed on to a shard of mirrored glass. Then Kassia's fingers connected with his.

There was a cone of light that seemed to emanate

from his body. It stretched out and engulfed Kassia in a blazing shaft of brilliance. A second of total stillness and then the light retracted like backdraught in a tunnel, suddenly swelling again and flinging Kassia across the room.

She crashed into the far wall, her back crunching against the brickwork. Air surged from her lungs as she slid down into a crumpled heap on the floor. Slivers of broken mirror crunched into her legs and arms, her cheek pressed hard against the ground. She blinked against the swirling dust and grit as it lifted. And it was as if the dust rose and took shape, swirling and twisting in front of her. A black dragon, turning and turning, closing in and getting nearer and nearer.

She covered her eyes as light flashed like flame from the mouth of the dragon, scorching her skin as she cowered in the corner. And in the darkness behind her eyelids she saw the sun circling and circling, a ball of fire in a blackening sky; there was the sound of an engine, a train perhaps, careering towards her getting louder and louder; she saw a street littered with bodies, trees bending down, pummelled by incredible wind.

And then the wind was not just behind her eyes. It filled the room, whipping at the pages of the discarded books and chasing the dragon so that the beast of dust was close enough to touch. Its eyes were rings of light, blazing forward. Not eyes at all, but headlights. Of a car. Out of control and about to crash. Kassia pressed her back against the wall. She pulled her head down to her chest. And the image of the car exploded, cleaving the dust dragon into a million pieces.

It was silent.

Everything was still.

And Kassia could see that Jed was lying, unmoving, spread-eagled on the floor.

'Jed! Please!' she screamed as she scrambled across the floor towards him. She grabbed for his hand, pressing her fingers against the blood that trickled down his wrist, searching desperately for a pulse. Nothing!

She tried to focus. Knew that every second counted. She rolled him so that he was flat on the ground, his arms spread wide now, like he was pinned to a cross. She held her face above his. His eyes were rolled back, unseeing in his head. She couldn't feel any breath. So she fumbled her lips against his and tried to breathe for him. *Was this right? Was this how you did it?* She tried to think of all the medical books her mum had made her study, but her mind was centring only on what was wrong: Jed's heart had stopped beating.

She pulled back from his face and ran her fingers down his chest, feeling for where his ribs knotted together. She balled her hand into a fist and thumped down hard. Then she linked her fingers together, pushing down on his sternum. 'Come on, Jed! Please!' Again and again she pressed, her own heart thumping the repetitions.

Nothing. It wasn't working. This could not be happening.

They were alone, in the underground of a city that wasn't home. And with no one there to help her, the boy who was supposed to live for ever was just about to die.

She didn't know how long she tried to bully his heart into beating again. She wasn't sure how many of her own breaths she poured into his lungs. She was only sure that her arms were shaking and that every muscle in her body was screaming out for her to stop. But she didn't. She pressed down again and again and again. Because giving up was not something she did.

The room grew darker. And the pain in her arms was so intense that she finally tipped forward so that her body fell across his as exhaustion overwhelmed her.

And then, so tiny and fragile she was sure she was imagining it, she felt his chest flicker. She clutched at the side of his face. The barest of breaths, like the finest lace on her skin. His eyes glimmered as if they searched for hers in the darkness. And they locked on tight.

Suddenly, Kassia and Jed were no longer alone. Dante was behind them. Giseppi shouting for others to come and help. Then hands moved around her, lifting Jed from the floor and carrying him to the makeshift bed in the corner.

Kassia didn't have the energy to move. It was as if all the strength she'd had, she'd emptied into him.

Giseppi put Jed down on the bed. And from her position still crumpled on the floor, Kassia saw something fall from Jed's pocket. It was a silver watch. The one which had once belonged to her father and which she'd given to Jed when she thought he was leaving her, back in London. The watch rocked on the ground amongst the dusting of broken glass and crumpled paper. The swallow bird engraved on the casing of the watch glinted and flickered. And even above the noise and the commotion of people battling round Jed's bed to help him, Kassia was sure that the watch was still ticking.

'He's burning up,' Kassia yelled in sign language. Her fingers moved so close to her brother's face that Dante pushed her arms away, holding on to her for a moment as if he sensed that even though she'd climbed up from the floor there was every chance she'd fall down again.

Jed was thrashing about as if he was fighting his

way out of some terrible nightmare. His lips were moving frantically, churning words, but none of them made sense.

Kassia yanked her hands free of her brother's hold. 'What's the matter with him?'

Dante's unmoving hands made it clear he didn't have a clue.

Kassia shook her head as if trying to settle all the words that were clamouring for her attention. But, like her brother, she said nothing now that could be heard by other people.

Jed was over a hundred years old. His body had undergone linear reprogramming like some sort of immortal jellyfish, flipping his system back in time. He'd been studying Giseppi's books for weeks, trying to make the change to his system permanent. And there had been no answers.

'Exhaustion?' Dante signed at last.

'It's more than that. He stopped breathing and . . .' Her signs tailed away.

Dante pushed her shoulder, his face furrowed in annoyance, demanding she go on.

But Kassia struggled to find the signs she needed.

Dante stamped his foot hard.

The noise of his shoe against the flagstones, shocked her hands back into moving. 'There was this light.

It was so bright.' She gestured, trying to show how the light had swelled, surged outwards and then folded. 'And I got flung across the room and . . .'

'You're OK?' Dante's signs interrupted.

She hesitated. This time Dante gave her the time she needed. 'It's like we were connected. And I saw things.'

'What things?'

'Pictures. Like from his memory.' She knew the words sounded weird so the signs were small as if she was trying to whisper them.

Dante nodded. He didn't look confused. Or questioning. And this was enough for Kassia to fling herself forward and hug him.

He held her tight and then eased her gently away so he could look at her.

'You don't think I'm mad,' she signed.

'Oh, yeah. As nutty as a box of frogs. But I believe you. About what happened.'

They turned towards the bed. Amelie was sponging Jed's forehead with a wet cloth. As she moved, the belt of coins she wore across her waist jangled softly. She mumbled in time with the sound, her soft French accent making her words almost like song as she tried to soothe Jed. Kassia felt a spike of emotion she didn't fully understand.

Jed's arms flailed against the covers of the bed.

Kassia looked at the mess of broken glass and shattered wood still strewn across the ground. Then she bent down and picked up her father's pocket watch.

Suddenly, its tick was no longer reassuring.

'What?' signed Dante.

Kassia grabbed the newspaper that had been under the fallen watch. She jabbed at the top of the page.

'I don't understand,' signed Dante.

'The date.'

Dante was still confused.

'It's over half a year ago,' said Kassia slowly, 'since Jed climbed out of the Thames. It means he's got less than six months left to find the elixir.'

Dante was still struggling to understand why this scared her so much.

Kassia signs were faltering and awkward and as she moved, she dropped the newspaper and it fluttered to the floor. 'He's closer now, to death, than he is to life.'

Kassia had been pacing up and down for nearly an hour. She could feel Dante watching her. But she avoided catching his eye. If she looked at him, then he'd ask what she was thinking. And she was scared to turn her thoughts into signs that she could see.

Suddenly, Jed called out from the bed again. The

words were fragmented and jumbled. Rambling on and on about a man dying. And as she watched him, his eyes looked beyond hers as if he was seeing something far away.

Kassia couldn't stand it any longer.

She grabbed Dante's arm and steered him to the corner of the room, turning her back on all the others who circled Jed's bed, so that the words she made with her hands were for her brother alone. 'He needs a doctor.'

Dante flung his arms wide, as if he was throwing away any signs he had.

Kassia stood her ground. 'We have to. Look at him!'

Dante folded his arms, refusing to answer – and then suddenly, as if the words were exploding out of him, his hands churned the air in frantic reply. 'You think we just bowl up to a hospital and say, "Excuse me. I know he doesn't look like it, but our friend is actually a hundred-year-old alchemist and he's taken five doses of the elixir of life which have totally messed up his life span but he needs to take a sixth dose of the stuff or, instead of living for ever, he's just going to die." And you think we'll say all that and they'll just run off to the pharmacy and come back with a bottle of the good stuff. Job done?'

Kassia scowled. Jed was calling out again. She

couldn't bear to hear it. 'I'm not talking about a hospital.'

'What then?'

'I want to ring home. Ask Nat? He might know what to do.'

'*Are you crazy?*' Dante flung his hands around. 'All this! Months living underground, out of sight, off the radar so NOAH couldn't get to us and you want to risk telling Nat everything. There are rules, Kass! About home and messages. You *know* we can never talk about Jed! If the call gets intercepted. If NOAH put two and two together, our cover could be blown. It could all be over.'

Kassia looked across at the bed and then she looked back at her brother and signed her answer slowly and precisely. 'If we don't ask a doctor what to do, it could all be over anyway.'

NOCEROS, CANIS MINOR,

Gomel

AND ATELIER TYPOGR

NAVIS

Le Bon Marchan

WEBCAFÉ

2 Rue Chanoinesse
75004 Paris

wifi mot de passe
notrefemme

DAY 193

8th September

Victor reared up, woken from the deepest dream by a piercing, ringing noise like a fire alarm. He reached out for the clock beside the bed and squinted to make the time come into focus. 03.17. Really? They had to be kidding. Didn't this state-of-the-art city in the sky have a sprinkler system to put out fires? With over eighty floors, surely the one he was on was safe.

He swung his legs around and down from the bed and pressed his feet to the floor. It wasn't warm. That was surely a good sign.

There was a thumping on the door. 'OK. OK,' he yelled, as he struggled into his T-shirt and fought into the jeans that he dragged, crumpled, from the floor. 'Where's the fire?' He laughed at his own joke. And then, just in case he really was about to be toasted alive as the London Shard burnt to the ground,

18

he hurried to the door and flung it open.

Cole Carter was leaning against the door jamb, his fist raised ready to thump again. He was wearing his long leather coat. His hair was slicked into place, his shirt neatly buttoned. Did this guy ever look hassled?

Victor shoved the end of his T-shirt into his jeans and then rubbed his buzz cut hair with his hands and frowned. 'So there's *actually* a fire?'

Cole laughed. 'Don't be ridiculous.'

'But the alarm?'

'My way of making you get out of your pit.'

Victor didn't have the energy to argue.

'You've been doing nothing but kip for the last three months. And now it's time for action.'

Victor was suddenly interested but before he could ask any details, Carter had begun to stride down the hallway, the tails of his leather coat floating out behind him like thick black wings.

They took the elevator to the fifty-fifth floor. Victor did not feel comfortable. In the past, bad things had happened here. Things he'd tried hard to forget. And when Cole led the way into the laboratory he began to feel more than a little unwell.

The cage was still there. Empty now of course, the door bolted shut. Victor remembered how they'd kept the boy in there. The boy they were sure was going to live for ever. And he remembered how the boy had convinced him to unlock the cage. It had not gone down well with those in charge.

That had been at the beginning. When everything at NOAH had been new. Victor understood things more clearly now. Almost compulsively, he rubbed his hand against the top part of his arm. He couldn't feel the tattoo of the unicorn in chains but he knew it was there. He knew which side he was on.

At the counter, beside the empty cage, two figures stood with their backs to the room. A walking cane was leaning against the worktop.

It had been a while since Victor had seen either Montgomery or Martha Quinn. And they didn't turn to acknowledge him. But Cole led the way over to join them, so Victor followed.

On the centre of the counter was a small metal canister. It looked a bit like an ice bucket that Victor imagined they used in fancy hotels. It was steaming, great wafts of smoke billowing from the lid. Beside the canister was some sort of centrifuge machine. Victor had seen those in a science lab at one of the many schools he'd attended. He had no idea what it did though. He'd never stayed long enough in lessons to find out. The centrifuge was filled with test-tubes. Martha Quinn was holding one of the tubes in her hand and the way she and Montgomery were staring at it suggested that Victor should somehow be impressed.

'What *is* that?' he said eventually, when it was clear that no one was going to explain anything to him without prompting.

'It's the blood Carter took from that boy on the Petrin tower,' said Montgomery without looking up.

'You still have that?' Victor didn't manage to hide the surprise in his voice. The confrontation in Petrin had not gone well either. Montgomery had not been happy that they'd let the Riverboy get away for a second time. But they had managed to snatch a small glass bottle from him that contained his blood. They'd no idea why he had that with him. Their job wasn't to question Riverboy's motivation. It was to question the blood. And scientists in the lab in The Shard had apparently been doing that for months.

'Of course.' Victor was surprised to find that Martha was talking now. 'We've continued to monitor the sample. We've been carrying out tests.'

This didn't really give Victor much to go on. And he still had no idea why the alarm had sounded and why any of this couldn't have waited until the morning. 'And?' he said hopefully.

'It's proof,' said Montgomery, his face obscured a little by the drifts of smoke rising from the canister. 'That he's Fulcanelli.'

'How?'

Martha Quinn held the glass tube up a little towards the light. The blood blazed deep red as she explained. 'It keeps regenerating. Cells reproducing. Endlessly. They should have stopped by now. If the blood was mortal.'

'So that's good then,' said Victor. He still didn't get why there had been the early wake-up call. Everyone here figured the boy was the unicorn they were chasing so why the sudden urgency?

'Something's changed,' said Martha Quinn, as if reading Victor's unspoken question. 'And it makes it even more important that we find the boy quickly.'

'I'm sending you and Carter back to Paris,' cut in Montgomery.

'Seriously? There's not an inch of that city we haven't searched. I'm telling you the guy's gone underground.'

Something in Victor's answer seemed to amuse Montgomery. 'Well, whatever's happening to this blood suggests that sometime soon, Fulcanelli's going to have to come up again for air.'

* * *

Kassia and Dante slid soundlessly along the banquette seating in the end booth of the internet café. Kassia looked over her shoulder, checking again that they hadn't been followed.

She took the small piece of paper from the café owner. It listed the password he'd given her for ten minutes' use of online connection. Then she took the silver pocket watch and put in on the table, tracing the engraving of the swallow on the casing before opening the watch so she could see the face.

Usually, she and Dante bought time slots in blocks of five minutes. They'd never risked this long a connection before.

They had a system for contacting home. Everything was about maintaining secrecy. Since being betrayed by Jacob, they did everything they could to keep the risk of discovery as small as possible. They'd plan a message for their mum and uncle. They'd write it in BSL so the sentences weren't the same as usual speech. Dante's sign language had a grammar all of its own and so writing down the words as if he was signing the message was a start. Then they'd cut the message in half. Dante would send every other word in an email to his uncle. Kassia would send every alternate word to her mum. Only when the two halves were put together could the whole message be read. And even then, they used no names. And they certainly never spoke about Jed.

'Are you sure I can't talk you out of this?' Dante signed silently.

Kassia shook her head. She needed to do this. For Jed. And maybe more than that. For herself.

They'd agreed she should be the one to do the talking. Dante was to stay out of shot, so the whole thing did not become overwhelming or complicated. If her mum saw both of them on screen, then they'd never get to the question they needed to ask. It was supposed to be simplest this way.

Kassia plugged the earphones into the socket, typed in the password to get the internet connection and pressed the Skype icon.

Then she waited. And her heart raced like it had done hours earlier back underground.

The screen flickered. An image appeared, frozen at first, trapped in a moment of time. Her uncle's sitting room. It hurt to remember that her own front room had been destroyed by fire in some crazy act of revenge by NOAH.

The face in the image was her mother's, tilted forward as if attempting to escape the confines of the screen. In that second of stillness it was possible to see that her mother's forehead was creased with lines, purple circles skirting the thin skin under her eyes. Kassia reached out her hand, grazing the screen with the tip of her finger. When her hand pulled away, there was a circle cut in the dust on the screen and her mother was moving, the image animated now.

'Mum?' The word fell from her mouth.

'Kassia?' Anna reached forward too. 'My God. I nearly rejected the call. I thought it was a trick.'

'No trick, Mum.' Kassia's voice faltered. There was so much she wanted to say. She touched the screen again and this time she let her hand stay a little longer. 'You're OK?'

It was a stupid question.

'You need to come home, Kass.' Her mother's voice was tight. 'Both of you. Dante too.' She finger-spelled his name and Kassia could tell the movement hurt her. Kassia wondered if this was lack of practice, or maybe because she'd been signing her children's names over and over again in a hope they'd come home. Kassia could hardly bear to look at her but neither could she bear to look away.

'Kassia, please. We can work something out. With the exams, I mean. I'll try and make it work. Be easier on you, I promise. I was just building a future, you know. Something you could work for—'

'Mum, please don't.' Kassia could feel tears burning

and she wiped her cheek and focused for a moment on the thick black edging of the computer screen.

'Tell me what you need me to do and we'll sort it.' Her mother was nodding. 'Please. We can do this. I can change. You can do the exams later. Wait for university. I can alter the timetable if that . . .' She checked herself. 'Just please come home.'

Kassia shoulders were rising and falling, sobs choking in her throat. She rubbed her face again and blew out a breath, nodding as Dante pointed to the watch on the table. 'Mum, please. You have to listen. We don't have long. It's too dangerous.'

'Kassia . . .'

'Mum, please!'

'OK. OK. I'm sorry. I just . . .' Anna reached out again and touched the screen.

Kassia fiddled with the medallion she wore around her neck. 'Mum, I'm sorry but I need to speak to Nat.'

The pain in her mother's face was overwhelming.

'Please, Mum. If you love me then you have to trust that what we're doing is important, and that we need Nat's help.'

Her mother stumbled up from the chair and called out until Kassia's uncle appeared beside her. He was still in his scrubs from the hospital, confusion written in every line of his skin.

'Kass. Is that you?' He peered into the screen and then back again at his sister who was sobbing openly now.

Dante tapped the face of the watch again.

'We don't have long,' blurted Kassia.

'You're coming home, right. Your mum's out of her mind with worry.'

'Please!' Kassia yelled at the screen, and even Dante recoiled as if the sound was evident from her desperation. 'We have so little time,' Kassia said again.

'OK. Where are you?'

Kassia shook her head. 'Still in Hugo's Court. But that's not important.'

'Go on.'

'It's Jed,' Kassia said at last. 'He had this sort of seizure and his heart stopped and now he's all kind of sick and rambling and . . .'

'His heart stopped?'

'We got it going again.'

'But he's still sick?'

'He has a fever and he's not making sense. And . . .' Telling her brother about the light and the images had been one thing, but to say it out loud to her uncle and not cloaked in sign, made it even more real than before. 'I don't know how to explain it. I held his hand and it was like I could feel what he was feeling

27

and there was just this rush of memories and I think I saw things that he could see, like from inside his head . . .'

Nat's eyes narrowed. 'It sounds like Jed's system has been overloaded. The stress of what he's going through, suddenly too much.'

'And the fever? What do we do?'

'I think it must be his body's way of coping with the return of those memories you saw.' Kassia could see he was struggling to know what to say next. Her mother was still standing behind him, her face pressed close to the screen. 'When we found Jed, he remembered nothing. And now he has all these memories jostling for space. Maybe that's what happened before?'

'You think he could lose all his memories again? Forget what happened? What he needs to do? Forget us even?' A new surge of pain fought for Kassia's attention and her shoulders heaved again.

'Kassia, the mind and the heart have a complicated connection,' Nat went on.

Dante tapped the face of the watch. They had one minute left.

'So what do we do to help him?' Kassia blurted.

'I think he's got to face those memories, Kass. Instead of drowning them out like he did before, he's got to face them.'

The hand on the watch clicked on. And the bar on the internet connection faded, the picture on the screen freezing as suddenly as it had burst into life. Kassia pressed the flat of her palm against the trace of her mum and her uncle, still hanging like an afterthought of all that had gone before. She pleaded silently for them to stay. But the image dissolved.

Kassia curled her fingers into a fist and slid her hand down the empty screen. Dante put his arm around her, but it was not enough to stop her from crying.

'I've told you.' Kassia was going through it again, although to be fair to her brother, her first explanation of her conversation with her uncle had been so interrupted by sobbing, it was little wonder that he'd struggled to follow what exactly had been said. 'Nat says he's got to face his memories.'

They were back in the Court of Miracles, though there had been no evidence of any miracles since they'd been away. Jed was still propped on the bed, his body slick with sweat, his eyes rolled back into his head. Amelie was kneeling beside him. She was murmuring gently again, songlike in his ear, just as she'd done before, mopping tenderly at his forehead with a wet cloth.

'Here, let me do that,' Kassia snapped, taking the

cloth from Amelie's hand and wringing it out in the bowl and then pressing it gently just above Jed's eyes. Water ran on to the pillow and it looked to Kassia as if it steamed. 'We have to do something,' she said. 'None of this is helping.'

Dante pulled at her arm so that she was turned round to face him. 'Which memories exactly? There's over a hundred years' worth in there. How do we know which ones he's got to tackle?'

Kassia had no idea. She stood still for a moment and then wrung out the cloth again and pressed it to Jed's forehead. His eyes squinted as if some part of him was responding to the attempt to cool him, but he began to mumble, words mixing in English and French in a jumbled muddle of sound.

'What's he saying?' Dante demanded.

'He keeps saying "He didn't die. He didn't die".'

Giseppi looked up from the chair at the end of the bed. 'And he keeps saying the name Bergier.'

'You think he's talking about you?' Kassia asked.

'No. I think he's talking about my grandfather.'

'What? THE Bergier? The guy Fulcanelli met in the gasworks in 1937. But he *did* die, right? In the seventies?'

Giseppi shrugged. 'Ahh. About that.'

'*About that?*' grimaced Kassia. 'What d'you mean,

about that? All those books you gave Jed on alchemy,' she said, waving her hands towards the mess of papers still strewn across the floor, 'say that Bergier died over thirty years ago.'

Giseppi looked embarrassed. The bracelets on his wrists rattled. 'Look, my grandfather. He confused.'

'Not as confused as I am right now,' snapped Kassia.

'Grandfather start talking about Fulcanelli and the meeting of him. And he wrote the things. And it was, how you say, awkward.'

'Awkward?' Kassia spat the word.

'Grandfather was at the risk, you see.' Giseppi fiddled with the shark tooth necklace that rested at the base of his throat.

'Risk of what?'

'The NOAH.'

Kassia could hardly cope with where this conversation was going.

'It's not the new thing, you know, the following of Fulcanelli. The CIA too, do the searching for him. It not be safe to know too much. And my grandfather, he was doing the speaking and we were scared of what would happen. Being a Brother of Heliopolis is not without risks.'

Kassia felt her face colouring. As a Brother of

Heliopolis himself, Giseppi had explained that he was part of a secret organisation doing all it could to help Fulcanelli and protect the details of his search for immortality. And Kassia knew first-hand how much Giseppi had risked since Prague to help them, even if he couldn't give them the answers about how to make the elixir. But this still didn't explain what had happened with Bergier. 'So what did you do?' she said at last. 'You killed your grandad to shut him up?' She flung her hands around frantically to try and keep Dante up to speed with what was happening. 'These people killed an old man to stop him talking,' she yelled with her fingers.

'We didn't kill anybody!' Giseppi yelled back, waving his own hands and carving a definite negative in the air, the bracelets on his wrists jangling like bells. 'That's the whole point of what Jed is saying!'

'I don't understand.'

'We let the world *think* my grandfather was dead,' Giseppi explained. 'All part of his cover. That's what Jed is doing the mumbling about.'

'So what you're saying is,' Kassia turned to face her brother, speaking and signing so there could be no doubt about what she said, 'Bergier is still alive. Jed needs to see him then! That's the memory he needs to deal with.'

'Hold on,' Giseppi said slowly. 'It's true my grandfather is alive. He is in the home for the nursing by the Seine. But he's 104 years old now. And he hasn't spoken a word for years.'

Kassia shrugged her shoulders. 'Well I think maybe it's time the old man started talking.'

Le Bon Marchand

WEBCAFÉ

2 Rue Chanoinesse
75004 Paris

Victor quite enjoyed being back in Paris. The air had a crispness to it as he made his way to the Institute de France. It was the edge of autumn. It felt as if things were about to change.

Montgomery was standing at the table in the boardroom. He wore a faded Def Leppard T-shirt tucked into jeans. The suit jacket he wore on top seemed a little on the large side. There was the familiar map of Paris spread out in front of him. Victor shot a look across the room at Cole, who'd got there before him. This had better be good. He and Cole had searched every part of the city after the social worker's fall from Notre Dame. Montgomery better have reliable information they could follow up on, if he was going to ask them both to pound the streets again.

He looked across at the older man as he fiddled with the end of his walking cane and stared down at the map.

In your own time, Victor said playfully inside his head, although he knew better than to say anything out loud. Instead, he wrapped his hand round the photograph of his father he kept inside his pocket and pressed the heel of his thumb against the corner. It was strangely reassuring.

'There was some internet activity,' Montgomery said, without looking up from the map. 'A Skype call. From the girl to her mother. We couldn't reclaim visuals from the connection. 'But we have some name recognition facilities and there was definite use of the words Kassia, Dante and Jed.' He spat the final name as if it left a bad taste in his mouth.

'Can't we find out where the Skype call came from?' pressed Victor.

'They used some fancy blocking system to hide the IP address,' Montgomery grumbled. 'Probably some internet café or hotel which promises secrecy.'

'But we're sure they're in the city then?' confirmed Victor.

'Oh, yes. But I don't think we ever really doubted that was the case.'

Victor didn't respond to the veiled mocking of his

and Carter's attempts to track Jed down. Instead he pressed his thumb more tightly against the edge of the photograph.

'The name recognition gave us something else,' Montgomery said. 'The name Hugo.'

Carter blew a rather large bubble with his chewing gum, snapping his lips together as the bubble popped. 'You reckon they've got a new friend?' he said, chewing vigorously. 'Sounds like a dog's name. You reckon they've gone and got themselves a poodle?'

Montgomery was not impressed with the suggestion. He took a large copy of a book from the cabinet next to him. Then he slammed it down on top of the map, making the edges flutter and lift from the table. '*The Hunchback of Notre Dame*,' he said, as if this should be enough to clarify the situation.

Victor reached for the book. 'Nice. Was going to give that a go sometime. You've got to love a story about abandoned babies and nutty priests. And the author has a great name. *Victor* Hugo.'

Montgomery grabbed the book back. 'Point is, the name "Hugo" was used in connection with the word "Court".'

He wasn't really making things any clearer as far as Victor was concerned.

'At first the software thought it was a full name –

Hugo Court. But it's much deeper than that.' He laughed as if impressed with his own cleverness. 'So deep, in fact, it's underground.' He peeled the map from the surface of the table and instead of revealing the polished wood below, there was another map.

Victor peered in more closely. It was hard to be sure but this new map seemed to be showing a series of tunnels and dungeons. A network of interconnected spaces.

'Hugo talked about a Court of Miracles in his book,' Montgomery said, lifting his cane and tapping it against the newly revealed drawing. 'A hidden place below the city of Paris.' He tapped the cane again. 'This is where they are.'

Victor was excited. A genuine lead then, and so a chance to find them. But there was something about this news that troubled him. 'Sir, we got this information from a conversation between the girl and her mum,' he said, his thumb once more pressed to the corner of the photo. 'It's a little low to use it, isn't it?'

Montgomery looked up at him for the first time since Victor had entered the room. His eyes were steely blue. 'All's fair in love and war, Victor. And this is most definitely war.'

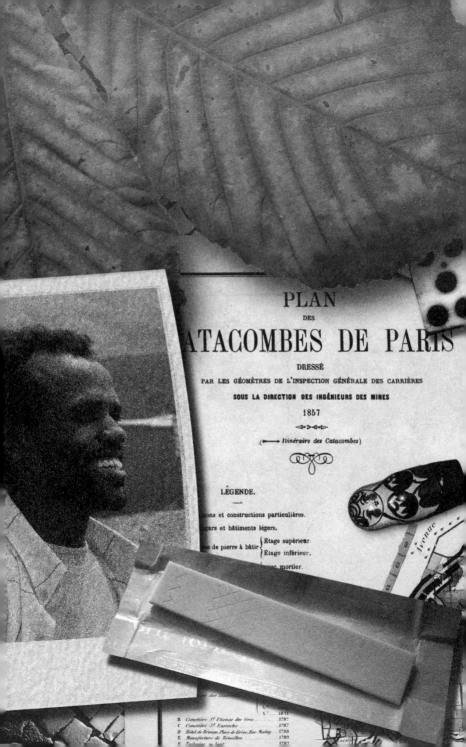

DAY 214
29th September

It had been nearly three weeks since Jed's collapse. He'd continued to flit in and out of consciousness, calling out in words that mixed French and English. Kassia sat with him, sponging his forehead to try and get his fever down and helping him take sips of water when he was strong enough to drink. There'd been no more flashes of light. No more connections to memories locked deep inside. And as Kassia watched him, she began to doubt he'd ever be strong enough to do what Nat said he needed to.

Days bled into night, time lost all sense of meaning and order and so Kassia had no idea what day it was when she woke to find that, as she'd been sleeping in the chair, her arms draped across Jed's bed, he'd slipped his hand into hers.

'We will only do this if you feel strong enough,' she

reassured him, as Giseppi went over the plan with them again.

Jed's hand tightened on hers.

Giseppi arranged for a taxi to be at the entrance of the catacombs to meet them. He and Kassia supported Jed, one of them each side. Progress through the tunnels was slow. He stopped frequently to steady his breathing and dragged his feet as if he no longer had the strength to lift them. As if every step in the darkness hurt him.

When they finally made it out into the street, Jed blinked his eyes against the light of the sun. He squinted and turned his head from the window as they clambered into the waiting car. And he said nothing as they made their way along the banks of the Seine.

When they reached the nursing home, Giseppi helped ease Jed from the car and steer him up the steps. It reminded Kassia of the way Jed had made his way so shakily towards St Paul's when they'd gone looking for answers back in London. And she wondered if the answers they found here would be as difficult to deal with as those they'd found in the cathedral.

Giseppi left them for a moment at reception as he chatted to a nurse, gesturing occasionally in their direction.

'You all right?' Kassia asked nervously.

'Not really.' Jed's voice was gravelly. It had been so long since he'd used it properly.

'But you want to do this?'

'Not really,' he said, and for the first time in weeks she saw something like the smallest flicker of a laugh pass across his eyes.

Giseppi returned and led the way down the wide, open corridor to a room at the end. It was large and airy, floor to ceiling windows with a view down to the river. And in the corner, propped up on pillows and cushions, was the man they'd come to see.

Bergier's body had twisted awkwardly, and the cushions had been jammed underneath him in a desperate attempt to keep him sliding free of the bed and on to the floor. His skin was shrivelled, like a fruit that had been left too long in the sun. His eyes were open but both irises were covered with a milky skin of cataract, which must have made vision out of them almost totally impossible.

Giseppi angled his head to the side. It was, Kassia guessed, his way of saying, *I told you so – nothing good will come of this meeting*. So she turned away and stared only at the old man in the bed.

'He's been this way for the years now,' confirmed Giseppi. 'The nurses are just doing the keeping him comfortable.' He hesitated for a moment and then made his way back towards the door. 'I'll leave you. See if you can find your answers,' he added, and he shut the door behind him.

Kassia could feel Jed's weight bearing down on her arm so she guided him to the chair at the end of the bed and helped him sit.

'Do you recognise him?' she asked at last.

Jed shook his head.

'Yeah, well, the person he was, is still inside,' she offered. 'We just have to see if we can find him.'

Jed looked away from her awkwardly.

Kassia moved round to the side of the bed. The room was deathly quiet except for the ticking of the clock on the mantle and the rasping of air in Bergier's ancient lungs. Kassia leant forward over the mountain of pillows. She didn't want Jed to hear and she wasn't even sure her amateur French would be good enough to say all she needed to. But there were certain phrases a novice in any language should learn. 'Please,' she whispered to the old man. 'We need help.'

The milky eyes looked back at her, unseeing.

So she pulled herself back to standing, the Brothers of Heliopolis medallion she wore round her neck swinging freely and brushing lightly against Bergier's forehead.

Suddenly, the old man reared up in the bed, and the extra cushions that supported him tumbled to the floor. He clawed the air, grabbed the medallion and locked his gnarled fingers around it.

Jed reared upright too in the chair in which he'd been slumped to gain his breath. It was as if a golden chain from the medallion connected the man in the bed and the boy in the chair. There was a fire and an energy in Jed's eyes that Kassia hadn't seen for weeks. And when she looked, she saw Bergier's eyes were sparkling too now, the milky skins vanished as if he had somehow blinked them away. His eyes were locked on Jed's.

'The Philosopher's Stone. Fulcanelli. It's you!' Bergier spoke with the voice of someone half his age, no glimpse of a tremor or hesitation.

'You remember?' Jed blurted, his own voice suddenly stronger too, as if the weeks of frailty had fallen away like the scales on the old man's eyes.

'You came to warn us,' Bergier said, his face hardening suddenly. 'But we didn't listen.'

'Warn you about what?' Jed pleaded.

'Danger!'

'For who?'

'Everyone,' Bergier cried out. 'You said it would change everything.'

'The elixir?' suggested Jed.

'The changing,' Bergier corrected, and then he stared hard at Jed, his eyes piercing and sharp now. 'The Phoenix Man in the church on the edge of two worlds.'

'Who's that?' begged Jed. 'Does he have the answers? Does he have the Philosopher's Stone?' His confusion drove him up from the chair so he was leaning over the bed.

'It's you,' Bergier said, and then he sank back into the diminished pile of pillows, his eyes staring upwards.

Kassia panicked. She leant down, suddenly sure that the old man must have died. But he looked directly at her, and his face softened into a smile.

'Zoe,' he said gently. 'You brought Zoe with you. You loved Zoe.'

Kassia felt colour rushing to her face. She looked at Jed and his awkwardness seemed as clear as her embarrassment.

Jed leant in closer, obviously desperate to keep the conversation on target. 'We need your help,' he pressed. 'The elixir of life. Did I talk to you about it? Tell you anything about how I got the recipe?'

The old man pulled himself up on his elbows, his face hardening again. 'The Emerald Tablet.'

Jed's eyes flitted backwards and forwards. 'What's that?'

The old man's eyes were wide now. 'The alchemical magnum opus.'

Kassia grabbed a piece of paper from the cabinet beside the bed and began to scribble down the message. It made little sense to her and the way that Jed was staring at the old man seemed to make it pretty clear he wasn't sure what it meant either.

'So where is this tablet?' Jed pleaded. 'I don't understand.'

The old man's breath seemed to be catching now in his chest. He was sinking back on to the bed. His eyes, so wide only moments before, were narrowing. The final words he spoke were barely audible at all. A breathless whisper. 'It's you, Fulcanelli,' he said. And then his eyes seemed to cloud again as he sank into the protection of the pillows.

'It's unbelievable,' said Giseppi, looking down at his grandfather.

'He honestly spoke to us,' Kassia said for the third time since Giseppi had come back into the room.

'That I find hard to do the believing of,' said Giseppi, smoothing the blankets across his grandfather's chest and rearranging the pillows behind the old man's head, as his milky white eyes gazed up at the ceiling. 'But this,' he said, waving his hand towards Jed, 'is more difficult to argue with. You look . . .'

'Different?' suggested Jed, shrugging awkwardly.

'Young again,' said Giseppi.

Jed pushed his hands deep into pockets. His hand latched over the silver pocket watch and somehow it made him calm.

'We were thinking, back in the Court of Miracles, when your heart did the stopping and the fever came, that the living for ever had lost its hold even before the year was up. It looked for a while as if you would, you know,' Giseppi ran his hand in a cutting movement across the shark tooth necklace that hung at the base of his neck, pulling a face as he did so. 'But now you look stronger than ever.'

Jed nodded again. He didn't understand the change either. But he certainly knew that standing here discussing it was making him feel ever more awkward. 'I think I need some air,' he blurted.

Giseppi's face was suddenly stern again. 'Oh, I think we should now be doing the return to Court of Miracles. I think streets of the city are no place for you, even now.'

Jed tightened his hand on the watch and forced himself to stay composed. 'Please, mate.' He took a deep breath and tried to organise his argument. 'I've been out of things for so long down there. All I'm asking is for a little time, just to *breathe*, you know.' He forced his lips into a hopeful half smile.

Giseppi seemed to weigh the idea. He blew out a laboured breath of his own and then turned to Kassia. 'Take the most direct route you can back to the catacombs. Don't do any of the drawing of attention to yourselves. And be on the watch all the time for suspicious things. Agreed?'

'Agreed,' said Kassia.

Jed smiled his appreciation and then he stooped down a final time at the bed of the old man and whispered gently, 'Thank you.'

There was a tiny track beside the Seine. They walked for a while without talking. Jed was aware that Kassia was looking up at him every now and then. 'You really feel OK?' she asked at last, when she could obviously no longer bear the silence.

'Not OK,' he laughed. 'I feel as if my body hasn't moved properly for weeks; a bit rusty, I guess. But I feel,' he searched for the word he needed, 'alive.'

Her hands were in her pockets but their elbows were so close that their arms brushed against each other with every stride. Neither of them did anything to stop this.

'I thought it was over,' Kassia added, this time her eyes looking firmly down at the track. 'And I was so scared.'

Jed stopped walking. He turned her by the shoulders so she had to face him. 'I was so scared too. I saw things that . . .'

'I know.'

He looked confused and tightened his hold on her. 'I could hear you, you know. Talking to me.'

She tried to laugh. 'Yeah, well. You weren't making much sense yourself, so one of us had to.'

'Thank you,' he said.

'For what?'

'Not giving up on me.'

'Oh, it was Nat's idea that we spoke to Bergier.'

This wasn't what he'd meant. He hesitated for a moment. 'Nat?'

'We spoke to him.' She looked embarrassed. 'We were careful. But he said that what you had to do was face your memories.'

Jed kept his hands on her shoulders. 'Well, we've made a start,' he said, trying to make his voice sound as light as possible.

Kassia pulled away a little.

'Although not much of what that old man said back there made any sense to me. Magnus opus.

51

The Great Work. We've heard that before. My book about the recipe for the elixir was supposed to be the Great Work, remember? And Bergier seems to be saying I got the idea from some sort of Emerald Tablet.'

Kassia scuffed her feet against the ground.

Now it was his turn to ask if she was OK.

'Of course. Why wouldn't I be?'

He eased her back to face him again. 'Kassia? What is it?'

She pulled out of his grasp and folded her arms across herself. 'It's stupid. I don't want to say. Forget it.'

He stepped in front of her, blocking her way. 'I thought this whole thing was about *not* forgetting.'

'Yeah, well.' She scuffed the ground again.

'Is this . . . ?' He wasn't sure if he should say it out loud. 'Is this about Zoe?'

She shrugged again, trying to make her face look dismissive. But there was a faint colouring of her cheeks.

'I don't know who this Zoe is,' he pleaded.

'But you loved her.'

'So some old man says,' he pressed urgently. 'He said all sorts of other stuff that was pretty weird too.'

Kassia's face was harder now, the blush more of anger than embarrassment. 'It's OK,' she said. 'You don't have to explain anything to me. I want you to remember. It's just I was surprised, I suppose. Hadn't thought the memories would be about things like that.' She sank down so that she was sitting on the curb, her feet in the gutter. 'See, I told you it was stupid.'

He sat down beside her, their arms close again, but not touching this time. 'I don't remember her.'

'But you loved her.'

'Maybe.'

Kassia lifted a stone and rolled it in her hand before dropping it again in front of their feet. 'Isn't that sad? That there are all these parts of your life you can't connect to, even now?'

He kicked the stone and it skittered away. 'When I came out of the Thames, that was the hardest thing. I didn't know who I was, but worse than that, I didn't know who cared.'

'And now?'

'Now that's not so difficult.'

They sat for a moment in silence, aware of the city moving all around them and the river carving its route behind them.

'Do you know what any of the other stuff Bergier said meant?' Kassia said eventually.

'Phoenix Man. Church on the edge of two worlds.' He laughed. 'Nope. No idea.'

'So what d'we do?'

Jed took another deep breath and stood, holding his hand out to help her up. 'We'll work it out,' he said. 'But right now, it feels so good to be above ground. To be out of the cage, if you know what I mean.'

She allowed herself to be pulled up reluctantly. 'You know we have to get back.'

'I know,' he mocked. 'Orders from Giseppi. I get that.'

'We promised we'd take no risks.'

'I know. But I'm the one with only six months left.'

She thumped him hard on the arm. 'Don't talk like that!'

'What? Because it suddenly isn't true?'

'No.' Her cheeks were violent red now and this time he was sure it was anger. 'Because my heart can't handle it,' she said forcefully.

He stared at her and she didn't look away. 'You're a good friend, Kassia.'

'Better than Zoe?' she said playfully.

'I think the best I've ever had,' he said.

She watched him for a moment, but she said nothing else.

'Come on. We're in Paris. The seasons are changing. We've spent a whole summer underground. I think Giseppi will allow us a little time. Just to *be*.'

Her face was wrinkled as if she was fighting against answers she knew she should give.

'Maybe we shouldn't just face old memories but make new ones,' he said.

They turned from the track beside the river and found themselves in a network of cobbled streets and alleyways. The buildings were so close they almost touched. It seemed so strange to Kassia that these people were hurrying through their normal, everyday lives. And it seemed even stranger that all this had been happening when everything had seemed so desperate and scary underground. She felt her shoulders lift a little, warmer air fill her lungs, and she realised that she was breathing deeply for the first time in ages, the breath no longer catching in her chest.

They stopped for a moment outside a small café. French flags on a string of bunting fluttered round the doorway. A stall laden with baskets of rolls and baguettes crowded for room in the narrow streetway. In the window, a stand of cakes rotated slowly, weighed down with choux buns crammed with coffee-coloured cream, long éclairs with shiny chocolate icing, apple tarts topped with latticed pastry, crispy cones flecked with sugar and stuffed with custard, bulging croissants and outsized meringues.

A tray of sugar mice arranged like an advancing army stared up at them.

'Come on,' said Jed. 'Let's live a little.'

Kassia snuffled a laugh. Her stomach rumbled. It had been weeks since she'd eaten properly and the hunger she felt was suddenly overwhelming. 'Really?'

'Really! Which one do you want?'

He dragged her into the café and she pointed out a coffee choux bun from the window. Jed chose a custard slice from the display on the counter and the waiter waved them over to a table in the corner. He brought the cakes and a jug of sparkling water topped with lemon and lime slices. Jed poured Kassia a glass and, as she sipped, the bubbles went up her nose. She giggled and wiped her face nervously. She couldn't believe they were doing this. It felt so wrong. And so right.

'It's Paris,' said Jed, licking a smear of custard from his finger. 'They call it the city of dreams. So tell me your dream.'

The cream from her coffee bun sat a little heavy in Kassia's stomach.

'No talk about unicorns or phoenixes or dragons,' Jed said forcefully. 'Just about you now.'

She wiped the edge of her mouth and took another

sip of water. She wasn't sure what to say. She wasn't sure if she had dreams that weren't bound up in all that had happened in the last six months. But Jed seemed so determined they shouldn't talk about that. That this stolen moment was just about now.

'What do you dream of being?' he encouraged.

'A writer, I think,' she said shakily. She wasn't sure what had made her say that. The rush of bubbles to her head. The sudden surge of sugar in her blood.

'Not a doctor?' Jed said, his confusion obvious.

It felt strangely wonderful to shake her head. 'I think that's my mum's dream.'

'So the notebooks I found. Back in London, when I shouldn't have been looking?'

She blushed to think about how angry that had made her then. And how unimportant his looking seemed now. 'My dad and I used to make stuff up. Write stories together. But I suppose the doctor thing. That's more serious. It's more important.' She bit into the bun again and flakes of pastry cascaded into her lap. 'Do you remember what you wanted to do?'

Jed seemed to give the thought some consideration. 'I liked changing things, I think. The cooking I did. That was about change.'

Kassia remembered that too and how cross her mum had been when they hadn't tidied away as she wanted. She tried not to think about her mum. And how in the Skype call her mum had begged them to come home. Jed had said this was about *now* so Kassia tried to push the memory of her mother's pleading face away. 'You were good at cooking,' she blurted.

He finished the custard slice and rubbed his hands together. 'I don't know what else I wanted, though.'

His face seemed to darken a little and she could tell, that like her, even when fighting to keep in the moment of what was happening, memories were tugging at the edge of his mind. He might be free of the fever now. But nothing had changed about the time limit on his life.

He smiled at her, though she could tell that the smile was struggling to reach his eyes.

'If you could have one perfect hour,' she said quietly. 'No dragons. No unicorns. What would it be?'

He leant forward and he wiped a flake of pastry from the corner of her mouth. 'I've just had it,' he said.

He paid the waiter and then they found their way back to the track beside the river. They reached the Pont des Arts bridge. The love-locks had been cleared. The bridge looked stark and bare. Just a functional walkway for getting from one place to another, no longer a groaning symbol of undying love. It made Kassia sad to see it like this.

Jed was struggling, as if the energy surge he'd had since meeting Bergier was waning. She leant on the railings and looked down into the water and it surged like oil beneath them. Jed did not hold on to the railings. He stood behind her and she could feel his breath on her back as he spoke. 'We need to face things now, right?'

She gripped tighter as she answered. 'Yeah.'

'So I guess we try and make sense of Bergier's riddle then?'

She took the piece of paper from her pocket and it fluttered in the breeze as she read from it. *'Phoenix Man. Hidden church resting on the border of two worlds. Emerald Tablet.'* It wasn't much to go on. But it was all they had.

'Where have you been?' Dante's signs were so frantic and sharp, Kassia felt as if they were cutting her skin. The relief of seeing Jed looking well again and the fun of the hour they'd spent together above ground evaporated.

'We've been waiting. We thought . . .' Dante didn't finish his signs. He was clearly too angry.

Kassia tried to compose herself. Had they really walked too slowly back through the tunnels? Her brother had the same look that her mother wore when she was a minute late for dinner. Kassia felt a surge of anger. Didn't Dante realise they had things to think through? Ideas to work out? What was his problem?

But as she glanced around the Court of Miracles, it suddenly became clear that there *was* a problem. A serious one.

Giseppi was at the line of cases in the corner, frantically grabbing things and stuffing them into smaller bags. Amelie was beside him. Neither looked up to acknowledge them.

'What's going on?' Kassia pleaded.

'NOAH,' Dante's fingers blurted. 'Here in the tunnels.'

Kassia felt as if someone had punched her hard in the stomach. She was aware of Jed beside her. He reached out to use the wall to steady himself, clamping the other hand hard across his mouth.

'But where? How d'you know it's them?'

Her brother started to pace. He threw his signs so the energy they contained bounced and rattled off the walls. 'I was so worried, Kassia. You should have come straight back. You can't just go up there and be gone and . . .'

Kassia batted her brother's hands to stop him signing. To make him see her words. 'How do you know?'

Dante's jaw was clenched.

'Dante!' She used no signs because now her hands were holding his.

He pulled free and dragged her across the space and towards another entrance to the Court. He walked so quickly down the narrow passageway that she had to run to keep up. She could feel Jed hurrying behind her. Then Dante stopped, and jabbed his hand towards the rough stone.

A second thumping sensation in her stomach, this one deeper and harder than before.

She lifted her hand to the wall. Painted on the stone was a picture of a unicorn. Around the leg of the unicorn, scrawled with thick black paint, was a chain.

Kassia withdrew her hand. The fingertips were stained with paint. The picture was so freshly done, it hadn't dried. 'Why would they paint this?' she blurted.

'To show they've checked this area, perhaps?' signed Dante. 'A way of marking off the sections their teams have searched, so they get more ground covered.'

She nodded and let him lead her back into the main space of the Court.

61

Giseppi was facing her when she returned. He threw a rucksack at Jed, who caught it. Another at Kassia, which she fumbled and then strapped firmly to her back. 'So they haven't found this place yet?' she blurted.

'We've been lucky so far. They must have followed the other path. But they could return at any time,' said Giseppi. 'So I have the thinking it's best to do the leaving.'

Jed nodded and turned towards the exit, but Giseppi grabbed his arm. 'Not that way, mate. We heard them doing the talking, about sealing the exits. It's a miracle you didn't get the caught by them on your way down here. What did you do? Take the long way round?'

Kassia could feel herself blushing. But Giseppi obviously had no intention of waiting for their answer.

'We can't risk doing the going that way too,' Giseppi said.

'So what, then?'

Giseppi grabbed a torch and switched it on. 'We go deep under cover,' he said. And he added emphasis to the way he said 'deep'.

The tunnels were narrow, twisting again and again without warning. Every now and then, the light of the torch cast shadows on the piles of bones stacked in alcoves that lined the warren of passages. Kassia had been so shocked to see these when she'd first been brought down to the catacombs. Horrific sculptures of death. But now they simply marked their progress through the tunnels. And now she was no longer scared of those who were already dead. She was scared of those who were alive and in the tunnels somewhere, searching for them.

They reached a section of passageways that spanned out. There was some sort of well in the centre of the space, ringed by a metal fence. Kassia supposed the well had been used by workers as they'd built the tunnels or stacked away the dead for safe keeping. Giseppi stopped for a moment. The five of them circled the fence: Amelie next to Giseppi; Dante next to Jed. Kassia completed the ring. She looked at Giseppi as he scanned the space, trying to decide which way to take them. And then she froze. Giseppi's eyes widened, sparking in the light of the torch he held. She turned and looked in the direction he was staring. Behind her, painted on the wall, another symbol. A unicorn. And a newly painted chain which dripped with wet paint.

Suddenly, Jed raised his arm. He moved his hand slowly so that his finger was pressed against his lips, begging them all to make no noise. Giseppi nodded and extinguished the torch. The darkness was all consuming.

Kassia was scared the noise of her heart would betray them.

She reached out her hand, and grabbed hold of Jed. A human chain. Giseppi steered them round behind the well and into a small alcove. The five of them pressed so tight together that they were like one in the darkness. Something sharp dug into Kassia's shoulder in the space not protected by the bag she wore. She tried not to think that it could be bones.

She could hear water dripping, the slight movement of air in the void of the underground shaft of the well. Nothing else, except her own heart beating.

They pressed their bodies tighter. Kassia held her breath.

Then footsteps. A line of people, marching together. And, finally, the swoosh of a long leather coat, its hem skirting the ground. A shaft of torch-light, swelling, and engulfing the space.

Then darkness again.

Kassia turned Jed's hand in hers and she spelt her question, letter by letter into his palm. 'Are they gone?'

It was an eternity before he answered. Just a squeeze of her hand which told her not to move.

Finally, when Kassia's knees were so cramped she

could hardly bear the pain, Giseppi switched on the torch. In the light of the single beam, he pointed down the furthest walkway. Then, hand in hand, the five of them crawled out of the space and in the direction of the light.

The passageway Giseppi had chosen was even narrower than before. And, suddenly, as the tunnel turned a little and the ground beneath their feet got steeper, the light bounced back at them. A dead end. Kassia tightened her hand on Jed's. What did they do now? Should they turn back? She was sure it had been Carter in the tunnel by the well. And he wasn't alone. There must be teams of them, closing in.

But instead of turning back, Giseppi passed the torch to Amelie, gesturing silently for her to hold its glow on him as he fumbled in the flickering beam. He began to grab at the wall of boxes and wooden panels which barred the end of the tunnel. Finally, as the panelling and boxes were pushed aside, Kassia saw a door.

Gispeppi nodded and tugged the handle.

The rush of cold air was immediate. The space beyond the opening enormous. A vast cavern. But this was no cave. It was organised like some sort of office.

'What is this?' whispered Jed, as Giseppi hurried them all inside, pulling as many boxes and panels back into position as he could to hide their route, and then shutting the door behind them.

'FFHQ,' said Giseppi, as if this was an answer everyone should understand. 'French Freedom Fighters Headquarters,' he explained, after checking for a second time that the door was firmly closed and therefore it was safe enough to risk using his regular voice. 'During World War Two, when Paris was being the occupied, this was the place of the Resistance. Bergier was part of the Resistance.'

The mention of the old man made Kassia feel uncomfortable. 'They fought against the Nazis?' she said awkwardly.

'Yes,' went on Giseppi. 'Right under the sight of the noses of the Gestapo.' He gestured to the spread of the ancient office. 'We under now the Denfert Rochereau Place in the Fourteenth District. The German Kommandant had his offices just above. We always had the knowing that if the Court of Miracles became unsafe, then we'd come to this place.'

'But we can't stay here,' gasped Kassia.

'And we can't leave the catacombs the way we always do,' said Amelie. 'We heard them talk of the exit. If we leave that way, we walk straight into a trap.'

Dante banged his fist against the table. Everyone

was so stressed that no one was signing what was said. 'I don't know what we do?' Kassia signed apologetically to her brother's angry question.

Giseppi reached into a cupboard, threw them each a head-torch and then unrolled a huge yellowed map across the table. 'What we do,' he said slowly enough for Kassia to convert into sign, 'is what my grandfather did here in the war. We use this place to make the plan of our liberation,' he said.

The yellowed map covered the table like a sheet. Across it ran a thin network of scrawling lines and loops. Words and phrases labelled the lines, making it look like a street map.

'This map is of Paris?' asked Dante.

Giseppi made a yes and no movement with his head. 'This is the dark side of the city of light,' he said, smoothing the map, trying to force it to lie flat on the table. 'A reflection of what is above, below.'

'It's huge,' said Kassia.

'As big as the city. But even more complicated,' said Amelie.

Kassia peered at the map. She could see sections marked with crosses where she guessed bones were stored, but there were other vast sections of rooms and spaces.

'Bodies of those who'd died were moved here long

ago,' said Giseppi, as if noting the crosses on the map too. 'Paris was so full of the dead that they were doing the breaking out of their overstuffed graves. And so underground storage of the bones was good. But there is much more than the bones being kept beneath the pavements.' He ran his hand along the length of the map. 'Two hundred and twenty-two miles of the tunnels,' he said, almost proudly. 'We even have the police of the underground. To do the stopping of those who hide here.' He smiled. 'They not too good. Court of Miracles beyond their reach. But that doesn't mean they don't do the looking for underground travellers. And if we go further into the tunnels we've rarely used, then we have the chance of doing the being seen by them.'

Kassia looked more closely. As well as street names she could see metro stations marked and even sections which were labelled as disused quarries.

Giseppi smoothed the curling map again with his hand and the page fluttered a little. 'It is a not safe place. You need to know that. In 1791, the doorman of the Val de Grace hospital decided to do the exploring of the underground city here.' He showed the connection to the hospital on the map. 'And so down the carved staircase he came and into the tunnels. But he never did the findings of the way back.'

'That's horrible,' blurted Kassia, suddenly aware of how cold she was. 'They never found him?'

'Oh yes, they found him. Just his bones though, and the key to the hospital that proved it was him.'

Kassia wasn't sure if Giseppi was deliberately trying to scare her, but he was doing a very good job of it.

'We need to get away from NOAH,' Giseppi went on, 'and so to do that we have to go deep into the belly of the underground city. But,' he looked up to be sure that Kassia was making his words tangible for Dante, 'we do the staying together. Understood?'

Kassia had absolutely no intention of going anywhere without the others.

Then because they'd all already done so, she slipped the head-torch on to her forehead and snapped on the beam.

Jed adjusted his head-torch and strode forward into the tunnels. Giseppi was leading the way and it had been agreed that Jed should be at the end of the line, keeping a watch to check whether they were being followed.

They had walked the tunnels that led to the Court of Miracles so often in their three months of hiding that Jed felt he knew every turn and twist. Now he knew nothing. These new tunnels were smaller. The narrow walls pressed in, uneven in places so that he had to keep his arms close to his body to prevent catching his shoulders against the rough stone. The ceilings were lower too, so that every now and then the head-torch grazed against the overhang and the light faltered and flickered. The ground below foot was rough and uneven. It was littered with debris and rubbish. And human remains.

Giseppi had explained that further away from the Court of Miracles, the 'Keeper of the Bones' had less control. Skeletons in this older part of the tunnels had not been organised or nicely arranged, stacked up in an Empire of the Dead. Here the bodies had just been tipped. Thrown away, out of sight of the city, so out of mind. The thought sickened Jed. Maybe dying wasn't the great leveller after all. Maybe there was a hierarchy in death too. And the bones he tried so hard not to walk on now were, he reasoned, the very lowest of the low. He wondered if anyone had grieved for these people who'd been scattered amongst the rubbish.

Jed tried not to look down. But looking up didn't make him feel much better either. Pressed into the side of the wall was a human skull. It had been covered with plaster and paint to look like the devil and Jed was sure the empty eyes followed him as he hurried onwards.

Suddenly, the front of the line stopped. Giseppi called them together in a huddle, the light from their head-torches swirling in an amber mix. They'd reached a curved metal gate. And beyond that was a narrow stone staircase.

Giseppi pointed upwards, then clambered over the gate and began to climb. The others followed.

Jed was aware of a sudden blast of noise from ahead, and a deluge of water which cascaded down the steps and soaked his legs. Giseppi had opened a huge metal door at the top of the stairs and the filthy water had rushed from the chamber beyond.

Jed reached the top of the stairs and pressed his hands to his ears. The noise was so loud it hurt. Only Dante was unphased, so he took the lead into the chamber.

The space was filled with huge metal canisters, each of which was as tall as a door and as wide across as about three rather large men. These connected to pumps that seemed to be sucking up the water that sloshed around the floor, and forcing it into pipes that drilled into the curved ceiling.

Giseppi cupped his hand around his mouth and shouted an explanation. 'The tunnels aren't fully watertight.'

This was not something Jed was very keen to know.

'This pumping station,' Giseppi shouted, 'is to do the keeping of water from the Seine flooding the metro!'

Jed pushed on with the others through the pumping station and towards another metal door as quickly as he could.

This time, instead of being met by water, they were pushed back by a pummelling of air. There was a roaring. It sounded like an animal in pain.

The space they'd entered was like some sort of wind tunnel, lined with huge circular fans that channelled great gusts of cold air towards them. Long metal fins had been secured to the walls in an attempt to funnel the air in the direction it was needed.

Jed bent his head into the force of air. He could feel the skin around his face pulling backwards; his hair tugging at the roots. His eyes were watering, making it almost impossible to see. But he could tell that Kassia was struggling to even stay upright. He linked his arm round her and tried to steer them both forward. He guessed these fans were to manage the heat of the underground train. But the ferocity of the wind meant it was almost impossible to keep walking.

Suddenly, just behind them, Amelie was blasted over, her body thrown first into the long metal fins and then tossed aside like crumpled paper, hard against the floor.

Jed manoeuvred Kassia towards the wall. 'Hang on here!' he yelled, but his voice was ripped away unheard.

He turned back into the wind, bent down low and scrabbled with his hand along the wall, trying desperately not to fall himself. He flung his arm out towards Amelie. 'Grab on!' he yelled, louder this time, but his voice was still tossed away into the wind.

Amelie fought against the blast of air. She strained to reach Jed's hand.

Jed pressed his feet down hard, trying to anchor himself. She couldn't reach him.

Suddenly, Dante flung himself into the funnel of wind. He allowed his body to be thrown sideways too, so that he landed in a heap beside Amelie. Then he wrapped his arm around her and grabbed Jed's hand, dragging Amelie with him, until the three of them were beside the wall.

Giseppi was shouting instructions. Jed could hear nothing but the roar of the wind. The circular fans turned backwards and forwards, like giant heads mocking their struggle to move on.

Jed could barely put one foot in front of the other. The surge of energy he'd felt after meeting Bergier had long since drained away. And now, fighting just to keep moving required every ounce of strength he had. But there was no alternative.

They had to keep driving forwards. They had to get out of the wind.

Giseppi clawed his way towards another doorway. The force of the air against it meant he couldn't pull it open. Dante pushed ahead to join him, clawing at the join where the door met the wall. Together they yanked it open. Kassia grabbed her brother's arm and pushed through the gap, reaching back to help drag Jed and Amelie through too.

Dante slammed the door shut. He leant against it and Jed doubled forward, trying to catch his breath. The sound of roaring surged behind them, but the space they'd entered now was quieter. Jed looked up and tried to make sense of where they were.

In front of them were two huge, red metal wheels, both taller than a fully grown man. Some sort of gear system, connected to pulleys, pistons and levers, reached either side of the wheels. 'The Eiffel Tower,' Giseppi explained. 'We're right below it. Elevators connect to the pillars of the Tower.'

There was a rushing noise. This time not a frantic wind but air channelled and directed inside a hydraulic system. An elevator was coming down from the ceiling. And there was someone in it.

Giseppi lurched to the left and the others followed, ducking behind a line of pistons which pressed up and down urgently, squirting oil and steam into the air as they moved. But Dante had missed the sound of the falling elevator. He stood rooted to the spot as the door of the elevator opened, and a man in overalls stepped out.

From her crouched position behind the pistons, Kassia reached towards her brother. Giseppi tugged her back. Amelie clamped her hand round Kassia's mouth, even though calling out would have been futile.

Jed couldn't bear to watch.

The man from the elevator stared at Dante. He creased his face in confusion, two narrow ridges forming above the bridge of his nose. He opened his hands wide, mumbling in French.

Dante didn't answer.

Jed looked across at Giseppi. *What should they do?*

The man from the elevator spoke again, this time his voice was sharper, more clipped. He stepped forward. He was close enough to touch Dante if he just reached out his hand. Was he going to grab him? Turn him in for trespassing?

Jed wanted to burst free and drag Dante clear. But revealing that Dante was not alone might make things worse.

Giseppi shook his head. All eyes were on Dante.

And then Dante did something odd. He pointed to

his hearing aids and then waved his hands around in elaborate signs.

The man from the elevator looked embarrassed. His face reddened. He didn't know how to answer. So Dante nodded and strode calmly across the room in front of the line of pistons where the others were hiding. He winked as he passed.

The man from the elevator scanned the room quickly, shrugged and then picked up a toolbox from the floor in front of him.

Then he stepped back into the elevator, and disappeared as the elevator slid up and away from view into the base of the Eiffel Tower.

Kassia leapt out from her hiding place and thumped Dante hard on the shoulder.

He yelped, his only sign language a frantic rubbing of his arm.

'You could have got us caught!' Kassia shouted with her hands. 'He could have taken you away!'

Dante stopped rubbing his shoulder. 'Yeah, well. Lucky for you, you're stuck with me.'

Kassia thumped him again, but this time a little more gently.

'He could come back, you know,' Jed urged, looking over to the far corner and another closed door.

'So we better not be here when he does,' signed Dante.

There was no blast of air beyond the next door, no whining machinery, no men at work. This exit led to another staircase which was older than the others they'd used. The steps were worn and the treads uneven. It reminded Jed of the stairs down to the lab they'd found hidden underground in the Museum of Alchemy in Prague.

The tunnel at the bottom of the stairs was more like a small elongated cave. It was impossible to walk without stooping fully. The head-torches banged and scraped the ceiling. Water dripped down the stone, making greasy pools at their feet. The air was heavy and stale. Jed found it hard to fill his lungs and the pressure of the walls closing in unnerved him. He wanted to burst the surface and take in great gulps of air. They seemed to be being forced downwards into the earth and there seemed no clear purpose to the route. 'What is this place?' he yelled out towards the front of the line.

Giseppi's reply was muffled and delayed. Jed caught only the word 'quarry', and so he guessed that this part of the tunnels was where the stones to make the buildings of Paris had been hacked out of the earth. It didn't feel like there had been a proper plan to the cutting. Great sections of the walls crumbled away to the side of him and, in places, rocks had been heaped into piles covered with calcified water. Nothing about this felt safe. In fact, the air felt too thin, and the walls pressed in so close, he felt like he was drowning.

'Watch your step,' shouted Giseppi.

They'd reached a fork in the path. The tunnel diverged: the smaller, narrower section continued to the left and a broader path turned right. Jed wanted to take the path to the right but Giseppi ploughed forward. Jed supposed he was trying to make it as difficult as possible for them to be followed. But Jed didn't like it.

Suddenly, the path opened out again, cutting across a smoother, wider walkway. The ceiling seemed higher.

Jed liked what he saw now even less than the claustrophobic tunnels of the quarry.

Kassia grabbed his arm. 'Who are they?' she hissed.

Slightly ahead, two men in uniform were walking together, locked tight in conversation.

'Police,' cut in Giseppi.

'Why here?' whispered Jed.

Giseppi frowned. 'We must be under Hospital Boulevard. It's the Police Data Base Centre building.'

'And you led us directly here!' hissed Jed.

'Hey,' said Giseppi defensively. 'Trying to avoid NOAH and workmen on the Tower as well, you know. I am doing of my best here!'

Jed nodded begrudgingly but there wasn't really time to say it was OK. It was far from OK. The policemen had stopped walking. They'd turned. Any second now they were bound to face their way.

'Quick,' hissed Giseppi, turning back into the quarry tunnels and hurrying forward.

'Do you think they saw us?' blurted Kassia.

'Not sure,' called Jed, 'But I don't think it's a good idea to hang around to find out.'

They splashed through the pools of stagnant water, hardly flinching as the rocks above bashed at their torches. Jed's arm cracked against a sharp shard of rock sticking out from the wall. But there was no time to even stop and register the pain.

They reached the fork in the tunnel again and this time they took the path Giseppi had rejected. It was wider, the ceiling higher, and Jed was annoyed they hadn't taken it in the first place. This was clearly the better route.

Until the tunnel ended. A pile of stone and boulders barred their way.

'Great,' groaned Amelie. 'What now?'

They couldn't hear any footsteps behind them but, still, the police might be on to them soon.

Dante scrunched his hands into fists and groaned.

There didn't seem to be a better answer. Then, as if even this was not enough, he kicked out at the pile of rubble.

There was a rumbling sound. A tremor beyond the rocks. A boulder fell free and rolled across the ground, stopping at their feet.

Dante scrabbled closer again to the pile of rocks barring the way. A hole now stared back at him, a shaft of what looked like natural light spilling through.

'Help me,' he signed wildly.

The four of them crushed next to him, pulling at the rocks and boulders and tossing them behind until an opening appeared in the barricade that was wide enough for Jed to push his head and shoulders into.

The view through the hole was confusing. It was a wide space with lots of light but the perspective seemed all wrong. Jed took a stone from the discarded pile of rubble and pitched it through the hole.

Silence. Then a splashing sound.

Giseppi reached into his bag and pulled out the map.

'I think through the hole leads to the Canal St Martin,' he said. 'The light we can see is from manhole covers in the streets.'

'And this is good?' said Jed.

Giseppi re-rolled the map and stuffed it back in his

bag. 'Yes. The canal is close to the ground of Paris. It means we are near the escaping.'

'So we climb through that hole?' gasped Kassia. 'You sure?'

Giseppi did his yes and no face again but a glance over his shoulder was all that was really needed to remind them that in the other direction were NOAH and the police.

'We do it,' said Jed, scrabbling at the hole again and making it wider. 'All good with this?'

He wasn't entirely sure he was good with the idea himself. But the canal was the route they needed for escape and they were running out of options.

Jed eased his shoulders through the hole first, wiggling his hips so that the circle of rocks cut into his stomach.

The ground fell away beyond the gap, and way below him he could hear the sound of water rushing in the canal. But just beneath the hole, attached to the wall, was what looked like a tiny wooden balcony. A viewing platform, he supposed, for the underground waterway.

'Is it safe?' Kassia's voice filtered through the hole.

'It's fine,' he lied.

The distance between the opening they'd made in the wall and the balcony was fairly large. He squeezed further through, then tossed the bag he carried down on to the balcony. There was a muffled thud, which suggested the drop was even greater than he'd thought. But there wasn't time to overthink this. He wriggled further, his waist sliding over the ridge of rock so that more of him was through the hole than still inside the quarry tunnel. It was like he was on a see-saw. He was toppling forward, his body lowering so it felt like he was performing some sort of crazy handstand manoeuvre. 'Hold on to my feet,' he yelled hopefully. He felt a tug on his shoes, but this did nothing to reassure him. His shoe was loose. Whoever was holding on needed to grab his leg, not the part of him that was detachable! But it was too late. His impetus had carried him so far through the opening that there was no stopping his trajectory. He closed his eyes. He crumpled forward. The descent seemed to last for ever. Until he landed, in a heap, shoeless, on the balcony.

'Are you OK?' Kassia's voice again.

He took a moment before he answered. He'd fallen on to something hard and slatted. The pain in his shoulder was so intense he wasn't sure he'd be able to speak and when he did use his voice, it sounded several octaves higher than usual. 'I'm OK,' he squeaked.

He wasn't. And neither was he sure how the others

would manage the descent with or without someone holding on to their feet.

But as he pulled himself up to try and warn them that copying what he'd done was not the best idea in the world, he realised that the hard thing he'd fallen on was a ladder. 'Hold on!' he yelled, in a pitch that sounded much more normal. 'It's going to be OK.'

It took a while for them all to get down the ladder and Jed wasn't totally sure that the balcony would support them. So they didn't leave it long before they used the ladder for what it was originally intended and swung it down to the walkway below them.

The walkway ran alongside the canal. Once they were on it, Jed could appreciate the smooth flooring below his feet and the light spilling in through the latticed manhole covers above them. Everything felt infinitely safer than when they'd been pressed inside the quarry tunnels and Jed allowed himself for the first time since the Freedom Fighters Offices to feel something that felt a little bit like hope.

But all hope faded when they saw a small rowboat moving towards them.

'Seriously?' groaned Kassia. 'They use boats down here?'

'Run!' yelled Amelie, leading the charge along the canal path.

The five of them jostled beside each other, bags banging on their shoulders, head-torches spilling light across the water.

But surely they could outrun a rowboat? It was out of sight around a bend in the canal now. Surely they were safe?

And maybe they would have been if, when the walkway had turned another corner, they hadn't been greeted by the sight of a second boat. This one was travelling straight towards them!

'Who are these people?' yelped Kassia. 'Police?' The figures on the boats were indistinct, but any moment now they would be clearer. And if the figures on the boats were clear to them, then . . .

'Maybe workers just getting from place to place,' said Jed, trying desperately to ease the tension.

'But being seen by anyone is not a good idea!' added Giseppi.

'What do we do?' gasped Kassia, looking frantically one way and then the other. The other boat had appeared round the bend and they were trapped between the two.

'Don't panic,' hissed Giseppi.

'Great idea!' Jed hissed back. 'And after we've not panicked, then what?'

The boats were getting closer. There was no escape

in either direction. Only the water below them. And the latticed manhole covers flinging down light above them. But surely these were far too high to reach and scramble through to make a getaway?

Jed ran his hand along the wall, searching for a handhold. Maybe they would just have to climb. Make for the openings up to the street. But there was nothing secure enough to hold on to. The climb was clearly too far.

What should they do? The boats were getting closer. The figures unblurring and coming into focus.

And then, suddenly, Jed felt a draught on his back.

It was only the walkway wall behind him. Air was flowing down from the shafts of light. But this was different. A definite blast of cold air against his spine.

He turned to face the wall. Peered more closely. Stone slick with slime, but smoother here behind him than elsewhere. He pressed his hand against the wall. Not stone. Something else. Metal maybe.

He thumped his fist against it hard. A rattle.

Yes, definitely metal. Some sort of opening.

He wrenched his fingers down the join and the panel shuddered and then swung open. There was a cavity beyond the metal door.

'Hurry,' he begged, directing the others as they

clambered inside. 'Come on!'

And he flung himself in afterwards and tugged the door shut behind them.

'Nice one,' said Dante, his fingers moving in the light of the torch. 'That was close.'

The way Jed's heart was racing inside him confirmed that it had been. He smiled. 'Yeah, well, it's good to live on the edge.'

Kassia looked at him reassuringly, but he noticed her face was still too scared to smile.

'It's OK,' he said gently. 'They didn't see us. We got away.'

She nodded. 'But where exactly are we?'

Giseppi reached into his bag and unfurled the map. It took him a while to locate where they were but when it looked like he'd worked it out, his forehead wrinkled a little. He looked up and down from the map and then into the space beyond them. 'I'm not sure,' he said, crawling in front of them and further away from the opening. 'But if the map is doing the correct then . . .'

He thumped his shoulder hard against the end of the crawl space. There was another rattling sound. Giseppi tapped the map happily against the wall, braced himself and thumped on the end of the space again. This time the shuddering was followed by a gentle creak. And a second metal panel rocked free.

'Nice,' said Giseppi, clambering through the opening. 'Very nice indeed.'

The others scuttled after him. 'Wow,' said Kassia, getting up. 'What is this place?'

'The Louvre,' said Giseppi.

Jed stood up too and looked around the huge room they'd entered. 'We're in the museum?' he said.

'Sort of,' said Giseppi, re-stowing the map in his bag. 'We're actually being under the Colonne de Juillet. Map says this is some sort of the storage room for exhibits.'

'So let's get out of here,' said Jed, moving to the front of the group and stepping out from behind a huge row of packing cases that were barring the way.

He lurched back again, just as quickly.

'What?' said Kassia.

'A problem,' he whispered.

They peered round the wall of cases. The view of the exit door was clear. But between that and them was a line of workers grouped round a long table. Ringing the table was a circle of ancient sarcophagi, each standing on end. A static procession of ancient coffins. One was empty. The workers watched as a woman wearing some sort of protective face-mask tended carefully to a bandage clad mummy.

'We can't risk it,' signed Jed, back behind the safety of the cases.

'But how come they didn't hear us,' signed Kassia. 'That door crashed down really loudly when it came free?'

Jed wasn't sure. He peered round the cases again. The answer was soon clear. 'Headphones in,' he said with his hands. 'Looks like someone is talking them through the work and what they are saying is being translated. Egyptian to French, I guess.'

'So?'

'So, they can't *hear* us,' Jed hissed. 'But they'll *see* us if we go piling past them.'

He rubbed his face with his hands. Beyond that door was freedom. But disturb these museum workers and they'd have the full weight of Louvre security called to deal with them.

Amelie had turned her back on him. Great. That was all they needed. Her having a strop about what to do next. But when Amelie turned, it was clear she wasn't angry or sulking.

'Up there,' she said, pointing to a metal grille just below the line of the ceiling. 'Leads into a metal ventilation tube, look.'

'And?'

'I am doing the thinking that it is wide enough to

88

crawl through,' she said.

Jed wasn't entirely happy about the idea of more crawling.

'Have you got another idea?' Amelie whispered huffily, clear that a strop wasn't altogether out of the question.

Jed didn't. But he had no idea how they would get up to the vent either. Amelie was ahead of him though. There was another row of packing cases, stacked by the wall below it. With a little bit of clever angling, they could make a sort of staircase which would take them directly up to the metal grille.

And the plan worked. Initially.

Amelie had climbed up first and the metal grille had been easy to remove. She'd hoisted herself into the crawl space and the others had followed. This time Jed was to be last. Waiting for the others to disappear made him anxious. And it made him careless.

He was on the top box. He was in reach of the shaft. All he had to do was take the final step. But having no shoes made the climbing awkward. His wet socks slipped on the final tread of the packing case. The tower of packing cases wobbled. Jed lurched backwards. Dante flung his arms out of the metal shaft and grabbed hold of Jed as he faltered. His foot slipped again. The packing case shook. It rocked. There was a moment as Jed straddled the opening to the hole and as Dante pulled him towards them that he thought they'd got away with it.

But the case rocked back again. A millimetre beyond its centre of gravity. A second longer than it should.

Then it fell. The tower of cases toppled and tumbled, crashing down hard into the opposite line of cases. But these cases were clearly empty and this made them so light that they scattered like dominoes. They crashed against the table. They hit the museum workers, felling them like skittles in a bowling alley. And they followed through so that the sarcophagi that lined the room fell too, turning and tumbling, splitting and splintering, as they crashed to the floor.

The last thing Jed saw as he plunged deep into the metal tubing of the ventilation shaft was a pile of Egyptian mummies sprawled amongst a group of screaming museum guides.

But he had no time to process the chaos. The line had stopped moving in front of him. 'Why have we stopped?' he yelled.

Amelie's voice drifted back. 'The shaft is blocked!'

'Well, unblock it then!' he yelled. 'It must go somewhere.'

There was a thumping noise. Yet more crunching of

metal. And then the sound of voices falling, carrying their owners with them.

Jed hurried after them.

Then he fell too.

And the stink that greeted him made it absolutely obvious which part of Paris's underground network they'd fallen into now.

Jed pulled himself to his feet and covered his nose with his hand and tried to choke back the nausea that surged inside him. 'You have *got* to be kidding me!'

Dante was gesticulating wildly. It was clear his language was as filthy as the sewer they'd landed in.

Amelie looked like she was going to pass out. Human waste hung from her skirt and was smeared on her face. Giseppi's long hair was caked in excrement.

Jed looked across at Kassia.

And she was laughing. 'My God. My mother would die down here,' she spluttered.

She wasn't wrong about that. The woman had had a fit about egg shells being placed in the wrong bin; she insisted shoes deemed clean enough to wear in an operating theatre were stored on sheets of plastic in her home and she never went anywhere without a bottle of hand sanitiser. If she saw her daughter covered in the contents of the toilet system of Paris, it was true she'd probably have a heart attack right there and then.

Jed was just contemplating this fact when he noticed that Kassia had stopped laughing.

Instead she was holding her arm out and pointing.

Jed was aware of a grinding noise behind him. Metal against stone. And as he turned he began to understand why the noise was getting louder by the second.

Behind them, moving forward in the sewer tunnel, was an enormous metal ball. It was twice the height of a person and so wide that it touched the walls, grinding against them. It filled every inch of space as it careered towards them, crushing and clearing the waste in its path.

'What is that?' yelled Amelie.

'Some sort of filtering thing,' Jed yelled back. 'Used to get rid of blockages.'

And as he turned to run towards her and away from the advancing ball, it dawned on everyone that the blockage the enormous ball was destined to clear from the sewers at the moment was ... them!

It was difficult to run. Water and excrement splashed on their legs. Debris drifted in waves in the wake of the advancing metal ball. And the rumbling got louder and louder. The gap between them and the ball was shrinking. It was bearing down on them and there was no way of escaping its path.

'I can't outrun it,' screamed Kassia, grabbing for Jed's hand.

'We have to! Come on!'

But the water was getting deeper. The ball getting closer. The sides of the tunnel closing in.

Suddenly, Dante veered to the left. He flung out his hand to stop the others passing and pulled them towards him into a small alcove built into the wall.

'Breathe in,' yelled Giseppi. But there wasn't room. The ball was metres away. Jed pressed his back against the alcove. It wasn't deep enough. They were going to be crushed. Smeared like human waste along the wall of the sewer.

Jed tightened his grip on Kassia's hand. He pressed his back harder against the alcove. Tried to pull his stomach in. But there wasn't room. The ball had been designed to press against the wall. There was no margin of error. No place to hide.

Then, with a shudder, the wall gave way behind them and the crushing ball pummelled past.

It took several moments before any of them felt brave enough to say anything.

'Did that just really happen?' Amelie said, pulling herself up from the ground, her skirt still dripping.

Jed gagged again with the smell. It was great they hadn't been pulverised, but he was pretty sure that if they didn't get out of here quickly they'd be overcome with fumes. The space they'd fallen into reeked of oil and cleaning fluid.

But he couldn't stand up. Here, it was shallower than the section of quarry they'd clambered through earlier. Pipes and cables pressed down on them now, just like the metal ball had borne down on them earlier, and the only way to move forward was to slither on your stomach like a snake.

Jed ducked his head and began to drag himself along. His elbows dug into the ground. His torch caught again on the overhead piping. The pipes rattled and thrummed with the noise of whatever was surging through them. Cables dragged downwards, sparking every now and then as they moved past. The relief of not being crushed evaporated. If they weren't careful, there was a very good chance they'd be electrocuted.

But beyond the piping and the cabling, Jed could see another doorway. He gestured with his hand so the others kept moving in his direction. Then he thumped the door open and crawled into the space beyond.

The room was empty. And silent.

There was no machinery, no furniture, no pipework. The walls were covered in large white tiles and here and there messages had been scrawled in graffiti. Apart from that, the space was bare. Jed shivered. It was eerily and unnaturally cold.

He looked across at Giseppi for explanation. 'La Cage aux Fous,' Giseppi said quietly.

'What's one of them?' asked Kassia.

'It means cage for the crazy. We must be underneath Sainte Anne hospital and this is where they did the locking up of dangerous patients.'

Jed felt another wave of nausea but it had nothing to do with the stench of the sewers this time.

They walked around in silence. Doors led from empty space to empty space. 'How many people did they keep down here?' Jed said.

'I guess they thought there was a lot of danger,' said Amelie.

'Look,' said Kassia, leading the way into the final room. This one was not empty. Instead, shelves were stacked with clothes, and a row of showers lined the walls.

Giseppi nodded. 'I guess we should do the taking of the time to wash away the filth,' he said. 'I think we will be safe for a while. No one will follow us here.'

And Jed was pretty sure that this was true. Of

all the places in the underground, this one scared him the most.

'Let's get cleaned up and come up with a plan,' he said.

Kassia let the water from the shower pummel down on to her. It was cold. This didn't matter. She wasn't sure she'd ever feel clean again.

The clothes from the shelves were old and threadbare. She didn't want to think about who had worn them before. Like the clothes she'd worn months earlier in the death wagon, she knew the stories woven into the cloth could not be happy ones. And the thin fabric did little to stop her shaking.

Jed was sitting with his back against the tiled wall. He tried to smile when he saw her, but it was clear that his face wasn't doing as he wanted it to.

She sank down to sit beside him, twisting her wet hair into a knot. It dripped down her back. 'This is a terrible place,' she said quietly.

'At least we're safe here for a while,' he said, but she knew that he agreed with her.

Their legs were so close together they were almost touching. Kassia didn't pull away.

'Everyone thought Bergier was mad because he said I could live for ever,' Jed said without turning to face her. 'Do you think they ever kept him in a place like this?'

'It's not your fault, Jed.'

'And what about the mess we're in now?'

'Hey, I feel pretty clean after that shower,' she tried to joke. He gave her a half smile in return and she let her leg rest against his now. 'None of this is your fault either. We're in this together. You can't blame yourself.'

She fiddled with the cuff of the shirt she was wearing. The material was itchy on her skin. 'Anyway,' she said, directing her words to her sleeve, 'if this is anyone's fault, it's mine.'

'How d'you work that one out?' said Jed.

'NOAH. Being in the tunnels. D'you think I gave something away when I was talking to Nat?' She lowered her hands and rested them on her knees.

'If you did lead them here, then it was worth it,' Jed said quietly.

'Really?'

'I was drowning, Kass. You taking me to see Bergier kind of saved me.'

A smile flickered on her lips. 'But it meant NOAH found out where we were hiding and led to all this.'

He rested his hand on his leg and his little finger

was almost close enough to link round hers. He kept looking forward. 'You did what you had to, Kass. And so we're on the run again. But at least we're not sitting still any more.'

She wanted to thank him. But she said nothing. Instead, her little finger brushed his and he smiled.

'And so?' he said at last. 'What do we do now?'

'We find a way out of here,' she said quietly.

Giseppi had been the last to shower, but after he'd joined them again, he unfurled the map and spread it as flat as he could on the ground. Kassia watched as he traced with his finger the route they'd taken across the underground of the city. The Court of Miracles seemed miles away, and in fact, she could see now that it really was. They'd done well to put so much distance between them and where NOAH had obviously been searching. But they were trapped. In a cage for the mad. And now they needed to find a way to escape.

'We have, what you say, backed ourselves into a corner,' said Giseppi, looking up from the map apologetically.

Great, Kassia said silently to herself. He scared them half to death with stories about getting lost in the tunnels; he'd made them crawl through a wind tunnel, swim in a sewer and eskimo roll under live electric cables and now he was telling them they weren't any closer to being free.

'We could do the going back the way we've come,' he said half-heartedly. 'Just hope the canal is empty and try somehow to get up to those manhole covers and do the climbing into the street.'

This didn't sound like the most thorough of plans as far as Kassia was concerned. She couldn't help thinking that if her mother had been here, there would have been a colour-coded chart of options and some sort of spreadsheet to organise the strategy. She smiled as she thought about that, and then she remembered the sewers, and the thought of her mother's reaction to having to swim through human excrement reminded her that even her mother might not have had a colour-coded chart to cover this scenario.

'There is another way,' said Giseppi. 'It's harder, but the chances of doing the escape are much better. You'd get much further away from the centre of Paris and so probably out of range of the NOAH more quickly. But there is, with this plan, a risk. And a, how do you say, *adaption* to our arrangement.'

'So you're going to explain that then,' said Jed impatiently.

Giseppi pointed at the map. 'Just to the left of us

here are two areas that are the being vital to the living of Paris,' he said, almost proudly. 'They give Paris its water and they do the keeping of the time.'

Kassia was vaguely interested, but she didn't quite understand why they needed to know this or how it would help them.

Giseppi drew a circle with his finger on the map. 'Time chamber,' he said. 'ITA.'

Another collection of letters like the ones he'd used for the Freedom Fighters Office. He obviously had a thing about them.

'International Atomic Time,' he said when it was clear that no one knew what he was on about. 'There is a chamber.' He drew the circle on the map again. 'And they keep atomic clocks there. Use them for the basis of the Universal Time. There's even a nineteenth-century clock in the chamber and this they have the name of the Time Keeper. Time around the world is being based on the clocks stored here.'

'Time is based on clocks kept in sewers?' said Jed.

Giseppi looked slightly annoyed. 'Underground, yes, but not in sewers. The clocks are kept out of contamination so the timing can be always be the accurate. That is where our risk comes in.' He didn't stop yet to explain. 'People are careful with time. Make decisions based on time. It does the controlling of all

100

things.' He looked across again at Jed. 'You of all the peoples should know this, Fulcanelli.'

Jed's face coloured a little. Kassia wasn't sure if it was due to embarrassment or anger but she didn't have time to work this out before Giseppi continued. 'I think the plan that is the best for you, is to do the entering of the Time Chamber.'

'And then?' pressed Kassia, keen to get to the idea of risk Giseppi was so clearly avoiding.

'Beyond the Time Chamber is the entrance to the Reservoir of Montsouris,' said Giseppi, widening the circle on the map. 'If you can get through the Time Chamber and into the reservoir that does the supplying of water for so much of Paris, then you will have the exit, here.' He jabbed the map and smiled decisively.

It sounded like a good plan to Kassia. No quarries, no sewers, just a few clocks and a load of clean water. 'So what's the catch?' she said at last.

Giseppi looked awkward. 'The Chamber is a controlled environment. Doing the bursting in there and you will trigger alarms.'

This didn't sound like a great idea. The whole point of coming this deep underground was to make their exit as discreet as possible, not to sound a warning for NOAH about where they were.

'But I have the idea.'

Kassia leant forward to hear more clearly, flexing her fingers to make sure she'd be able to sign quickly for Dante to keep up.

'We have to do the separating now,' said Giseppi.

'Hold on,' said Kassia. 'You said we were to stick together.'

'That was then,' said Giseppi. 'Now we need the having of another plan.'

Kassia did not feel good about this. When they'd separated at Notre Dame all sorts of awful things had happened.

'Amelie and I stay and take responsibility for the alarm. It should then do the distracting for your exit.'

'What will happen to you?' Dante was signing wildly and Kassia was surprised that he seemed so desperately keen not to split up. But the way her brother was looking across at Amelie made it suddenly clear why. How could she have been so stupid? Three months underground and she'd been so worried about Jed she hadn't really wondered about why Dante and Amelie were always together. She could have kicked herself for not working it out sooner. But Giseppi was clearly oblivious as well. The looks that were being passed between Amelie and Dante required no sign language to translate them. Giseppi was ploughing on regardless in his attempt to explain.

'We will be arrested, probably. They'll presume we are the law breakers who did the entering of the underground city for the thrill.'

'And then what?' urged Dante, hardly able to hide his horror.

'A fine, maybe,' said Giseppi. 'I have the lots of money.' And with that he drew a neatly packaged plastic envelope from the bottom of his bag. It was bulging with bank notes. Jed was sure he'd never seen so much cash. 'But we will take the custodial sentence because the money should be yours.' He handed it over to Jed.

'What?' Jed fumbled the money awkwardly. 'We can't take this.'

'You must,' said Giseppi. 'Use it to do the buying of your airline tickets out of Paris.'

'But . . .'

'You must go to Bernard Ruan,' Giseppi continued. 'He's on l'avenue Reille. He will arrange everything. Papers. The transport. All you need.'

'Why are you doing this?' pressed Jed.

Giseppi took a deep breath. 'Because, Fulcanelli, I always knew my grandfather wasn't mad. And you've done the proving of it for me.' He shook himself a little as if he was determined to go on without allowing his voice to waver. 'His work is complete now. And if I have failed to help you to do the finding of the elixir then at least I can help you find your freedom to keep doing the looking.' He tapped the shoulder of his arm, the tattoo hidden by his sleeve. 'As a Brother of Heliopolis I'm honoured to have served you. And I believe there will be other Brothers out there, waiting to do the helpings too. If you are lucky enough to find them.'

Jed closed his hand around the plastic wallet. Then he took Giseppi's hand and shook it hard.

Giseppi nodded his thanks and rolled up the map. 'Now go,' he said. 'That Chamber might control time, but it does not do the meaning that time is unlimited.'

A corridor of white tiles led eventually to an ordinary looking wooden door. There was a glass panel making it possible to see the room beyond. It was bare of furniture apart from six wooden crates. Sitting on each crate was a metal box about the size of a shoe box, each covered with an array of levers and dials. Jed supposed these were the atomic clocks Giseppi had told them about. In the corner of the room, fixed to the wall, was a bronze-coloured cylindrical machine, attached to wires and cabling. This, unlike the silver boxes, had an actual clock face. The Time Keeper, Jed reasoned. Somehow, the thought of time being managed in such a clinical setting made him want to laugh. It looked so simple and ordered and safe. As he peered through the glass, it misted with the traces of his breath. When he stepped away, the glass looked smeary.

Behind him, Dante was hugging Amelie goodbye; Kassia was saying thank you to Giseppi. He could see Kassia searching for the right words, and this time it wasn't the fact that Giseppi spoke a different language that was making it so difficult. How did she thank him when he'd done so much to help? And how did anyone say goodbye when they didn't want to?

Jed couldn't believe it had come to this so quickly. For three months he'd believed the pair who'd led them to safety on *The Phoenix* train would be able to give them answers. And here they were looking at time marching on relentlessly with order and precision, and they had hardly come any closer to answers at all.

He hugged Amelie awkwardly after she'd peeled herself away from Dante, and then he shook Giseppi's hand again. He wanted to say something sensible, meaningful or important. But any words he had were clogging his throat and making it impossible to swallow, let alone speak. Giseppi nodded as if Jed had managed to deliver a message that was coherent and made perfect sense. Then he gestured towards the Time Chamber.

'There's an alarm,' he said, 'but you have to do the ignoring and keep moving. Beyond the Chamber, if the map is being correct, you'll do the finding of the entrance to the reservoir.'

'*If* the map's correct?' stuttered Jed.

The yes and no movement of Giseppi's head again. The shark tooth necklace bounced at the base of his neck. 'I'm thinking any guards alerted by an alarm will come through the hospital. It looks like the quickest entry point for them.'

'Looks like?'

'So it is important you do the keeping going.' He rubbed his hands together as if he was planning a Sunday afternoon tea party, not the breaking and entering of some secure scientific environment which he was actively hoping would lead to his arrest.

Jed glanced across at Kassia. She nodded. And then Dante turned to join them, his hand lingering for a second in Amelie's before he pulled away.

Jed thumped hard on the door of the Time Chamber.

Three shoulder barges later, the door had split from it hinges. The alarm was ripping the air apart and the lights on the ceiling were flashing red.

'Shame we've messed with time,' Jed shouted as he raced through the Chamber, but somehow, even to him, the words didn't seem funny.

Giseppi had said to keep going. So they did.

Beyond the room of atomic clocks was another corridor and this one snaked back and forth until it opened up into a wider space and a set of double doors. Jed braced himself to shoulder barge these open too, but there was no resistance this time as the doors weren't locked. He staggered forward, the weight of the rucksack on his back forcing him to stumble. The doors swung open, and he found himself on a high stone balcony. Kassia and Dante burst through to stand beside him. Behind them, the alarm still screeched and the air flashed red. Jed supposed the guards had reached Giseppi and Amelie. He prayed they would convince them they were alone. But as he looked down from the balcony, he realised that there was something else he should probably start praying about.

They'd certainly reached the reservoir. Below the balcony, a great pool of water stretched in front of them. Above, domed and arched ceilings spread across the indoor lake like the roof of a huge cathedral. The water went on and on. Jed could barely see the end. Neither could he see any way down from the balcony.

No stairs, no ladders, nothing.

'What d'we do?' yelped Kassia, glancing behind her.

There was only one answer.

Kassia was shaking her head. 'I can't! I can't!'

Dante was peering over the edge of the balcony. 'We have to. It looks deep enough.'

Kassia shook her head again. 'You think it's *good* that it's deep,' she yelled with her hands.

Jed was beginning to panic. Supposing the guards didn't believe Giseppi and Amelie were alone? Supposing they were after them now, metres beyond the double doors?

Jed grabbed Kassia's hand. 'Do you trust me?' he yelled.

'Yes. But . . .'

That was all he needed. He clambered up on to the wall of the balcony and reached back his hand. Kassia grabbed hold, reaching for Dante's hand too. The three of them stood on the edge of the wall, facing the water. 'Ready?' Jed said.

He didn't wait for her to answer. He stepped forward and Kassia and Dante followed. Hand in hand, the three of them plunged into the water.

The water was so cold it took Jed's breath away. He lost all sense of orientation. Kassia's hand slipped from his. He kicked and fought to get to the surface. The memories from the Thames and the Neckar pressing in on his chest so that he was sure his lungs would tear. And then, when he burst through the surface, only Dante had come up for air before him.

Jed turned and struggled in the water, spluttering Kassia's name.

Had she hurt herself, been pulled down too deep? He spun round in the water, kicking wildly. 'Kassia!'

Suddenly the surface shattered. She punched up through the water, spluttering and coughing. He grabbed on to her and they kicked water together to keep afloat.

'I've got you,' he breathed into her hair.

She could only cough in answer as he steered her forward, following Dante's lead.

The water stretched on and on, under the canopy of stone, but it was clear that Dante had seen something. He was ploughing ahead, checking now and then that they followed.

At the edge of the great lake, a flight of metal stairs was attached to the wall. Dante climbed up it, turning to help Kassia. The water dripped from Jed as he clambered out last and the rush of cold air made him shiver.

The steps led to a swing screen like an oversized cat-flap which swung into place as soon as they'd climbed through. There was another set of steps which took them down into a second chamber. This one was totally empty. A vast overflow space with thick stone walls, totally separate now from the manmade lake behind them.

Jed jumped the last two steps and looked around.

The sound of his feet on the stone echoed.

In front of them, a metal doorway led to an exit.

'You OK?' he asked.

Kassia nodded in reply as Dante waited for them to catch up with him. But then they stood completely still.

Jed was suddenly aware of a creaking noise. The metal door to the exit was being lowered.

The three of them raced towards it but it crashed to the ground before they could reach it, sealing the chamber completely.

But the creaking continued. The door was not the only thing that had started to move.

The noise was a turning of giant gears, perhaps. Jed looked up at the ceiling. Above them was a vast line of metal-headed sprinklers. They had started to rotate. A single drop of water splashed down on his face. He wiped it away. Another, this time on his shoulder. Then one more.

And then, suddenly, a great gush of water deluged down from above. Sprinklers on the walls began to throw water towards them. Water streamed from every direction.

Jed sloshed across the once empty chamber, searching desperately for another exit. Kassia and Dante scrabbled at the flap they'd clambered through from the indoor lake, but some sort of suction system was sealing the flap closed from the other side. There was no returning that way. The metal door barred the only other exit. And as far as Jed could see, there was no other way out anywhere!

In seconds the water was up to their waists. Then shoulders. They fought to keep standing but the onslaught was so intense that before long they were floating – fighting to keep upright as the water churned around them.

And as the water rose, the ceiling got closer and closer.

'There must be a way out,' Kassia spluttered.

Jed couldn't see one.

There wasn't a section of the walls or ceiling from which water wasn't pouring.

Except one!

Dante saw it first, and waved his arm wildly in its direction. An overflow pipe, Jed presumed, high up in the far corner of the chamber.

He battled his way towards it, the surging water

pummelling his shoulders. The gap between his head and the ceiling shrinking by the second.

'We don't know where it goes!' yelled Kassia, spluttering as she fought to keep her head above the water.

'We don't have a choice!' yelled back Jed.

Dante churned through the water beside them, grabbing hold of the edge of the pipe and clambering into its opening. He reached out his hand and dragged Kassia towards him. Her hand slipped free. She sank below the water. Jed plunged down and pushed her upwards. He felt a fierce tugging on his shoulder, but his focus was on Kassia and steering her towards her brother.

Kassia grabbed Dante's hand and scrabbled on to the lip of the pipe, slithering beside him and then out of sight into the depths of the plumbing.

The water level was edging close to the opening. If Jed didn't clamber through now, the pipe would be filled with water and he wouldn't be able to breathe. But in diving down to rescue Kassia, Jed's bag had been ripped from his shoulder. The money they needed for escape was floating away. Though if he didn't make it through the pipe, the money would be useless anyway.

Jed looked from the pipe to the bag which bobbed

out of reach behind him just under the surface. The bag was getting heavier. It was going to sink completely! Reaching the bag would take precious seconds. Seconds Jed wasn't sure he had.

Jed took the deepest breath he could, dived under the water, flinging his hands out wildly. He couldn't see the bag. He had no idea where it was. He'd wasted time for nothing.

And then, his hand caught on the strap.

His chest was burning. He fought to find the edge of the pipe. His hands slipped. His feet scraped against the wall.

And then with one last enormous heave, he flung himself into the opening of the pipe and slithered through, dragging the water-logged bag behind him.

The pipe ran like a water slide. Jed dragged himself along on his stomach, the bag back on his shoulder, thumping and grinding into the roof of the pipe as he moved.

Suddenly, without any warning, the pipe dipped down.

Jed tumbled forward, sliding and slipping until he landed in another pool of water.

Dante and Kassia were bobbing beside him. But this time they weren't alone.

The pool was full of fish.

'Why?' Jed yelled.

'A way of testing how clean it is?' suggested Kassia, treading water frantically.

'Well, the results aren't good,' said Jed urgently. When he'd recovered enough from the fall from the pipe to steady himself in the water, it became totally clear to him that all the fish in the pool had one thing in common. They were dead. Somehow, whatever the three of them had done to the water flow had not worked out well for the marine life.

Kassia thrashed her way through the water, fish unmoving in her wake.

Things might be over for the fish, but Jed saw a glimmer of hope in front of him. A spiral staircase in the corner of the pool wound upwards and out of the reservoir. And above it, now the only obstacle between them and the streets of Paris, was a glass skylight.

And better than that, a section of the skylight was propped open. A doorway to freedom was finally within their reach.

PÂTISSERIE DU PARADIS
RUE DU SUCRE
75117 PARIS

CAFÉ AU LAIT
CAFÉ AU LAIT
PÂTE À CHOUX
MILLE-FEUILLE

€3
€3
€4
€5

June 29th 1927

DAY 216
1st October

'How could you have let this happen?'

To say that Montgomery was unhappy was a little bit like saying snowmen aren't that keen on heatwaves. The man cracked his walking cane through the air like a whip then banged it down on the table. 'Too late! Always too late!'

Victor couldn't argue with the man's reasoning. It did seem they had a pretty disastrous record with regards to actually catching up with Fulcanelli and bringing him in.

'To be fair,' cut in Cole, 'there's a whole city's worth of hiding places underground. They were needles in a haystack, sir.'

Montgomery took the newspaper from the table and tossed it irritably through the air.

Victor caught the pages and held them crumpled against him. He didn't need to see the pictures. The story had been on the television news all morning. Dead fish in the reservoir, suggesting the water of Paris was contaminated, tended to make headline news. And that was without the total chaos caused because the environment which housed the atomic clocks had been messed with. Time itself had to be reset. Montgomery was not the only one in Paris who had reason to be angry.

But it did seem likely he was the only one who was unable to calm down.

Victor and Cole had been trying to pull out some positives from the situation and had been failing miserably. 'At least we've flushed them out, sir,' Victor said hopefully, with hardly any emphasis on the pun. 'Forcing them up for air might make them easier to catch in the long run.'

'And there's something else,' offered Cole, grabbing the newspaper from Victor and sneering at him dismissively. 'The cataphiles they arrested.'

Victor wasn't sure what that word meant but he knew it was some sort of term the authorities used for anyone who went underground in Paris without permission.

Montgomery stopped his pacing. 'The girl and the

boy who'd gone into the catacombs for a dare, you mean?'

Cole flicked through the paper to find the page he needed. 'There's something interesting about them, look.'

Victor didn't say a word but he failed to see how anything could really be more interesting than a boy who could live for ever. And they'd had one of those and let him go.

'The name's Bergier,' said Cole smugly.

Victor had to concede this *was* quite interesting. The months of research Montgomery had made him do on the Brothers of Heliopolis had certainly focused quite a lot on that name. Some poor mad man who'd died decades ago, after rambling about the elixir of life.

'Track down all friends, relatives and associates of this Bergier guy from the catacombs,' said Montgomery, his anger suddenly channelled towards forming a plan. 'Check out all the places the boy might have visited in the last year. Come up with a list of his favourite haunts.'

'You think there's a definite link?' asked Victor, cautiously.

'If there is, then you better make sure you find it,' said Montgomery, pressing the newspaper back against Victor's stomach.

It took a while for Victor to catch his breath and by the time he had, Montgomery had left the room.

DAY 217

2nd October

It had been three days since the escape from the reservoir.

It turned out that Bernard Ruan ran a very nice twenty-four-hour café with rooms to rent on l'avenue Reille and he was totally happy to do anything to help out his friend Giseppi Bergier, especially when he saw the enormous wad of soggy cash that Jed produced from his rather battered rucksack.

He'd given them three rooms in the attic area over the café and for a while all Jed could do was sleep. Now all he could do was eat. It felt like he hadn't had any real food for months, apart from the custard slice in the café with Kassia, which seemed stolen somehow from someone else's lifetime. Maybe things tasted better when they weren't eaten underground.

They used a table at the back of the café. It seemed

that despite being popular with those on the run from NOAH, hardly anyone else chose to eat here, so there was plenty of space to chomp their way through croissants, and try and come up with a plan.

The few books on alchemy they had salvaged from the Court of Miracles took a while to dry after their dunking in the reservoir. Their pages curled and puckered, but Jed was determined not to give up on finding the answers somewhere inside. Bernard Ruan had promised to arrange plane tickets for them to any destination. The problem was, that despite their efforts to pore over the books with renewed determination, they still had no idea where they should go.

Kassia had taken Bergier's cryptic message and dried that out on the radiator before tacking it to the wall above the table they worked at. '*Phoenix Man. Hidden church resting on the border of two worlds. Emerald Tablet.*' There seemed to be three parts to this puzzle.

Jed stared at the message morosely. Worse than having no idea where to go, they had no clue what Bergier's message meant either.

Suddenly, Dante walked into the café and slid into the seat next to them. He had a newspaper under his arm. 'You were careful, right?' signed Kassia.

'No.' He dropped the newspaper on to the table

making it possible to sign. 'I was ridiculously dangerous. I made a spectacle so everyone could see and drew as much attention to myself as possible.' He pulled a face worth a wealth of signs. '*Of course* I was careful.'

Kassia winced in apology. Jed couldn't blame her for being on edge. The longer they sat here waiting for answers, the greater the chance of being discovered by NOAH.

Dante grabbed the paper in an effort to avoid the awkward glare from his sister and flicked through the pages, with a speed that suggested he couldn't possibly be reading, but was just making a point.

Suddenly, the pages stopped turning. Dante pressed the newspaper down on to the table and poked at the photograph spread across the page. 'What does it say?' he signed.

Jed pulled the page round so he could see it more clearly. The photograph showed the Time Chamber, the atomic clocks highlighted with a separate picture of the bronze-coloured Time Keeper. The article, as far as he could make out, was talking about the problems involved in resetting the clocks. Seemed time was so sensitive it was dangerous to mess about with it. The irony wasn't lost on him and he did well not to laugh.

But the rest of the story wasn't so funny.

It mentioned Giseppi and Amelie and it explained they'd been taken into custody. Jed mumbled the details awkwardly and let Kassia turn them into sign. He didn't dare look up and see how Dante was taking the news, but it soon became clear from the way Dante shuffled violently beside him that the article had not gone down well.

'They risked everything,' Dante said eventually with his hands. 'Swam through sewage, went to prison. For what exactly? So we could sit here eating pastries?'

Jed folded the newspaper and, as if desperate for distraction, Dante grabbed one of the books from the table, stood up and began to pace.

Jed shot a glance at Kassia. He didn't need sign language to convey to her that he had no idea what to say.

Suddenly, the book Dante had taken thudded back on to the table. Jed supposed Dante had discarded it in annoyance, but the way he was smoothing the pages and angling the text directly under Jed's gaze suggested he wasn't dismissing the text. He wanted Jed to see it.

Jed lifted the book and peered in closely. 'The Emerald Tablet?' he breathed softly.

The picture was pencil-drawn. An artist's impression. 'It says here,' Jed went on, 'that this Tablet was some sort of emerald stone with writing on, which held the secret of transmutation.'

Kassia looked confused.

'Change,' signed Dante. 'You know. Of the Philosopher's Stone to the elixir of life.'

'Great,' said Kassia. 'We kind of got that. Jed must have used this tablet thing to help him with the recipe.'

Dante pulled a face. 'Well, it says here where the Tablet thing was initially discovered.'

Kassia waited.

'Turkey.'

Jed flicked through the pages of the book. 'That's great!' he said more loudly. 'Because look at this.' He put the book back on the table so that both of them could see. 'A cathedral.'

'Notre Dame?' asked Kassia.

Jed shook his head.

'St Paul's, then?'

Jed tapped the open page of the book. 'No. But there *is* a link to both.' He spoke the rest of his sentence more quietly. 'And to Zoe.' Again, it didn't seem sensible to look up and see how this statement had gone down. 'Great work, Dante,' he said in a transparent attempt to shift the focus. 'This church is on the border of two worlds. I reckon you could be on to something.'

126

Kassia grabbed the book from the table. 'You know where we're going then?'

Jed nodded. 'Yep. I know exactly where.'

DAY 218

3rd October

'Well it's so nice for the old man to have visitors,' the nurse said enthusiastically. 'I'm always sent to show round the English visitors. I was born in Croydon, you see. You're the second lot to visit him in less than a week.'

Victor looked across knowingly at Cole as they followed the nurse down the corridor. Victor felt uncomfortable. The smell of the nursing home reminded him of Etkin House, and anything that took him back to memories of his time in a care home churned his stomach. There was a pungent whiff of artificial air freshener, failing miserably to hide less pleasant smells.

'You have the names of the others who visited?' asked Cole.

The nurse hesitated for a moment. 'I'm not at

liberty to say,' she said, and grinned rather smugly, as if chuffed with herself for following official regulations. 'His grandson just said the boy was an old friend, which I thought was a little odd at the time as he looked under twenty.' Her face suddenly rushed with colour. 'The old guy seemed to respond nicely, though, but now, well, you'll see for yourself.'

Victor stared across the room to the oversized bed in the window. A man who looked to be at least one hundred was propped up on a tower of cushions and pillows. He was staring at the window but his eyes were so milky white it was clear he couldn't possibly see anything with them.

The nurse stepped awkwardly from foot to foot, and then moved back into the corridor, pulling the door to. 'I'll give you a few minutes alone,' she said.

Cole strode round by the bed. He lifted a framed picture from the cabinet and then put it back dismissively. He pulled open the bedside drawer and rummaged inside.

'Should you be doing that?' Victor hissed.

'What? You think we actually came here for a chat with the geezer?' Cole snorted. 'Get looking, Viccy boy. We have ground to make up with Montgomery.'

Victor peered around the room. 'Do we have any idea what we're searching for, exactly?' he pressed.

Cole slammed a sock drawer shut and looked up. 'Nope. No clue at all.'

'Great.' Victor scanned the wall unit. There were books, more photos, a scrapbook, tucked on the highest shelf. Victor hesitated before he reached for it, but the old man in the bed was snoring now so it seemed safe to have a look.

He was just flicking through the pages, covered with newspaper clippings and photos, when the quiet was shattered by the sound of a phone ringing. Cole scrabbled in his pocket and took out his mobile.

Victor could only hear one side of the conversation. There were lots of 'ahhas', 'OKs' and 'rights' and then he hung up. 'Let's get going, Hot Shot,' Cole said, slamming the cupboard shut.

'What was that, then?' said Victor, pointing to the phone.

'Consulate services. They've found security footage of three travellers at Charles de Gaulle airport.'

'Fulcanelli and his friends?'

Cole grimaced. 'Of course Fulcanelli and his friends. You think Interpol would be interested in the holiday plans of your great aunt Ethel and her knitting circle?'

'I was just wondering . . .'

'The images are already hours old,' Cole interrupted.

'That's going to make Montgomery even angrier than he was. But at least we have some sort of fix on them.' The tails of his leather coat skirted the edge of the old man's bed as he moved. 'So put that down,' he said, waving at the scrapbook. 'Old time memories aren't going to help us now. We've got real live people to track.'

Victor flipped the scrapbook closed and slid it back into position on the shelf, then he nodded at the old man in the bed and followed Cole out into the corridor.

CHRISTOPHER WREN, LORENZO GAFÀ

PARIS — La Tour Eiffel
le Panoramique

DEPART

BRILLANT

DAY 220

5th October

Kassia felt a bead of sweat trickle down the back of her neck, between her shoulder blades and towards her waist. The city was humming, her ears throbbed with the sound of traffic and people, and her eyes blinked against the flashes of light from the river that curved its way past them. They certainly weren't in Paris any more!

'Well, this is it then,' signed Dante. 'The border of two worlds.' He pointed backwards and forwards across the river. 'Europe one side and Asia the other.'

Kassia screwed up her eyes again, against the light. Months of hiding underground in Paris had failed to prepare her for the colours and sounds of Istanbul and she was totally overwhelmed. She hadn't been prepared for the smells either: sweet pomegranate juice, fish being cooked by the side of the river and warm bread rolls that were being carried through the streets on large wooden trays and sold to passers-by.

'River's called the Bosphorus,' said Dante, spelling out each letter of the name.

'Ooh, I read about Lord Byron swimming that,' said Kassia. 'He said it was his biggest achievement.'

'Kind of weird for a guy who wrote so many poems,' said Jed. 'But hey, good for him. How d'you know that anyway?'

'Guess it must have been on one of my mum's reading lists sometime,' she said, and for just a moment the excitement of being in the city of a country she'd never visited before dulled a little.

'Hey, come on,' interrupted Dante. 'I don't think we're going to get any answers about the elixir of life standing outside a church discussing poetry, do you?'

Kassia shook herself and tried to push away the worry about what her mum would make of all this. Somehow coming to Turkey seemed an even bigger step than anywhere else they'd been, and of course, it was just the three of them now. Her mum would be having a meltdown. This time they'd sent her and Nat a coded message. There was no way they could risk Skyping again.

'So this church then,' said Dante. 'Hardly hidden, is it? I'd pretty much say that this is one of the most beautiful and biggest churches in the world.'

Kassia looked up behind her. It would have taken someone very brave to disagree.

It was hard for Kassia to get her head round quite how amazing the building of the Hagia Sophia was. A huge central dome seemed to float above four enormous stone archways. Around the dome stretched a ribbon of windows. Other domes surrounded the main one and four tall minarets pierced the sky like giant spears. The whole place was enormous. More like a fabulous estate than just one building.

'Is it a church though?' asked Dante, as they hurried up the stairs towards it. 'Don't those tall towers make it a mosque?'

'That's the point,' laughed Jed, his stride widening as they got closer, as if demonstrating his urgency to get inside. 'The Hagia Sophia isn't actually a church *or* a mosque.'

Kassia was struggling to keep up, not only with Jed and her brother but also with the way the conversation was going. The bead of sweat soaked into the waistband of her jeans. She swept her hair behind her shoulders in a futile attempt to keep cool.

'It's a museum,' explained Jed. 'At least, it is now. Before that, it was a mosque and so they added the minarets. But before that, it was a cathedral. So, you could say the church is pretty hidden. Which,' he added with a grin, 'is why we're here.'

It took them ages to work their way through the crowds and get to the door. As soon as they were inside, Kassia felt her breath draining away. She spun around on the spot, her head lifted, trying to take in the majesty of what she saw. The ceiling of the dome seemed impossibly high and she couldn't work out how the whole weight of the canopy didn't come crashing down on them. It seemed to be resting on four enormous buttresses and it didn't look possible that these pillars wouldn't collapse and allow the roof to cave in.

Light flooded through the band of windows in the dome, giving the whole interior a warm coppery glow. The floor was amber marble, and pillars down the edge of either side held up beautiful balconies with intricate wrought iron railings that ran the length of the building. Colossal round black discs attached to the walls, decorated with golden Islamic lettering which gave away the building's past as a mosque. The higher walls and ceilings were painted in layered gold and intricate interconnected geometric designs.

People stood, faces upturned, to take in the beauty. Voices were hushed, movement slow, the frantic speed of the city totally slowed down here.

Dante's signing of the word 'beautiful' didn't have the strength to cover it, but signs felt better than spoken words somehow, as if strings of sounds wouldn't be enough.

Kassia wondered what sort of people came here. And she wondered if anyone ever got to a point where the magnificence of the place seemed ordinary.

She was particularly interested in a line of people stretched silently waiting, heads bowed as if they were in prayer.

'What are they doing?' she whispered to Jed.

Jed flicked through the guidebook he'd bought with their entry ticket. Giseppi had been more than generous with the funds, so they had lot of money even after their flights had been arranged.

'Erm, something to do with that pillar,' said Jed, pointing, and then reading more from the guidebook. 'Apparently this guy Emperor Justinian rested his aching head against the damp stone of the pillar one time.'

'And?' This still didn't make sense of the queue.

'Says here that he was instantly cured of his headache. So that's what everyone in the line is hoping for, I guess. A cure for something.'

Kassia shuffled her feet awkwardly. Another bead of sweat rolled down her back. 'If only finding our answer was as simple as looking up at some pillar inside a cathedral, hey?'

Jed closed the guidebook. 'Yep. If only.'

'Come on,' said Dante, who'd obviously completely missed the conversation, having spent the last few minutes gawping at the splendour of the space around him. 'We need to get serious about finding answers, so what exactly are we looking for here?'

'The Phoenix Man,' Kassia said in words and sign, and then she led the way deeper into the ancient cathedral.

Under the sweep of the great dome, Jed could see enormous painted pictures. There was one on each wall, just like there'd been a single word painted on each side of the domed ceiling in the museum of alchemy in Prague. Fire, earth, air and water. No words this time though. On the edge of each sweeping archway was a picture of what looked like a man, but each one was covered in feathers.

'What *are* they?' signed Dante.

Jed had to finger spell the word as there was no way he'd learnt the sign for 'seraphim' yet.

'OK. Some sort of angel then,' said Dante. 'Great.'

They walked on under the dome and made their way into what was signposted as the South Gallery.

Looking up this time, it was possible to see that high up, mosaic pictures had been pressed into the walls. The paint around the edge of each mosaic was flaky, making it look as if it was peeling off.

'You like our pictures?' came a voice from behind them.

Jed spun round a little too quickly and the man who had spoken looked taken aback and defensively tapped his 'guide' badge emblazoned with the British Union Jack flag.

'I just saw you looking at our mosaics,' he explained quickly.

'They're beautiful,' said Kassia, trying to make up for Jed's rather shocked reaction.

'And at last we can see that beauty again,' said the guide. 'For years the mosaics were covered over.'

'Seriously?'

'It was necessary, of course, when the cathedral changed its use,' said the guide. 'It is not appropriate to have images of faces inside a mosque. But what I find most fascinating about the revealed picture,' he went on, 'is the hidden man within the mosaic you see now.'

The guide's explanation was getting interesting and Jed stepped in closer to hear more. He was aware that Dante was getting restless, but he let Kassia turn the guide's words into sign.

'The man in the mosaic you see now was once the husband of the Empress, but there was another face placed over his. A later husband, replaced then with the original, as if he'd come back to life and escaped the shroud.' The guide looked rather pleased with himself for sharing this information. 'I like to call him the Phoenix Man. A husband reborn.'

Jed looked across at Kassia. Her hands were trying to turn this information into sign for Dante, but her fingers were fumbling. Dante was struggling to keep up.

'Who are the two men?' asked Jed urgently.

'Constantine,' said the guide, 'and the Phoenix Man who replaced him and came back from the dead is Romanos.'

The names meant nothing to Jed. 'And the Empress. Who's she?' he asked.

The guide looked surprised that anyone would have to ask this. He ran a finger around a golden chain at his neck and just for a second a medallion glinted in the light cast down by the mosaic. 'Zoe, of course.'

Jed felt a rush of adrenaline. Zoe? Bergier had said that name.

Jed looked across at Kassia and he was surprised to see that her hands had stopped signing completely.

* * *

'I don't know why he went on about Zoe,' said Jed defensively. They'd left the Hagia Sophia and were booked into a rather shabby apartment block in the back streets of Istanbul. They'd been trying to make sense of the conversation about the mosaic, but Kassia seemed to be bringing the discussion back again and again to an empress who lived centuries before.

'It's just odd,' said Kassia. 'That the guide used *that* name. Zoe, I mean. The same one Bergier mentioned.'

Jed was perfectly aware that the name had been mentioned before. And he felt just as uncomfortable now as he had the first time he'd heard it. 'I don't know who she is,' he said, banging his hands on the table.

'Fine.' Kassia folded her arms. 'I was just saying. It's weird, that's all.'

'More weird,' said Jed, determined to take the heat out of the situation, 'is that the guide just *happened* to be there, standing under the mosaic ready to talk about the Phoenix Man. It's as if he'd been waiting.'

Kassia grabbed a cube of Turkish delight from the bag on the table. They'd bought a few provisions for tea, but she seemed most keen to chomp her way through great doses of sugar and had ignored the fresh fruit and bread that was also arranged on the table.

'Does that stuff *really* help?' Jed said snappily.

Kassia chewed elaborately and then licked the dusting of sugar from her fingers. It was her only offer of an answer.

Dante grimaced at them both. 'Erm, Phoenix Man; hidden church; edge of two worlds. Can we focus here, please! I don't know how pictures on a cathedral wall can really help us. But it would be good to keep on task.'

Jed leant forward and took his own cube of Turkish delight. He hadn't even got it to his lips when he was aware of a thundering noise from the street outside.

'I mean we have to get a . . .' Dante was continuing to sign, but Jed had dashed with Kassia to stare out of the window.

The rumbling noise intensified and then there was a blinding flash.

Jed and Kassia rushed for the door of the apartment and Dante raced after them.

Out in the street it was difficult to work out at first exactly what had happened. A crowd had formed and people were shouting and charging in all directions. From the midst of the people, smoke was rising: thick and gagging, pungent with the smell of engine oil.

Jed battled to the front of the crowd.

A car had obviously lost control as it made its way

down the hill and had crashed into the side of a street vendor's stall that was little more than a wooden shack. The car had concertinaed itself so it now took up half the space it had done only moments before. Smoke was belching from the bonnet, thrown open with the impact. Workers from the food stall had scrambled free, the line of Kokoreç kebabs they'd been cooking tumbling with the coals from the open oven, out on to the street.

Those in the crowd, covered their faces. Partly in shock, partly to fight back the gag of fumes, and partly because of an inbuilt reflex not to look too closely at tragedy.

Jed wanted to look away too. But the detail he couldn't tear his eyes from was the slow and gentle dripping of petrol from the busted exhaust pipe.

Jed shouted, waving at people to get back.

He scanned for Kassia and Dante in the crowd but he couldn't see them. No one else seemed to have spotted the danger. Petrol pooled on the ground, inching closer to the burning coals from the debris of the food stall.

Jed flung himself towards the crumpled car. He tugged at the driver's door, frantically wrenching to pull it free. It wouldn't budge. It was too dented by the crash.

He clambered round to the passenger side, yanking this door open instead and then climbing inside the battered husk of the car.

The noise from outside somehow intensified. The reek of petrol was overwhelming. They had to be seconds away from an explosion but the driver was still belted in place.

Jed scrabbled for the release catch. This was crumpled too. So crushed it wouldn't give. The screams from outside were getting louder. He was aware the crowd had finally backed away as if they knew now what was bound to happen.

Jed ripped the catch out of the socket and tugged the driver free of the seat. He hauled him into the road, dragging his body as far away from the crash as he could.

There was a rushing sound. It cut through the screams of the crowd. Then a whooshing noise. For a second, silence. And then an almighty blast as the car exploded, flinging Jed and the driver into the crumpled food shack. Jed braced his body around the driver as shards of metal and glass rained down on him in a curtain of fire.

'You could have died!' screamed Kassia.

'Yeah, well, about that. Haven't we spent six

months working out that *can't* really happen?'

Kassia was washing a particularly deep laceration on Jed's shoulder. Her anger meant she wasn't being quite as gentle as he'd have liked to her to be.

He pulled his shirt sleeve over his arm and stood up. 'It's fine, honest.'

'Fine!'

The way she clenched the cotton wool in her hand made him exceptionally glad he'd got up when he had. 'Look, Kass, I'll heal. Quickly, like I did in London after the cage. That's what happens.'

She nodded and put the cotton wool back down in the dish. 'Promise?'

He grinned and buttoned up his shirt. 'I promise.'

She folded her arms. 'Maybe you really are totally immortal now,' she said without looking at him. 'I mean, we think you have to take a sixth elixir but the way you coped with the explosion and the fire, well, maybe that's it. Five doses might have been enough.'

He tucked his shirt into his jeans. She looked so believing and it felt wrong to crush her hope, but they were in this together, that's what she'd said. And there was no use pretending. He opened his hand. The life-line running from the top of his palm to the heel of his hand was open again and it was bleeding. 'Kassia, we might not know all the answers but we do know one thing for sure and we have to face that.' He was aware that he sounded braver than he felt. 'This immortality isn't fixed. I can't die. At the moment. But the clock is ticking.'

She lifted the bowl of water and cotton wool and took it into the kitchen. 'You were still very brave,' she said. The conversation was over.

Jed looked across at Dante. He had a face on. 'I guess you don't agree with your sister about the being brave bit,' he signed awkwardly, the blood from his hand, snaking down his wrist.

Dante was leaning back in the chair. For a moment Jed didn't think that he would answer. 'I think you were an idiot,' Dante signed.

'What?'

'You've given yourself away, mate. We might have got out of there before the ambulance arrived but it won't be long before NOAH track us down again after that little show of invulnerability.'

Suddenly the pain in Jed's hand was not the thing that hurt him most.

DAY 221

6th October

Dante dropped the newspaper on to the table along with the food he'd gone out to buy for breakfast. 'Told you!' he signed sharply.

Jed grabbed the newspaper. The picture on the front showed the crumpled car mangled in the debris of the Kokoreç kebab stall.

'You can read this?' said Jed, pointing at the Turkish text.

'Of course not,' signed Dante. 'But there's bound to be some mention of your dramatic rescue. We spend months underground to try and keep a low profile and then you do that.'

'You think I should have let the guy die?' said Jed, his own signs erratic now.

'Yes. No. I don't know. It's just . . .' Dante had stopped signing. He was leaning forward, winded

148

slightly. Kassia had thumped him hard in the stomach with the newspaper.

'Whatever happened, happened,' she said, her signs clinical and precise. 'I don't think the car crash is the thing we should be focusing on.'

Jed waited for her to explain.

She grabbed the newspaper from Dante and tossed it back down on the table. 'Where did you get this?' she said.

Dante rubbed his stomach.

So Kassia thumped him again on the arm.

Jed made a mental note not to upset either of them today. When they were angry, their signs became more physical. Words didn't seem to matter so much.

'Where did you buy the newspaper?' Kassia asked again.

'I didn't buy it,' signed Dante. 'It was outside. On the doormat. Why?'

Kassia smoothed the rather crumpled paper out on the table but this time the back page faced upwards. 'Look?'

Jed wasn't sure what he was supposed to be looking at, but he was too worried about Kassia's reaction to ask directly. He'd healed well from the explosion the night before but he was still a little sore.

She seemed to realise that neither Jed nor her brother had a clue what she was going on about. 'Here, look,' she said, pointing at a small hand-drawn picture on the far margins of the back page. It was the mark of the Brothers of Heliopolis, neatly sketched in pencil. A circle, a triangle and a square.

'What? Why? Who?' The questions tumbled from Jed's lips.

'And that's not all, look,' said Kassia. She pointed again, this time at an advert halfway down the page. It was for a stall selling lanterns at the Grand Bazaar. And across the advert in the same pencil as the symbol sketch above was that day's date. And a time. Eleven o'clock.

'We can't possibly go,' signed Dante. He'd been pacing up and down in front of the window and his signs seemed to be directed at the ceiling rather than Jed or Kassia.

'But the message might be there to help us,' said Kassia. It was the third time she'd made the suggestion.

'Or a trap,' signed Dante. 'I told you! NOAH could be on to us.'

'Maybe they are,' said Jed. 'But the symbol is from the Brothers. Maybe they are on our side?'

'Like the guy who claimed you were William Jones

back in London?' said Dante. 'Have you forgotten what he did to you?'

Jed didn't bother to sign his answer. 'No,' he said defiantly. 'I haven't forgotten what they did.'

Dante stopped pacing. 'Look, I'm sorry, mate. Now it's just the three of us, I feel that someone has got to be in charge and I feel like we have to be careful.'

'We do,' said Jed. 'But we have to be more than careful.'

Dante looked confused.

'We have to be *quick*. I've only got months left. And like you say, NOAH could very well be on to us now. So we can't take risks.'

'That's what I'm saying,' Dante signed desperately.

'No. You're not,' said Jed calmly. 'You don't want me to take the risk of going to the Bazaar. And I don't want to take the risk of *not* going there.'

'I've got a bad feeling about this.' Kassia knew she was mumbling. She also knew better than to convert her words into sign. Dante's feelings about responding to the cryptic notes on the newspaper had been made perfectly clear and she was wise enough not to add fuel to the fire.

'Well, I've got a bad feeling about dying,' Jed

mumbled quietly, as he checked the time on his watch and then slipped it back inside his pocket.

Kassia felt her stomach knot. 'It will be OK,' she said. But she had no idea if it would be or if they were about to walk into a trap.

It was certainly an enormous trap if it was one. The guidebook told them Istanbul's Grand Bazaar was one of the oldest and biggest covered markets in the world. Apparently there were sixty-one streets and over three thousand shops. It certainly felt like the whole of Turkey had come here to do their shopping.

They'd entered through one of the twenty-two gates and were now pretty much lost amongst a maze of vibrant colour and noise. The Bazaar smelt like Christmas and Kassia let the scent of nuts and spices soak into her, but it did little to help her feel calm. A shopkeeper held out a pair of brightly patterned slippers with curled toes, as another stall owner offered a tray bearing glasses of steaming tea. Kassia grabbed Jed's arm to avoid the crush and even when the path widened out again, she didn't let go.

'It's down there,' signed Dante, the map he'd been referring to tucked now under his arm, making his signs lopsided and rather small. 'Are you ready?'

Kassia wasn't sure she was. And Jed did nothing to get free of her hold on his arm.

The front of the shop was open. Carpets and scarves hung down like curtains, screening off the back of the stall from the kaleidoscope of glass lanterns that were suspended from the ceiling. They looked like ripe, plump fruit on tree branches, each lantern spilling waves of fragmented coloured light so that the whole space shone with dazzling brilliance. Interspersed between the lanterns were large blue discs. Like the lanterns, these were made of glass, each with a white circle in the centre, spiked with a small black dot. It felt to Kassia as if a hundred unblinking eyes stared down at her and she gripped even tighter to Jed's arm.

As far as Kassia could see, there were no customers inside the shop. Just a man seated on a stool, his back turned slightly so that his face was hidden behind the drape of hanging carpet.

Jed stepped forward. The man turned his head, thick black curls momentarily falling in front of his eyes. He scooped his hair back and then he lowered his hand and reached inside the open neck of his thin cotton shirt.

Kassia darted backwards. The man was reaching for a gun! Jed turned his body, his back braced around her like a shield.

But there was no gun shot.

No sound at all.

Kassia wriggled free of Jed's protection and looked up. The man was smiling. Looped around his finger and drawn from behind the folds of his shirt was a long golden chain that wound round his neck. And hanging on the chain, swinging against his finger, was a medallion. A circle, a triangle and a square. The mark of the Brothers of Heliopolis.

'I am Metin,' said the man with the medallion. 'You were brave to come.'

Jed didn't feel very brave. His legs were shaking, and he felt stupid for throwing himself over Kassia to protect her. The dark blue glass eyes hanging from the ceiling seemed to mock him. Jed had thought they were in danger and, despite the fact the man was smiling at them, it didn't mean they weren't. Jed had made that mistake before and he'd ended up in a cage in The Shard and then hanging from the roof of Notre Dame.

Metin tucked the medallion out of sight inside his shirt. 'But you have shown yourself to be brave already, Fulcanelli. I can call you that, can't I?'

Jed's throat was too tight to allow him to speak an answer. He wasn't sure what he would say anyway.

This didn't seem to deter Metin, who had got up from the stool and was reaching behind the counter.

'You have demonstrated who you *are*,' he said. 'But there are three stages to alchemy. Now you must demonstrate who you *were* and who you *are going to be*.' He'd obviously found what he was reaching for and withdrew his hand. He was holding a small thin rectangular box. The box was covered with writing. It was impossible to see what the writing said, but the print spread across the lid and down the sides. He put the box on top of the counter and smiled again, a bouncy black curl bobbing backwards and forwards in front of his eye.

'You saw the explosion?' Jed blurted.

'Of course.'

There was something about the way Metin answered that unnerved Jed. 'You *arranged* it?' he stuttered. 'Like some sort of test?'

Metin fiddled again with the medallion around his neck. The way he did this seemed vaguely familiar. 'Maybe? But perhaps it was chance? Like meeting a guide who could tell you all about the Phoenix Man.' He leant forward. 'Do you believe in chance, Fulcanelli?'

Jed's mind was spinning. Not with images of dragons, but twisting back through his mind to the Hagia Sophia and the guide who'd been so keen to talk.

Metin let the medallion fall against his chest. 'The Brothers have been waiting for years, Fulcanelli. We act as a golden chain linking across time to preserve a secret. And you want to know that secret. So the time of testing has begun.'

Jed did not like the mention of the word 'testing'. That had led to all sorts of disasters in Prague. But before he could get his head round this, Metin picked up the box he'd taken from under the counter and held it out.

Dante suddenly thrust out his arm, blocking Jed's hand. 'Hold on, mate! You sure?'

Jed hesitated then he nodded at Dante. Instead of signing his answer, he took the box from Metin's hand.

The box was light, made of thick cardboard. There were two discs on top and a cord of fabric snaked around these raised discs, keeping the box lid secure. Jed looked at Metin and he nodded encouragement, so Jed slipped the cord free of the fasteners. The lid, which had been scored in half across the diagonal line, popped open.

The inside of the box had been lined with blue velvet and, lying in chiselled-out containers, were three squat bottles, each one a different colour and each one sealed shut with a lid of dark wax. A golden

156

strand ran around the edge of each wax lid. Jed supposed you opened each bottle by tearing the strand of gold free.

'Ink,' explained Metin, nodding towards the bottles.

Jed lifted one and allowed the light from the lanterns to flow through the liquid. This bottle held red ink, but each container held a different colour. As well as red, there was black and white.

Jed placed the bottle of ink back inside its protective velvet casing. Set behind the three segmented sections for the ink was a fourth compartment. This one was long and thin. Inside this section was a spear of twisted glass. It bulged slightly in the centre and a ball of glass led down to a ridged point. The main body of the spear was made of black and white glass twisted together like two strands of a rope. As Jed rolled the spear in his hand, light from the lanterns above spiralled though it.

'What is it?' said Jed, turning it over and over in his hand.

'You dip the point into the ink and twist,' explained Metin. 'The ink is drawn up the outside edge of the shaft towards the ball. And then you write.'

'A glass pen?' said Jed. It was beautiful, but he had absolutely no idea why the shopowner had given it to him. 'Why would I need this?'

Metin sat back down. He flicked the hair once more away from his eyes, as if contemplating how best to answer. Then he rubbed his stubbled chin with his fingers. 'We can suppose, Fulcanelli, that you came to Istanbul for answers. And with this pen you will be able to write the answers you need.'

This didn't really help much.

'We've talked about the three stages of alchemy. Nigredo: black; Albedo: white; and finally Rubedo: red.'

This was sounding horribly familiar. Andel had told them about these stages in Prague.

Jed slotted the glass pen back into its velvet container. 'What has any of this got to do with me?'

Metin smiled. His hand slowed on his chin. He leant forward. 'We can play games, Fulcanelli, or you can take the pen and use it to deal with the stages of alchemy. The choice is yours.'

'And how do we know we can trust you?' cut in Kassia.

'You don't,' said Metin. 'But I think part of the reason for your journey here was to find something of a different colour to black or white or red.'

Jed felt the hairs on the back of his neck stand up. He tried to look noncommittal, stifling the excitement he felt flooding through him.

'If, as I predict, you are interested in the secret of the Emerald, then join me tomorrow at the Topkapi Palace, where I will have something to show you.'

DAY 222
7th October

'This is madness!' Dante was far from happy.

'This is the only lead we have. If you think NOAH might be on to us, then we have to take a chance.'

'And what about the crazy treasure hunt in Prague?' said Kassia, struggling to keep up as Jed strode ahead of her.

He stopped suddenly to face her as the crowds rushed past on either side. 'I know all that. I know this could be the worse decision ever.' He let the crowds charge past him. 'But supposing it's not?'

Kassia rested her hand on his arm. 'OK,' she said quietly. 'Let's do this. Together.'

Metin had given them instructions to meet him at the Topkapi Palace.

The estate had been used by the Ottoman sultans for nearly four hundred years. It was a sprawling spread of buildings and courtyards; a small town in itself beside the banks of the Bosphorus. There were mosques, a hospital, bakeries and even a royal mint all inside the palace walls. Metin had told them to meet him at the palace treasury.

The treasury consisted of four rooms. Jed hurried into the first, scanning the crowds of sightseers who were wandering around using hushed and reverential tones as they passed each of the splendid treasures on show. The place had the same feel as the treasury of Notre Dame cathedral. Hordes of tourists staring at things that were beautiful or old or strange. Or maybe all three at once.

One room held two gigantic golden candle sticks, each studded with precious gems. Another showcased a sultan's throne, this decorated with pearls. In the third room, most of the crowds were pressed around a cabinet displaying what was labelled as the Spoonmaker's Diamond. The enormous gem was set in silver and ringed by other smaller sparkling stones. But Jed found the exhibit next to this, which claimed to be the shrivelled hand of John the Baptist, to be more worthy of his staring.

Kassia steered him away from the gruesome exhibit. Her skin looked deathly pale. 'The hand?' he asked.

'It's like the thief's hand in Prague,' she said.

Jed was confused. There was much of the treasure hunt through the old town he couldn't remember, and those parts he could, he'd been trying to forget. Memories fought inside his mind for attention and the pain of pushing so many back down made his head throb.

'Here,' said Kassia taking the lead. 'The fourth room. We haven't tried here.'

But the door of the fourth room was closed. A sign in Turkish, which none of them could read, hung across the handle.

'Great!' signed Dante. 'A waste of time, I knew it!'

Jed felt a surge of dread. The promise of answers withdrawn again like so many times before. He raised his clenched fist to his forehead and then, because he had no idea what to do next, he lowered his hand and thumped it on the door.

And the door swung open.

Jed looked behind him. The rest of the crowd were pouring into the opposite room to see the pearl-studded throne. If he, Kassia and Dante were quick, there was a chance they could be inside the fourth room before anyone else noticed.

He dragged the other two in with him, pushed the door shut and leant his weight against it. He tipped his head back, breathing out nervously. And

162

when he finally looked around, he was aware of the sound of clapping.

Metin stood in the centre, in front of a large glass display cabinet. 'Well done,' he said, striking his hands together enthusiastically. 'I thought for a moment you would fail to join me.'

Jed was still not altogether sure he could trust the guy. The room was like the other three they'd visited. Except in this one, there were no crowds. And in this one, in the central cabinet, was a single exhibit sharing display space with absolutely nothing else. 'You said you would show us the Emerald Tablet,' Jed said nervously.

Metin began to laugh. 'That's not exactly what I said,' he clarified. 'You remember incorrectly. But memory can do that sometimes. Focus on things that want to be seen.'

Jed was growing impatient. Was this some cruel joke? Was this man playing with them?

Metin began to walk alongside the front of the display cabinet. 'I said I had something of emerald with a secret for you,' he said. 'You just hoped for more.'

'So the Tablet?' blurted Jed. 'You don't have that?'

'Not here,' said Metin, and his voice was teasing. 'I'm not saying that the Brothers of Heliopolis don't have the Tablet. I'm not saying that you won't eventually get to see it. But the search for answers is a journey, Fulcanelli, and one that cannot be rushed.'

This man was getting *really* irritating now.

'So this message of the Emerald you said you *have* got,' pressed Kassia. 'What's that then?'

Metin turned and pointed into the display cabinet.

Resting on a pillow of red satin was an ornate ceremonial dagger.

'The Topkapi Dagger,' said Metin dramatically, sweeping his hands across the top of the display cabinet, and unlocking the frontage. He reached inside, and lifted the dagger to show them.

'You can do that?' said Jed, scanning the room anxiously. If they'd set off alarms just by entering a chamber full of clocks back in Paris, then surely someone in Istanbul wouldn't be too happy about a golden dagger being taken out of a display case by some market trader from the Grand Bazaar.

'Relax, Fulcanelli. This is all arranged.'

Jed wasn't sure if Metin was referring to the security measures or that fact that they were meeting here to look at something which Jed presumed was somehow connected to the puzzle they were trying so hard to solve.

'That's beautiful,' said Kassia, stepping forward.

Metin held the dagger out so that they could see more clearly. The blade was gently curved, almost like a letter C. It was covered with a golden scabbard. The handle of the dagger was golden too, but decorated with three enormous emeralds. Jed saw that the top of the handle was also topped with a huge green stone, but Metin showed that with his thumb, this larger gem could be flicked back to reveal a watch face hidden beneath.

'Sultan Mahmud the First had the dagger made for Nader Shah of Persia, but the Shah was assassinated before the dagger was ever his, so the Sultan kept it,' said Metin, as if he was speaking to a room full of visitors who had paid for a guided tour.

'It's incredible,' said Jed, although he struggled to hide his confusion about why they were looking at a dagger when they were searching for answers about how to live for ever.

'But you're wondering how it can be the key to all your questions,' said Metin, placing the dagger back on the silk cushion.

'Yes. That's what I'm wondering.'

Metin slid the glass screen back into place on the cabinet. 'It's a symbol for you to read, Fulcanelli. I know you've been seeking those. And my job as a Brother of Heliopolis is to open doors for you to read messages you need to find.'

'Look, you know why we came to Turkey. The Emerald Tablet. The recipe for the elixir,' said Jed. 'You've got to tell me how *this* connects to *that*.'

Metin shook his head. 'I wish it was that simple. But anything of any worth must be won by some sort of struggle, Fulcanelli. You must realise that already.' He pointed to the golden dagger in the case. 'It is true the Brothers have been waiting to help you find what you seek. There is a silent army of them guarding the secrets you need. All part of the network you established yourself. And we are loyal to you and to your quest. You know better than any other that a true alchemist must work and be tested to win the prize he wants.'

'How do I do that, exactly?' Jed spluttered.

Metin replied slowly. 'That's not for me to say.'

'What? But you've just said the Brothers are here to help me?'

'I think part of the challenge will be you helping yourself,' Metin said.

Jed was floundering. This was ridiculous. They were getting nowhere!

'You talked about symbols,' cut in Kassia. 'What d'you mean about those?'

'Well, if we look at the dagger then maybe we

can read its symbols to help you in your quest. The emerald connection is obvious, of course. But what else do you read?'

'It's a dagger!' yelped Jed in frustration. 'What symbols can there be?'

'Now, now,' said Metin. 'This is not time for impatience. It is a dagger, yes. But what does that symbolise to you?'

'Danger,' said Kassia quietly, translating Dante's sign so it could be spoken aloud.

'You do well to remember the path you tread is one of danger,' said Metin. 'And what else?'

'You said the dagger wasn't ever used?' said Kassia, turning her statement into a question.

Metin nodded. 'You are doing well. And what about the hidden clock counting down your time?'

Jed could feel himself tensing, air thickening in his throat. The throbbing in his head was intensifying.

'But of course the most important thing about a dagger,' said Metin softly, 'is its blade. The ability to cut.'

'And how does that help us?' begged Jed.

'Maybe you will need to cut to the truth of all you remember if you are ever to get the chance to see the Emerald Tablet for yourself.'

Jed stumbled forward and pressed his hands against

the glass cabinet. Emerald Tablets, hidden clocks, daggers for assassinated Shahs. Dante had been right. This was madness. His hands touched the glass and heat surged through his fingers. He felt panic bubbling in the pit of his stomach.

'Please,' said Kassia urgently behind him. 'You haven't really made much sense. We don't understand what we should do.'

Metin took a small square postcard from his pocket. Printed across the front was a picture of the golden dagger. 'You have everything you need for now. And all else will be provided for you. If you weigh my words, I know you will find a way.'

Kassia took the postcard reluctantly and pushed it into her pocket. Then she touched Jed's shoulder in a gentle attempt to steer him away.

The surge of energy was immediate. A pain like the one he'd felt in Paris speared Jed's hand as if the dagger had been lifted from the silk cushion and plunged into his palm. He was flung back from the cabinet, and landed sprawled across the floor. Kassia fell crumpled beside him. His mind filled with smoke and he could hardly breathe.

Suddenly, Dante was bending over him, shaking him as if he'd been sleeping. Kassia's eyes were wide in panic.

Metin was striding for the door. 'You have to read the pieces of the puzzle now, Fulcanelli. And you have to enter the river of ink if you want to make sense of what lies just ahead and far behind. The light of extinguished stars reaches us eventually, if we focus and look carefully into the darkest of nights.'

Jed had no idea where the pain had come from or what Metin was talking about, and if Metin had answers, he wasn't hanging around to explain. He opened the door and walked out.

Within seconds, the room was full of tourists peering into the glass cabinet at the emerald-studded dagger. Not one of them seemed to notice the deaf boy helping his sister and their friend clamber up from the floor in the corner or see them together towards the exit.

DAY 223
8th October

Jed was seated with his back to Kassia. His shoulders were slumped, his elbows resting on the table, one hand drawn into a fist against his chin and the other gripped tightly around it.

'You can't sleep?' she said.

A tense shrug of his shoulders was the only answer he gave.

Dante came in from the kitchen. He was carrying mugs of tea.

Kassia pulled out a chair and sat down. Jed took a deep breath, but he faltered as he did so, as if he couldn't quite pull the air he needed inside of him.

'It's a mess,' he said, and then he laughed a little. 'I thought it was a mess in Paris, in the sewers, but this . . .' He spread his hands out and pressed them either side of his face, fingers splayed. It was clear he didn't have the energy to sign, but as Kassia glanced across at her brother who'd sat down too, it was equally as clear that Dante wasn't going to force things.

'I feel like we're back in those tunnels,' said Jed. 'And we're scrabbling around trying to find the exit and there are all these traps and I just can't find the way out.'

'But we *did* find the way out in Paris,' Kassia said gently. 'And we will do here.'

Jed raised his eyebrows. 'None of it makes sense! None of it. Phoenix Man; edge of two worlds; this.' He lifted the postcard of the dagger. 'What does any of it mean?'

Kassia reached forward and touched his hand. She felt a jolt, as if a cable had been pulled taut through her stomach and out the other side. Jed's face showed he felt it too.

He broke his hand free and scrabbled for his pocket watch, flipping open the case to see the time, then dropped it on to the table so that it landed on the postcard picture of the dagger. 'What am I supposed to do with any of this?' he said, waving his hand towards the box containing the ink and pen he'd been given at the Grand Bazaar.

Kassia looked again at her brother. Jed's mood was spiralling like the twisted glass on the shaft of the pen and she was scared that if they didn't do something soon then he'd become angry like he had in the Court of Miracles. And that had really not ended well for any of them.

She signed frantically to Dante, not sure whether she should make the suggestion aloud.

Dante shrugged, pulled a face, and then nodded. 'Maybe?' he said with his hands.

It was Kassia's turn to take a deep breath. 'OK. This is all crazy complicated. And I,' she paused and pointed at Dante, '*we*, have no idea what to do either. So maybe we should try and simplify the whole thing.'

Jed waited.

'*You* had the answer, Jed. You're the one who made the elixir in the first place and I think,' again she looked at Dante, '*we* think, that maybe the answers, in the end, are down to you. All these,' she said, gesturing to the stuff on the table, 'are maybe just clues to help you remember. And the one thing Metin said that made sense was that you had to remember the truth.'

'But I can't!'

She swallowed hard. 'I think you can.'

He looked confused.

'And I think you do. But I think you're so scared to think about what happened on the days that you took the elixir that you block out the memories.'

His look of confusion morphed into something else. Anger.

'What if that's the only way to make sense of it all? Jed, back in Paris, before you got really ill, I think you had started to see things more clearly.'

'How can you possibly know what I saw?'

Her voice and her signs were tiny. 'Because I saw them too.'

He stood up from the table, turning, so that his back was towards her again, his arms folded across his chest as if her words had hurt him.

Kassia stayed seated and continued to speak and sign. 'We were holding hands and somehow your memories were so intense that it was like they burst out of you and I saw them too. Nat said you had to deal with your memories. Seeing Bergier was the start. But all these extra clues are there, I think, to help you understand what happened to you.'

'So what are you saying?'

'I think you have to try and face the past.'

Jed's shoulders lifted again and time seemed to stretch before he turned. 'I can't! I'm not *me* in the memories,' he signed. 'I'm someone else. It's too difficult.'

'Just because you look different doesn't mean it's not you,' pleaded Kassia.

'I don't mean about how I look,' Jed blurted.

'But I think . . .'

'I can't, Kassia. I just can't.' And he staggered forward to grab his watch from the table, stumbling as he moved.

Dante reached out to steady him. Kassia grabbed for his hand. And the watch tumbled from his fingers.

There was a burst of light as the three of them connected: the edges of a triangle.

And the watch rocked backwards and forwards on the square postcard of the golden dagger.

And the hands of the watch began to spin backwards, carving a circle as they moved.

And in Jed's mind a dragon twisted and turned, again and again, like the hands of the watch, scoring the path to a memory. And Kassia and Dante held on to his hands. And they saw it too.

The sky is darkening.

A figure kneels on the ground, his shoulders stooped with age and weariness. A man, in front of a grave. He holds a white rose in his hand, twisting it between his fingers. A thorn nicks at his skin and blood beads on the petals. He leans forward and places the single bloom on top of the gravestone, letting his hand rest there a second longer than is necessary.

Suddenly, a small boy darts between the gravestones. He skids to a halt in front of the kneeling man and hesitates for just a second. 'Mr Fulcanelli, sir.'

The man looks up. His face is lined, the skin taut, dark mauve shadows under the eyes.

'Canseliet told me to tell you it is ready, sir.' The boy lowers his head as if suddenly acknowledging the presence of the gravestone. It is possible to see the writing carved there now. The name 'Zoe' and the date, '1910'.

The kneeling man presses his hand against the ground and stands up slowly, the effort etched deep on his face. He takes a small leather pouch from his pocket and tips a golden coin into the boy's hand.

'Thank you, sir! Canseliet said to hurry, but surely you'll be wanting to see the eclipse too.'

The man says nothing. He turns his back on the boy and the grave and the rose.

In the breeze, a single petal, stained with blood, falls free and flutters on the air like a bird taking flight.

The man hurries through the streets. It is clear to see now that he is in Paris. The cathedral of Notre Dame sends a shadow across the cobbles. The Seine winds beside the path he hurries down. The man does not look at the river. An anger surges inside him that he's unable to find words for, but he drives forward. The streets are full of people but they are crowding towards the river, heads raised, focused on the sky. The man fights against the current, his eyes on the ground.

He turns and enters a small courtyard, then fumbles in his pocket for a key. He unlocks a battered door and enters quickly. The door closes behind him and he slips the key into his pocket.

In the hallway, there is a mirror on the wall. Again the man averts his gaze. He is not interested in reflections, but hurries towards a flight of stairs that leads into the basement, steadying himself against the handrail as he descends.

The room is small, the ceiling low. There is little light, but the smell of herbs is overwhelming. Glass containers line the walls, bottles fill the rickety shelves, a marble pestle and mortar stands beside the door and a shabby wooden table spreads across the room. In the centre of the table is a set of bronze scales. One pan is laden with weights. The other stacked with gold.

A fire blazes in the corner. Two men stand either side of the fire. The older of the men points to a flask hoisted above the flames. The flask is shaped like a bird. A long glass neck reaches forward and from the neck a golden liquid bubbles and drips.

A third man appears from the shadows. 'Son, I'm not sure . . .' But the man from the graveyard says nothing. He holds a small glass bottle beneath the bubbling liquid.

The other men press closer. 'Does it have to be today?'

The man from the graveyard sets the bottle on the table and takes another from the shelf. 'It has to be today.'

'And you are sure about the number six?'

'I'm sure.'

'And . . .'

The man from the graveyard holds out his hand. 'This is what we've worked for, Julien.' The flask on the fire is nearly empty. Five bottles sit on the table. Each is filled with glimmering liquid. The man takes a sixth bottle now and he holds it under the spout of the flask. He catches the very last drip.

The man from the shadows steps across him. 'I can't watch,' he mumbles quietly.

'I'm doing this for us!' says the man from the graveyard. He holds up the sixth bottle, which is now full too, and he holds it high so that the golden liquid dances in the reflected light of the fire.

But the man from the shadows makes for the stairs.

The fire crackles. There is the sound of shouting from the street outside. Darkness presses in and the man from the graveyard lifts the glass to his lips. The golden liquid swirls as he drinks.

There is a blinding light. The flames of the fire stretch and grow and the glass falls from his fingers and shatters on the flagstone floor.

The two men by the fire cover their faces and draw back in fear, but the man from the graveyard stands tall. Light radiates from him, pulsing in time with his heart.

He turns to the table, scooping a handful of gold from the pan of the scales. He runs towards the stairs, taking them two at a time until he reaches the top.

In the hallway, he stops for just a second in front of the mirror. And he smiles.

Then he races out into the street.

The crowds are staring upwards at a blackened sun, but the man from the graveyard glows with the light of the fire. And he runs towards the river.

Jed pushed hard against the table, and his chair rocked violently backwards. The mugs toppled, spilling coffee on to the postcard. The pocket watch tumbled to the floor.

Jed clutched his hands to his body and doubled over, clawing at his chest.

Kassia leapt up too. 'Jed!'

His face contorted in pain.

'Jed! Please!'

'I can't, Kassia!' His words hissed through gritted teeth. And as he turned and made for the door, his foot caught against the pocket watch, sending it skidding and spinning across the floor.

DAY 224

9th October

'I'm not answering your questions about your father! I don't know anything. I've told you!' Cole Carter was champing vigorously on his chewing gum.

Victor groaned. 'Come on, mate. Anything. Anything at all.'

Cole slammed his hand down on the desk. 'Please, Victor. Will you give it a rest? We have a job to do here! Interpol's useless data search still hasn't registered the flights Fulcanelli and his friends took and you must've noticed that since we've been back in London, Montgomery's been even crankier than before!'

'So what are we supposed to do?' Victor said, leaning back in his chair, his fingers linked behind his head. 'Just sit here for months like we did in Paris. *He* might be able to live for ever but we're gonna die waiting for him at this rate!'

'This is what Department Nine does,' snapped Cole, spinning round on his chair. 'It waits for the unicorn. You knew that.' He thumped Victor hard on the shoulder. 'That mark on your arm shows you knew that. So do something useful, will you? And start looking through the stash of stuff I took from Bergier's.'

'You *took* stuff?' said Victor, fiddling nervously with the photo pressed inside his pocket.

'Hey, you think I wear this enormous coat in all weathers just to make a fashion statement?'

Victor looked at Cole with renewed appreciation. He wondered what else he'd had hidden away in those pockets.

Cole pushed a pile of papers across the table towards him.

'What am I looking for? Exactly?'

Cole reached a finger into his mouth, pulled the end of his chewing gum and then snapped it back between his lips. 'Tracks, I guess. Marks from the unicorn we might have missed.'

'Great. You gonna translate that?'

'Just get looking, Viccy boy. That's what we do here. Look for clues.'

Victor rubbed his shoulder awkwardly and then

turned to the papers on the top of the pile and began to flick through them. After a while, he leant back in his chair, his hands re-looped behind his head. 'The old guy was kind of out there,' he said. 'All sorts of theories in this book he wrote called *The Mornings of the Magicians*. Kind of weird.'

Cole didn't respond, so Victor turned to the notes again. His eyes hesitated for a moment over a name. Cockren. It seemed familiar, like he should recognise it. Why did that name seem important?

More importantly, why were they wasting their time being inside an office when they could be out there tracking Fulcanelli down. He sighed and stood up, walking across the room towards a board covered with notes and cuttings. There was a space in the corner. A photograph-shaped hole. Victor pressed his thumb against the corner of the photograph in his pocket. It had once been sharp and pointed but it was dulled now, worn down and blunt beneath the pressure of his thumb.

Suddenly, his eyes were drawn to a newspaper cutting in the centre of the board. He'd studied the article a hundred times. It was from the week everything changed. The week Martha Quinn had come to find him and Fulcanelli had climbed out of the Thames with no idea who he was or why he was in the river.

And there, in the centre of the article, was the name of the man who'd found him as he'd wondered alone and disorientated up the steps of St Paul's Cathedral. The Reverend Solomon Cockren.

There was a mirror in the corner of the bedroom. Jed stared at his reflection, winced, then pressed his fingertips gently against the skin at the base of his neck.

Suddenly, the door to the bedroom rattled.

'Just a minute,' he called, grabbing his shirt, forcing his arms inside and fumbling with the buttons. He bit his lip against the pain.

'Jed. Are you OK?'

'Just a minute,' Jed said again, tucking his shirt into his jeans and then opening the door.

Kassia hesitated in the doorway. 'Can I . . . ?'

'Yeah, of course.' Jed didn't look at her. Instead, he waved his hand towards the end of the bed. As she sat down, the springs in the mattress creaked.

'You OK?' she said again, more slowly.

It was almost funny. 'Define OK.'

She swung her feet a little. 'You know what I mean.'

He nodded, but he kept his eyes cast down firmly

at the floor.

'Are we going to even talk about what happened?'

'She was my sister,' Jed blurted. 'Zoe. I remembered.'

'Oh.'

He moved across the room and sat on the end of the bed too but this time he made sure there was a gap between them.

'Do you know how she died?'

His throat thickened. 'There was a flood. The River Seine burst its banks. The press said no one drowned. But they were wrong.' He closed his eyes. 'I remember her. Her laugh. The way she bossed me about.' He hesitated. 'Everything from that time is clearer now.'

'I'm so sorry. We shouldn't have done it. I just thought that . . .'

'She's the reason for the elixir. The reason I did it. That version of me you saw in the memory . . .' He tried to swallow but the muscles were pulling even tighter in his throat. 'I was so angry. And no one cared. They didn't even report her death. She didn't count, you see. And I wanted her to count.'

'Of course you did.'

'I think I did this for Zoe. And somehow the picture of the Empress and the Phoenix Man in the Hagia Sophia are connected to that.'

Kassia put her hand on the bed between them. An ocean of space, her fingers outstretched. 'So, it's good then,' she said. 'That you faced it. That you saw what happened. That we all saw.'

Jed sat very still. Maybe Kassia had seen what he'd seen. But he wasn't entirely sure she'd understood it as he had.

They sat for ages in the silence, the space between them unchanged, Jed's hands resting in his lap.

And when they looked up, Dante was standing in the doorway. He was holding three envelopes: one red, one black, one white.

'What are they?' Kassia said in sign.

Dante shrugged. He handed them to her. 'They were on the doormat,' he said. 'Like the newspaper was.'

Kassia turned the envelopes over. On the back of each was a small pencil-drawn symbol. The mark of the Brothers of Heliopolis.

'Part of the test?' signed Dante.

Kassia slid the envelopes open. Each contained some sort of ticket. These were coloured too.

'What are they for?' asked Jed, taking the red ticket.

'These are for an air balloon ride and some sort of mineral pool in a place called Pamukkale. What about that one?'

186

She took the red ticket but Jed had already begun to sign the answer. 'A place called the Maiden's Tower, here in Istanbul.'

ADMIT ONE
MAIDEN'S TOWER

This TICKET
Entitles the Bearer to One Passage
on the
ISTANBUL
FERRY

NOAH

DAY 225

10th October

The boat pulled gracefully into the mooring. Tourists scrambled out on to the small island that housed nothing except a tall building called the Maiden's Tower. The Bosphorus river washed her route around its base.

'Why do you think we needed to come here?' asked Kassia, following Jed as he climbed up the steps and entered the building at the base beside the water.

'All part of the puzzle,' said Jed. He looked round. The squat, red roofed building was used as a café, but he, Kassia and Dante hadn't come here to eat. He led the way between the crowded tables to the stairs that twisted inside the tower. Signs directed them to a viewing platform, but Jed knew they hadn't come here to look at the view either. He hoisted his bag on to his shoulder and began to climb the stairs.

The tower was rectangular and made of thick stone. Windows in the walls showed the river falling away as they climbed, and it wasn't long before they reached the entrance to a balcony that ran around the outside edge. Most tourists stopped here, but Jed was pretty sure they had to keep climbing.

There was a door preventing access any further. Jed checked over his shoulder to be sure they hadn't been followed, then he grabbed the handle. The door was locked. Jed checked behind him again and then pushed his shoulder hard against the door.

'What are you *doing*?' groaned Kassia.

Jed thudded the door again. 'From the boat you could see that there's another balcony on the very top of this thing.'

'And from *right here*,' reprimanded Kassia, 'you can see there's a door that says no one should go up there!'

Jed spun round to face her. 'Kass, you said yourself, we had to think about why we'd come. We weren't sent here to eat fish sandwiches and take selfies from the boat! You've got to see that.'

'You think we were sent here to break and enter, then?' she said defensively.

Jed thought back to Jacob and how he'd broken into the tower of Notre Dame. The memory was confusing. Jed had been sure then that they shouldn't do that, and yet the answers were just as Jacob had been convinced they would be – hidden out of reach of everybody else. 'I don't know, Kass. But we've always had to look beyond the obvious, so I reckon we should try.'

Dante stepped beside him and shoulder barged the door himself. There was the sound of wood splintering and the door swung open.

'Are you with us?' asked Jed, stepping through and nodding his thanks at Dante.

Kassia reluctantly followed them.

The stairs worked in a spiral, narrower this time as the tower reached a point. Another door led out on to a tiny balcony. This one ringed the very tip of the structure, which was wooden now, an enormous flag pole driving upwards, a huge Turkish flag blowing in the wind. The curve of the tower meant it wasn't possible to see down on to the lower balcony from this higher one and this made Jed feel more confident. If they could see no one else, then perhaps that meant no one could see them.

'Now what?' signed Dante.

Jed rubbed his hand across his chin, put his bag down and sat down on the floor. The climb had been exhausting and he was struggling to breathe. He knew

Kassia was watching him anxiously and so he tried as hard as he could to keep his back to her. The pain in his chest didn't help, but this had nothing to do with the shortness of breath.

'Jed?'

'I'm fine,' he snapped, almost too quickly. 'Honestly. I'm OK.' He reached into his bag and pulled out a guidebook they'd bought from the shop next to the apartment. 'Whoever the Brothers of Heliopolis are, it seems to me that they have a plan. And I guess we just have to work out what it is.'

'You trust them now?' said Kassia, sitting down beside him.

'No.'

Kassia looked surprised.

'Trusting anyone seems crazy . . . after Jacob. But we're running out of time. And if there's a chance that all these tickets and clues are going to help us, then maybe we just have to go with it.' He looked down through the railings at the surging flow of the river and the boats bobbing in the water and he wished he was as confident in his plan as he sounded.

'So you think someone from the Brotherhood is going to meet us here?' signed Dante, sitting down too.

Jed shook his head.

'Really? So what are we doing then?'

'Metin said we had all we need,' said Jed, taking the postcard and the box of inks from his bag. 'And I think this is all to do with the past again. And I think the past of this place is important. That's why we're here.'

Dante pointed to the guidebook. 'And there's stuff in there about this tower?' he said.

Jed flicked the pages open that he'd scanned quickly in the boat on the way over. 'It's a sad story,' he said. 'This emperor had a daughter. And someone made this wacky prophecy. Said she was going to die from a snake bite by her eighteenth birthday.'

'Nice,' signed Dante sarcastically.

'Exactly. So the emperor built this tower and he made his daughter live here. No snakes could get across the river, see.'

'Bit harsh,' Dante went on. 'But I see the logic.'

'So this girl was OK, then?' said Kassia.

'No,' said Jed. 'On her eighteenth birthday, her dad sailed out to visit her here and he brought a basket of presents and fruit. And this snake had got itself into the basket and . . .'

'Prophecy fulfilled then,' said Kassia.

'Yep. Girl died of a snake bite just like the Oracle had said she would.'

'And so what's the point of this story?' pressed Dante. 'For us, I mean.'

'I guess it's that you can't always escape what you have to face, even if you want to.'

Kassia leapt up from the ground. 'You're not going to die, Jed. We're not going to let that happen.'

Jed reached for her arm and pulled her back down beside him. 'That isn't what I meant.' His voice sounded shaky and he knew that she saw through the lie. 'I think what we did in the apartment with the memory was important. And you were right. Nat was right. I've been trying not to remember the past and I think after everything in Prague I just tried to push the memory of the elixir days away. But I think I have to face them.'

'What about the fact it hurt so much? And the stuff about Zoe and . . .'

Jed fiddled with the top button of his shirt. 'You wanted me to do this, Kassia.'

'But how do we go back to those memories? The postcard again? The watch?'

Jed took the box Metin had given him in the Grand Bazaar and opened it. The sun glinted on the shaft of the twisted glass pen. 'In the hospital after the Thames, Nat asked me to draw. Remember?'

'And you drew the ouroboros.'

'Except I didn't know it was that. You two helped. You fitted the pieces together.'

'And you think you've got to draw again?' signed Dante.

Jed took the bottle of black ink from the box. 'With these,' he said. 'The colours of the stages of alchemy.'

'But what about Prague?' said Kassia. 'We had to do all that stuff about the stages of alchemy there and it was all a waste of time.'

'It wasn't,' said Jed quietly. 'It's like those pieces of the ouroboros. When I drew them, I had no idea why. Just scribbles and scratches on page after page. But you helped me. And the pages fitted together. I think the stuff in Prague was just a beginning.' He smiled. 'And anyway, this time it will be different.'

'How?'

'This time I won't see the memories alone.'

He took a pad of plain paper from the bag. Then he pulled the golden cord that kept the wax lid secure on the bottle of black ink. The wax crumbled.

'How will it work?' signed Dante.

Jed took the pen and dipped it into the bottle.

'How will you know what to draw?'

Jed didn't answer. He wasn't sure he had the confidence to explain. The idea could be crazy. But maybe no more crazy than coming to Istanbul in the first place. They hadn't really been sure why they'd done that. But they'd trusted it was right. And so he trusted now, because the cold truth was that they were running out of options. And out of time.

He let the tip of the pen rest against the paper like he'd done so many months before in the hospital in London and he let his mind be free. 'Don't self-check,' Nat had said in those very first days after he'd clambered from the River Thames knowing absolutely nothing. 'Hold nothing back,' Nat had urged. And so Jed let his hand move slowly. At first, the glass pen scratched at the paper, the ink spluttered and smudged. But then the pen began to move fluidly and the ink ran like water.

Finally, his hand slowed. The ink from the spiral nib dried. Jed put down the pen.

On the paper in front of him was an image, not of a dragon, but a bird. 'It's a raven,' he said quietly and he had no idea why he felt so sure, but he was certain that it was.

Kassia took the pen and rested it back in the blue velvet lining of the box. 'Now what?' she said.

Jed reached into his pocket and took out the watch. He opened the front and put it on top of the picture of the raven. 'Ready?' he said.

Kassia put her hand on his. And Dante leant forward and completed the triangle.

A breeze blew in from the river and the hands of the watch began to spin. Mist, lifting from the water, thickened and darkened like smoke and began to turn. The body of a dragon boring a circle in a memory into which they all fell.

A signpost in the road declares the name of the village to be Lagny-Pomponne. A man stands alone in a quiet alleyway. He watches the fog swirl and the patterns made by ice, crisscrossing the windows of the house that corners the track. The man is Fulcanelli. He looks younger than in the first memory. His face is sharper. His eyes brighter, no mauve shadows ringing the skin beneath.

Another man enters the alley. He too was in the first memory but this man has aged; shadows now ring his eyes. His shoulders stoop as he walks.

Fulcanelli acknowledges his arrival with a nod. Canseliet nods back. He is struggling not to stare.

'You look,' the older man hesitates, 'well.'

'I feel well, Eugene.'

The older man struggles to find an answer, but no words come.

'How is Paris?' says Fulcanelli.

'Good. Life is good.' The older man is nervous but he cannot take his eyes from his companion. 'I think, perhaps, for you, that life is better.'

A smile twitches at the corner of Fulcanelli's lips.

For the first time since arriving, Canseliet looks away. 'Julien says he is sorry. His excitement about what you had done made him so keen to make idle chatter.'

The smile vanishes. 'Many of the good and the great have had to leave Paris and go into exile. Even Victor Hugo had to leave. And I am close enough to feel connected.' He takes a deep breath. 'Have you done what I asked? My parents' grave? And Zoe's?'

'Every week, new flowers.'

Fulcanelli acknowledges the response but it does not look much like a thank you, perhaps more of an acknowledgement of a bargain fulfilled. 'And the other thing I asked?'

Canseliet takes a small bottle from the inside pocket of his coat. A golden liquid churns inside.

Fulcanelli looks angry now. 'Just the one? You brought the others too?'

'No.' It is a simple answer but Canseliet looks scared to say it.

'But they make me feel so alive, so strong, so free.'

'We agreed, sir. The six doses must be spread across time. You agreed that timing is important. I should keep the other doses safe, sir. In case anything happens. There should be checks and balances at every stage. We decided that, before this ever began.'

Fulcanelli grabs the single bottle from the older man's hand. He twists it between his fingers. The fog circles the glass but the liquid inside does not dull.

'And the exchange, sir?' Canseliet's voice is shaking slightly. 'You said there would be a trade.'

With his other hand, Fulcanelli pulls a brown paper parcel from inside his own coat. It is tied with string.

'This is it? Your third manuscript?' says Canseliet. 'The Great Work? The answers for everyone to share?'

'I've changed my mind,' says Fulcanelli, and a smile plays again at the edge of his mouth. 'I think we should delay publication.'

Canseliet runs his finger under the string. 'Wait, sir? But for what? The recipe works. You are proof of that.'

'For safety, we should be sure. About possible side effects, you understand. We just need to be certain.'

Canseliet's voice is barely more than a whisper. 'But you want me to have the manuscript.'

'I want you to protect it, Eugene. To keep my secret safe.'

Canseliet hesitates. His jaw clenches. 'I will keep our secret safe, sir. Like the rest of the elixir.'

Fulcanelli's eyes flash but he is distracted by the weight of the tiny bottle in his hand.

'Are you scared?' says Canseliet.

'No!' There is a wildness about Fulcanelli's eyes.

He glances down the alley and then he pulls the cork from the bottle. He lifts the bottle to his lips. And a town clock strikes the hour of eleven as he drinks.

There is a flash of light. It roils through the fog as Fulcanelli collapses to the ground. He clutches at his chest, struggling to loosen his coat as if a fire burns inside.

The fog covers him like a shroud and when he stands, his coat open, his shirt loose, a golden medallion hanging at his neck, he is changed. A younger man, but still recognisable, where he once stood.

Canseliet steadies himself against the wall. Icy air swirls around them.

Fulcanelli flexes his hands. He feels the strength of youth flowing in his fingers. A warmth and an excitement that is overwhelming.

Suddenly a woman calls into the alley. 'Sirs, please. Come quickly. There's been an accident!' The woman is spluttering, her voice rasping in the cold. 'The eleven o'clock express train from Strasbourg! The ice on the rails. It couldn't stop. Please come.'

Canseliet tightens his hold on the parcel and turns to follow the woman. The sound of distant screaming drifts *in with the fog.*

Fulcanelli grabs Canseliet's arm. 'I can't, Eugene. If I am seen . . .'

Canseliet's forehead wrinkles in confusion. 'But you are changed, sir. Hardly recognisable now from the man you were in Paris. And there are people injured. People hurt.'

Fulcanelli looks down at his hands. 'I look now even more like the Fulcanelli the world is searching for. Do you want my exile to be for nothing? The time I missed with my parents, wasted for nothing?'

Canseliet face is drained of colour. 'But don't you see, sir? The time of the train?'

Fulcanelli is struggling to understand.

'Eleven o'clock.'

Fulcanelli staggers free. And the fog swirls. And the screams of the injured thunder in his head as the elixir surges in his veins.

Jed grabbed for the watch that rested on the picture of the raven. The hands stopped spinning. He folded forward, clutching at his chest.

'It's OK, Jed!' Kassia's voice cut through the fog that swirled in his head.

Jed scrambled to stand. He knocked the bottle of ink. It shattered on the ground, ink oozing like blood on the stones. 'It was my fault,' he yelled, his hand clawing at his chest.

'No!' Kassia pleaded. 'We've been through this. You taking the elixir is not the reason for the crash.'

'Eleven o'clock, Canseliet said,' Jed moaned, folded forward still, rocking against the pain in his chest.

'They can't be connected!' Kassia said, making a grab for him.

But he pulled away, his back pressed hard on the railings of the balcony. 'So why did I need to see that,' cried Jed. 'If it's all part of the puzzle, then why?'

Kassia looked across at her brother. She fumbled for words to answer Jed's question.

Dante tugged at Jed's arm and forced him to focus as he moved his hand in reply. 'Metin went on about the three stages of alchemy. Who you *are* and *were* and *wanted to be*.' He made his signs as gentle as possible. 'I think all this is about making you see what kind of man you were.'

Jed folded forward again, his shoulders heaving. And when he spoke, his signs were precise and clean, cutting the air like a knife. 'And what kind of man was I, then? You saw me. You watched me walk away from all those people.'

'You were protecting your secret!' said Kassia.

Jed used the railings to steady himself. He said

nothing as he stuffed the guidebook and the box of ink into his bag and made for the stairs.

The picture of the raven lifted on the wind. It rode the air for a moment and then it fell into the river.

Far below the top of the Maiden's Tower, the ink raven bled into the River Bosphorus, and drifted away.

DAY 226
11th October

'I'm not sure what you hope to get from this visit,' said Cole, blowing a bubble with his chewing gum and letting it pop on his lips.

'You told me to look for unicorn tracks and I found some,' said Victor.

They'd been back in London a few days now, but it had been Victor's idea to come to St Paul's. They were still no further forward with information from Interpol about flights from Paris. The net of options seemed to take in most of Europe, Africa and Australia. If it was possible, Montgomery was tetchier than ever. Getting outside and doing something seemed like a positive option as far as Victor was concerned.

'There's something that connects Fulcanelli and Bergier to this Reverend Cockren at St Paul's Cathedral and I want to find out what it is,' said Victor.

Cole blew another bubble. 'Well, I can bet you that old Riverboy's not hiding out at the cathedral. No chance we'll see him back here after Notre Dame.'

'Yeah, well, maybe this Cockren guy can shed some light on where he might be then.'

'I actually prefer the name Reverend Cockren,' said a voice from behind. The Reverend was wearing full regalia, a long white cassock billowing out behind him, a golden-edged blue stole around his neck.

Victor mumbled something that sounded like an apology. The guy was quiet. Sort of sneaky. This unnerved him.

'Oh, I'm used to being called all sorts,' Reverend Cockren laughed. 'Not all of it pleasant.' He straightened his arm so that the sleeve of his cassock fluttered. 'So, the verger told me you wanted to have a chat. Is there anything particular I can help you with? Any specific prayers I can offer?'

Victor began to feel even more uncomfortable. Maybe this was not such a good idea. Maybe searching flight plans like Martha Quinn had suggested would have been a better option. 'No. You're OK about the prayers, ta. It's just we wanted to ask about the Riverboy.'

The Reverend's smile vanished. His eyes drew closer together. His voice, when he spoke again was sharper, more clipped. 'That old chestnut. I thought we were over the story of the boy from the river.'

'Yes, well,' Victor tried to ignore the irritated look Cole was throwing in his direction or the excessive snapping noises he was making with his chewing gum. 'It's just there's this French bloke, Bergier,' Victor ploughed on, 'and I think he was connected to the Riverboy.'

Reverend Cockren linked his arms together, hiding his hands in the folds of his enormous sleeves. 'I'm afraid I fail to see how this involves me.'

'Bergier named you in some notes he'd made.' He fumbled for the folder he'd brought with him but the Reverend allowed him no time to open it.

Reverend Cockren steered them over to the closed east door of the cathedral. Victor noticed there was a section of the wall that was darker than the others. It threw an eerie shadow over the Reverend. 'I expect the mention was of my father and not me,' he said in barely more than a whisper as he stared down at the folder in Victor's hand. His narrowed eyes bore down on the insignia stamped in the corner.

Then he looked directly into Victor's face and it was as if he was seeing him for the first time. And there was something about the way Reverend Cockren looked at him. As if he was someone else. Someone he knew.

Victor felt his blood run cold.

'Now, you tell your bosses at NOAH that whatever Jaques Bergier has to say about the Riverboy has absolutely nothing to do with me.'

DAY 230
15th October

'I've brought Turkish delight.' Kassia stood in the doorway, her fingers gripped tightly to the top of a paper bag. It had been five days since the Tower. Jed had barely left the bedroom.

He was standing by the window looking out into the street and he didn't turn to face her. 'You think that will help?' he asked quietly.

'Probably not. But I like it. And in London, when you were stressed, you made biscuits. And I just thought that maybe the sugar . . .'

'We're a long way from London, Kassia.'

She sighed and walked into the room, closing the door behind her. She sat on the end of the bed and looked at the bag in her hand, but she didn't open it. When she turned, Jed was still staring out of the window. His hand was twitching. 'Where do we go from here?' she said.

He shrugged and something like a laugh escaped his lips. 'I don't know. I've lost sight of why we're doing this.'

Her fingers gripped the top of the bag so tightly that the paper tore. 'So that when the year is up, you don't die,' she said matter of factly.

He pulled his hand across himself but she could see that this didn't stop the shaking.

'Somehow looking for the recipe for the elixir made sense,' Jed said. 'But this messing around with the memories just hurts.' His voice cracked and he leant forward so that his forehead rested against the window pane. 'I don't like what I see, Kassia.'

Sugar leaked from the paper bag and dusted the ends of her fingers.

'I see this person and I know it's me. But . . .'

'I don't know how it works, Jed. But I read a book once and a mother was looking at her grown up child. And when she looked, she saw the baby and the child he'd once been as well as the man. And I couldn't understand how that could happen. But I think that when we see your memories, it's like that. We see who you were. All the versions of you. And I think if the Brothers of Heliopolis want you to face those, then it must be important.'

'But supposing I do all this and it doesn't lead to the recipe. Supposing I see all the versions of me and none of it helps?' He pushed against the window, his hand leaving a misty stain on the glass. 'You say what I did didn't cause the train accident, but how can you be sure? All those people, Kassia. And you know that every time I took the elixir something bad happened on that day.'

'But how can it be connected?' she begged.

'I messed with time! You're not supposed to do that!'

Kassia put the bag down on the end of the bed. 'Look at me,' she said quietly.

He shook his head.

'Please, Jed. Just look at me.'

He kept his hand pressed to the window.

'I've seen the same memories as you, but I'm still here.'

'For how long?'

'What?'

'What if the next version of myself is worse? What if the connection between what I did and the disasters can't be argued with next time? What if you really see who I am and . . .'

She got up from the bed and walked to the window, grabbing hold of his arms and trying to force him to

211

look at her. But he kept his head down. His eyes turned away.

'Jed, please look at me!'

He swallowed and lifted his head and she could see that his eyes were raw from crying.

Her words faltered a little but she pressed on. 'We've come this far, given up so much to try and make sense of this and to be sure you don't die. And you are not going to give up on me now! So this is difficult. And painful! But it's the only hope we have and I'm not going back to London without answers, you understand.'

He tried to turn away again but she shook his arms and made him focus on her.

'There are two bottles of ink left. Two more stages. And I don't care how hard it is or what we see that you have done. If doing this means you will work out how to keep on living, then I say we plough on!'

He stood for a moment, his eyes locked finally on hers.

'Now, my brother is out there in a strange city looking for a way to get us to where we need to be for the second invitation. And you can turn down my Turkish delight all you like, but if Dante comes back with a plan to get us out of here, then I am telling you that we have to take it. OK?'

Something like a smile twitched across Jed's lips. 'You know you can be quite persuasive when you're angry,' he said.

'Good,' said Kassia, finally letting go of Jed's arms and wiping her hands together so that dustings of sugar lifted on the air. 'All right then. Now which do you want? Lemon or rose?'

'What?'

'Turkish delight, you doughnut. If we don't have some before Dante gets back, then there won't be any left.'

Jed's smile flickered again and for just a second Kassia believed it reached his eyes.

'What *is* that thing?'

Jed and Kassia had heard the screeching of a car horn out in the road and had raced down the stairs to see. Kassia was half expecting another car crash. Instead, she saw Dante grinning widely and leaning against the bonnet of what looked to her like an oversized toy car.

Dante spelt four letters on his fingers. 'JEEP. Just every essential part,' he added proudly.

Kassia walked round the front of the vehicle. She guessed it was green but the thing was so caked in mud that it was hard to be completely sure. 'Is this thing even roadworthy?' she quizzed.

'What d'you expect when you send me out with such a small budget?' Dante laughed with his hands.

'Well, maybe something with a roof?'

'Hey!' Dante signed defensively. 'I don't even speak the language. In fact,' he added mockingly, 'I don't even speak. I think I did pretty amazingly to get anything. OK, they probably gave me this just to get rid of me, but I think the thing has history. Character, maybe.'

Kassia pulled a face. 'It hasn't even got doors,' she groaned.

'You sent me out to get a car. I got one. Next time you need to be specific.'

'I think it's fine,' said Jed. 'You did great.'

'Thank you! At least someone appreciates my efforts.'

Kassia pulled a face. 'It'll do,' she said grudgingly.

Dante winked at Jed. 'She does this when she thinks she's in charge. How's she been with you?'

Jed kicked the nearest tyre of the jeep and a clod of earth fell free. 'She's been,' he searched for the right word, 'decisive,' he said.

'So she's bossed you about too, hey? Oh well, if it means me and her don't have to look at each other for days and work out what to do with you

214

then that's fine by me.'

Jed looked like he was going to say something, but Kassia cut across him and made her signs so large they'd drown out any hand movements either of the others made. 'So the extra thing I asked you to get?' she said.

Dante reached into the open back of the jeep and pulled out a road map and spread it on the bonnet.

'Brilliant,' signed Kassia. 'Jed and I were just saying that we think it's time we tried to get to the second place the Brothers of Heliopolis are sending him to. So we should get serious and start planning a route.'

ember 23rd 1933

...th, be not proud, though some have called thee

...ghty and dreadful, for thou art not so;

...r those whom thou think'st thou dost overthrow

...ie not, poor Death, nor yet canst thou kill me.

From rest and sleep, which but thy pictures be,

Much pleasure; then from thee much more must flo...

And soonest our best men with thee do go,

Rest of their bones, and soul's delivery.

Thou art slave to fate, chance, kings, and desper...

And dost with poison, war, and sickness dwell,

And poppy or charms can make us sleep as well

And better than thy stroke; why swell'st thou

One short sleep past, we wake eternally

And death shall be no more; Death, thou shal...

John Donn...

DAY 242

27th October

Victor sat on the steps of St Paul's Cathedral. He pulled his jacket tighter around his neck. A cold wind was blowing up from the Thames and it was making him shiver.

He tried to think back to another time when the weather had been cold and he'd been at the cathedral. It had been February and it felt like a lifetime ago. But that day was scored into his mind. It was the day Martha Quinn had come to Etkin House, and everything had changed. It was also the day that his life had become intertwined somehow with the boy from the river.

And he had only just remembered now that the day had started at the cathedral.

He'd been hurrying past. And there had been a girl hurrying too. And he had bumped into her. And she had been carrying flowers. But the flowers were dead. And they had fallen to the ground.

Victor remembered the flowers. He couldn't see the face of the girl in his memory. It was blurred. A fleeting image that he hadn't fixed, because there had been no need to. And yet . . . Something bothered him about the memory. Something he felt was important. And so he fought to claw back her face from the dark and distant folds of his mind.

And suddenly he felt a surge of images. A jolt as recollections bombarded into his brain.

He *did* remember her face. Oh god, how could he have not made the connection?

The girl with the flowers was the girl he'd seen at Riverboy's home when they went to collect him. And so that meant that the girl with the flowers had been . . . He couldn't bear to remember. She'd been the girl from the Neckar. The girl NOAH had been willing to sacrifice for their cause.

How could it have taken him so long to put that piece of the puzzle together?

He tightened his coat again and shivered.

The pieces were connecting and he wasn't sure that he liked the picture they were forming.

And he knew that he hadn't been the only one at the cathedral to make a connection.

Reverend Cockren had put things together, Victor was sure now. The meeting with him and Cole, just over a week ago, had played over and over in Victor's mind. The man was scared by something, but Victor wasn't sure what it was. And he was hiding something too. That was totally obvious. But even more than that, Victor was sure that Reverend Cockren had recognised him when, as far as he knew, the man had never met him before.

And that's why Victor was waiting.

And that's why he'd been here every morning. Because, however long it took, he was going to get the man to give him some answers.

He rubbed his hands together against the cold and he tried to ignore the rumbling in his stomach. He was hungry. But today he was going to wait until Reverend Cockren finally agreed to see him.

It was nearly dark when he became aware of a figure standing on the steps behind him.

Victor scrambled up.

The Reverend's flowing black robes skirted the edge of the steps. The long white stole cut a line around his neck.

'You came?' Victor spluttered. 'I'd almost given up hope that you'd agree to see me. I've waited days and . . .'

'I'm sorry.' The Reverend's voice was cold and unforgiving. 'I said all I needed to you and your friend days ago. You need to leave here now.'

'Please,' Victor stuttered. 'If you could just tell me . . .'

Reverend Cockren had turned and begun to re-climb the steps to the cathedral. 'This is a house of God,' he said. 'And you are welcome here any time to pray or to worship. But I cannot be of more help to you.'

Victor scrabbled in his pocket. He thrust a photograph in front of Reverend Cockren. 'This is my father,' he said.

The Reverend stopped walking. His cassock still rippled in the breeze.

'But you know that, don't you?' Victor mumbled. 'I saw you recognise me. You knew him, didn't you? Please! You have to tell me what you know.' The photograph flapped backwards and forwards in the cold November wind. 'Please!'

Reverend Cockren winced, as if searching for what to say in answer caused him pain. 'Look, child, perhaps I *did* know your father. But that was in another lifetime. I want nothing to do with what he was involved in. I warned him back then and I thought he'd understood.'

221

'Understood what?' Victor spluttered.

Reverend Cockren turned so that he was finally facing him. 'That there was a reason the unicorn missed the ark.'

DAY 249
3rd November

They'd been driving on and off for nearly three weeks. They'd stopped and spent the nights in terrible bed and breakfasts. The beds were so cramped and hard they left bruises after sleeping and the breakfasts consisted of unrecognisable pickled foods and doughy concoctions smothered in syrupy sauces that made their teeth feel gritty for hours. The jeep had broken down twice. They'd had a puncture and had had to change a wheel. And when it rained, the lack of roof or windows at the side meant they got soaked.

But somehow, despite it all, Kassia felt better than she'd done for months. They were breathing fresh air and weren't trapped underground. And they were moving forward, so there was a sense of purpose and direction.

Jed looked different. His skin coloured with

windburn as they drove, and his eyes looked brighter in the sun. She could tell his muscles had relaxed. The tension in his shoulders was less obvious and the tremor in his hand was barely noticeable for days at a time.

Kassia didn't allow hope to overwhelm her, but she clung on to the tiniest glimmer of chance that things might be OK.

The rain that morning came heavily.

They'd given up trying to protect themselves against it. There was no point.

'So this is living?' laughed Jed, as Dante pulled the jeep into the car park of a roadside motel.

Kassia grinned back and clambered down after him. He held his hand out to help her jump to the ground and she let herself hold on for a second longer than she needed to.

Jed's T-shirt was soaked and clinging to his chest.

Kassia reached out and pressed her fingers gently at the space below his throat. His eyes narrowed a fraction as if the pressure of her hand hurt him. 'And your heart can cope with it?' she asked.

Since Paris they'd hardly talked about what had happened in the Court of Miracles but the way his clothes clung to him now, as they had done months before with the sweat of a fever, had reminded her, and like the rain, some memories could not be avoided.

He pulled away gently. 'My heart's fine.'

She knew she'd spoilt the moment and she was angry with herself. But memories ebbed and flowed like the ripples on a river and, sometimes, when she least expected it, their waves pulled her under.

She fiddled awkwardly with her hair. It hung wet on her shoulders and so she pulled it to the side, twisting it into a plait.

Jed's eyes sparkled again, as if the awkwardness of the seconds before had washed away in the rain. 'You look like you did when I first saw you,' he said. 'So organised and in charge. Hair all tied up as if not a strand could afford to be out of place.'

She reached up and ruffled his own hair like he was a puppy. 'Yeah, well, you look like you did when I first met you too. This mane is out of control and could do with a trim.'

He laughed and it was OK again.

Kassia was suddenly aware of water splashing up her legs. Dante had kicked hard against a puddle in an obvious attempt to make them realise that he was still there. 'When you're both ready,' he signed clumsily, one hand carrying a bag from the back of the jeep, making it difficult for him to say what he needed to with any fluidity. The intention behind his words was clear in his eyes, though.

Kassia pulled a face in apology and grinned at Jed conspiratorially, then she and Jed grabbed their things from the back of the jeep and followed Dante to the motel reception to check in.

Kassia made use of the shower after they'd eaten a rather thin yogurt soup served in plastic cups and available for sale in the motel lobby. She'd probably got wetter in the rain, though, and the banging and spluttering from the ensuite plumbing was so unnerving that she hadn't taken long before getting out and clambering into bed. This mattress was marginally more comfortable than any of the others since Istanbul. But she couldn't sleep. She was lying instead looking up at the ceiling, trying to see patterns in the eruptions of mould on the paintwork.

She could hear rain on the window, a light drizzle now. It was gently reassuring.

Suddenly the noise of the drizzle was driven out by the sound of tapping.

Her heart reared in her chest and pummelled the back of her throat. Had NOAH found them?

But then a voice joined with the tapping. And she realised it was Jed.

'You trying to give me a heart attack?' she hissed, throwing open the window. And then, because the irony of both their hearts having stopped before wasn't lost on her, she thumped him with the pillow which she'd clutched against her as she'd leapt up from the bed.

'Whoah, watch it, tiger,' Jed laughed, steadying himself on the rickety balcony that stretched along the front of the motel.

Kassia dropped the pillow. 'You got a thing about using the door?' she said.

He shrugged. 'I like being in the rain,' he said. 'It makes me feel alive.'

Kassia wasn't quite sure how to answer.

'Hey, don't look so sad. I *am* still alive. Or is that the reason for the frown?'

Kassia thumped him again with the pillow. 'Don't joke. It's not funny.'

He grabbed the pillow from her, sat down and slid the pillow behind his back so that he was resting against the wall beside the window, looking out on to the road. A line of tail lights snaked red across the valley and towards the nearest town.

'Coming out here to sit in the rain too?' he asked.

'Nah. You're all right. I'm good in here thanks.'

'Suit yourself.' He nestled further back into the support of the pillow.

'So, your own stretch of balcony not comfy enough,

then?' Kassia said at last, having pulled a chair up to the window so she could sit.

'Maybe I didn't want to be alone.'

Kassia twisted her hands together. Without Dante here it felt strange not to need to sign.

'But about the being alone bit,' Jed said quietly, and his voice sounded strangely heavier as if the words suddenly were harder to say. 'I've been thinking about the next memory.'

She said nothing to interrupt him.

'We're not far from the mineral terraces now. The second ticket and all that. Could be there in an hour, Dante says.'

'So tomorrow, then?'

He sighed. 'Yep. Tomorrow. Time to face the next memory.'

'And are you ready?'

'No.'

Again she had no answer.

'And so I've been thinking about the alone bit,' he said again.

She finally saw where this was going. And she felt something like anger bubble in her mouth. 'You're going to do the whole *I want to do this on my own* thing, aren't you?' she snapped. 'That's what this is all about.'

He was struggling now to find the words to say.

'Jed, haven't you thought that just like there are three stage of alchemy, maybe it's important that there are three of us to see the memories?' She wasn't sure if this made sense. But then none of what they were doing really seemed that sensible and all she knew for certain was that she couldn't bear the thought of Jed seeing the memories on his own.

'I don't know, Kass.'

She turned away from the window, facing into the room, but she could still hear his breathing. 'Look, we're here together. That's the deal. And so tomorrow when we go to the mineral pools, we face the memory like we have done the others. Together. Understand?'

He didn't speak an answer.

'You do know that nodding or signing doesn't work if I can't see you,' she said gently.

She thought she heard a soft laugh. And then, suddenly, she saw his hand pressed to the window.

She knew it was his way of agreeing with her. But as his hand slid downwards she could see that the lifeline running across his palm was still unhealed. It left a smear of blood against the glass.

DAY 250
4th November

Just as Dante had predicted, it took them an hour to get to Pamukkale. The signs told them the name of the mineral pools meant 'cotton castle' and as the jeep trundled closer, it was easy to see why the place had got that name. There was an enormous stretch of hills, but whereas the surrounding area was green and fertile, the hills here were terraced and completely white. It looked to Kassia as if snow had fallen though as they got closer, it was clear it wasn't snow. Instead, terraces of spring water had solidified as white crystals. The light bouncing off the terraces was sharp and cold.

Dante found a parking space and then they used the ticket from the envelope to enter through a visitors' gate that formed a barrier to the whole expanse of otherworldly terrain.

'It looks kind of manmade,' said Kassia.

'Could man really have done this?' said Jed. 'God or man, you tell me?'

'No deep discussions yet, please,' signed Dante. 'We've only just got here.'

Kassia winked at Jed and they followed the signs towards an area where the rules for the terraces were clearly set out in a variety of languages. 'No shoes allowed,' said Jed, taking off his trainers and slipping them into his bag. 'They're really going along with the place of God thing.'

Kassia fumbled with her shoe laces. The solidified spa water felt rough beneath her feet, sharp and cold like the reflected light.

They walked through the pools, following the other visitors. People were speaking in hushed voices. It really did feel like being inside some sort of temple to a higher power.

As Kassia walked on, she noticed how, close up, the solid spa water looked like layers of candle wax spilling down the hillside. They rarely used candles at home. The mess they made had, as far as her mother was concerned, no purpose. But once Kassia had persuaded her mum to allow them to have a special candle at advent. It was lit every day in December and burnt down by a section each time; one notch for each day moving closer to Christmas. After a while, Kassia hadn't liked the candle. There was something sad about watching it burn down in increments, the patterns on the shaft being destroyed day by day. She never asked her mother to buy another one.

She shook away the memory.

'So where to?' asked Dante, stopping for a moment and surveying the terraces.

Jed overtook him, water splashing on their bare feet as he passed.

'Oh, so we just keep going then?' said Dante, taking Jed's movement as an answer.

'I think we should be somewhere more private,' said Jed. He was distracted and anxious, and his signs were clumsy, as if he couldn't concentrate on looking and signing at the same time.

Kassia hurried to keep up.

The terraces stretched down the hillside but the mineral springs weren't the only things people came to Pamukkale to see. There was a town of Hierapolis too, but it was in ruins, deserted and abandoned centuries ago. Jed led the way towards the rubble and mass of crumbling stone.

There were huge archways, and small squat houses with long flat rooves. Flowers grew between the cracks, and grass pushed up in between the stones. Around the buildings were pools for bathing in, and into these had crumbled statues and ornate pillars which poked out of the water like rocks in the sea. Set back on the hill, there was even a huge amphitheatre.

'This place must have been so busy,' said Jed. 'But it looks like everyone just picked up and left.'

'There was an earthquake,' said Dante, gesturing towards noticeboards that told the story of the town.

'And did everyone die?' said Kassia, moving in closer to read for herself. 'Oh, that's tragic, listen.' She converted the main bit of information into signs. 'People who lived here thought they would be safe from death because they believed the mineral pools had the power to give them long life.'

'So people have always believed in the power of an elixir,' cut in Jed.

'Yep. Seems so. And they believed it so much here, that they built mausoleums just for show. But the tombs were sealed up as they had no intention of ever using them.'

Jed looked around at the crumbling sepulchres that lined the pavements. At the nearest one, wild flowers sprawled across the top. He pulled a single yellow bloom and handed it to Kassia. 'Come on,' he said. 'I think the place to find the memory is near here.'

'Close to the empty graves?' Kassia said.

Jed nodded and hurried further down the walkway.

The path fell away a little to the left and led down towards a large bricked up gateway. The air grew colder.

Kassia turned the flower Jed had given her between her fingers and the petals seemed to shrivel as if the bloom had been left out too long in the sun. 'What *is* this place?' she said nervously.

It was Dante's turn to read from the noticeboard. 'It was called Plutonion in Greek, apparently.' He spelt the name letter by letter.

'And in English?'

He spelt this letter by letter too, but his fingers fumbled when they hadn't done before. 'It says it is the Gate of Hell.'

There were steps leading down to the bricked-up doorway and the smell that drifted between the stone prickled at Kassia's nose. 'Oh no, look,' she stuttered, stumbling forward and dropping the flower from her hand.

On the ground in front of the blocked gate was the body of a dead bird.

Jed moved forward too, but as Kassia looked at him she could see that something else was wrong. He was gazing beyond the bird, as if something was fighting from behind the boarded gate and trying to get out.

'The dragon?' she said. 'Can you see the dragon?'

His teeth were clenched and his hands didn't sign an answer but she knew what he was saying.

'So it's here then? The place for the next memory?'

Jed knelt down on the ground and Dante scrabbled in the bag to pull out the ink and pen and the paper to draw on. The paper was black this time. And the ink was white. And as Jed broke the wax that stoppered the bottle, smoke began to swirl. Kassia didn't know if the smoke was real, but the twisting body of the dragon in front of her eyes looked real enough.

Jed dipped the tip of the pen into the ink. He looked up and Kassia nodded reassuringly. And his hand moved backwards and forwards, scratching lines of white across the black.

'What is it?' said Dante when the image was finished. 'Another bird?'

'It's a swan,' said Jed, as if suddenly understanding. 'Those books Giseppi gave me about alchemy. The three stages. I remember now. The raven and then the swan stood for stages one and two.' He took the watch from his pocket and fumbled nervously with the catch. Then he put the watch on top of the picture.

'We can do this,' reassured Kassia. And as time spun backwards and the dragon circled in front of them, they joined hands and tumbled into something else that Jed fought to remember.

There is a cage, a lockup of sorts, like a prison cell. A man sits in rags in the corner, head bowed, knees pulled in to his chest.

A woman appears at the bars. She is dressed in white. A uniform; perhaps a nurse.

With one hand, she fumbles in the pocket of her dress and takes out a small glass bottle. With the other, she holds a metal dinner plate. There is a hunk of bread lying across it, dusted with mould.

The man in the corner looks up. It is Fulcanelli. He scrambles to his feet and lurches towards the bars. 'You brought it?'

The nurse nods quickly and pushes her hand through the bars. 'I need the medallion in return,' she says, glancing left and right to ensure she is not overheard. There are other cells along the corridor. A sound of moaning, a shuffling of feet as, out of sight, people pace like caged animals in a zoo.

Fulcanelli takes the bottle, greedily twisting it in his hand so that the liquid flickers with flecks of light inside. He takes the bread on the battered metal plate and he puts both on the floor at his feet. Then he opens the neck of his shirt and unclasps a golden chain. A medallion swings to and fro as he passes it between the bars.

'I could lose my job for doing this,' breathes the nurse, tucking the golden necklace into her pocket.

'I could have lost much more, if you hadn't,' says Fulcanelli.

She presses her hands on the bars. 'You're a sick man,' she says.

He lifts the bottle from the floor and rocks it in his hand. 'I've told you before that I'm going to live for ever,' he says.

The nurse laughs. 'It's wicked talk like that which got you locked away in here in the first place,' she says.

'The man who brought the bottle,' Fulcanelli says, stepping closer to the bars. 'He is still outside?'

'In the village of Pont-Saint-Esprit,' says the nurse. 'But you know visitors are forbidden.'

Fulcanelli looks down at the ground. He is hungry but the bread looks uninviting.

The nurse fiddles once more with the newly traded necklace in her pocket, her eyes glinting in the light reflected from the bars. 'There are others to feed,' she says.

'And others to bargain with, no doubt,' says Fulcanelli.

She does not grace him with an answer but walks off down the corridor.

Now alone, Fulcanelli takes the stopper from the bottle. There is no hesitation as he drinks, even though the light, when it comes, is brighter than ever before. He falls to the ground, the rags burning on his chest and he pulls them away, clutching at his skin as if trying to dampen a fire that rages there. He lies for what seems an eternity against the cold stone. And then, when the light has faded completely, he eats the bread as if he has never eaten before.

It is the screaming that wakes him. Curled on the floor of his cell, he scrambles upwards, kicking the empty plate so that is bounces against the bars. There is running in the corridor, voices raised. He clings to the wall of the cage and stares out into the darkness.

'What's happened?' he yells, tugging frantically at the bars.

The nurse returns. Her voice is clogging in her throat so that the words are strangled. 'You!' she screams. And he turns his face away from her, trying to hide the change. But she opens the cage and scoops the empty plate from the ground, her foot shattering the discarded bottle and grinding it into the stone. 'You!' she says again, grabbing him by the edge of his rags and making him face her. 'What work of the devil is this?' she screams.

'I don't understand.' He pleads again.

'Poison,' she yells, waving the empty plate. 'All others lie dying because of poison in the bread. But you . . . !'

Fulcanelli bursts free and clutches at the bars.

'You've eaten the same bread as them,' yells the nurse. 'And you look . . .' She is spluttering, struggling to breathe, scanning his face to make sense of what she sees.

238

Fulcanelli sinks to the floor but the nurse grabs at his collar and hoists him to his feet. 'Get out,' she yells. 'You need to leave.'

He wrestles away from her and cowers in the corner. 'But I'm safe here. Please.'

'What have you done?' she shouts again and steers him towards the open door of the cell.

Fulcanelli staggers, clutching at the bars and then he turns. He runs into the chaos of the corridor and then out into the streets of Pont-Saint-Esprit.

As he rounds the corner of the asylum, a man pitches forward out of the shadows.

Fulcanelli struggles to get free. But the arms that hold him are strong. He falls to the ground sobbing.

And when he looks up an old man is looking down at him.

'Devaux? Is that you?'

The older man sinks to his knees on the cobbles. 'You took the next dose of the elixir?' the older man says.

And Fulcanelli trembles as he nods his answer.

Jed pulled his hand free and staggered to his feet. Kassia's face was drained of all colour. 'I called that man Devaux,' he stammered. 'That's your name.'

Kassia scrambled up and reached for his arm. But he pulled away. 'That man. The one who brought me

239

the elixir. Who was he?'

Kassia looked down at her brother, stumbling in words and sign. 'Our grandfather,' she said. 'I think he was a Brother of Heliopolis.'

'And you *knew* that?'

'Please Jed, wait.'

'You *knew* your grandfather was involved and you said nothing.'

Kassia looked again at her brother. 'He helped you, Jed.'

'But I was in an asylum. People thought I was mad. How long had I been there? How long had he made me wait for the elixir?' He was gripping tightly now to the picture of the swan and the black paper was bulging between his fingers, the white of the ink, leaking on to his skin.

'Look, wait!' Dante had stood up too. 'Maybe that's why the three of us were needed. The connection in the past.'

'But I'm so confused,' said Jed, letting the crumpled picture fall to the ground so he could sign. 'I don't understand what I'm supposed to be seeing.'

Dante grabbed the paper from the ground. He flapped it in front of Jed's face and then let it fall again. 'That picture is white ink on black,' he said angrily. 'And you want it all to be that simple, don't you?

Right versus wrong. Good or bad. And it's *never* that simple, Jed. It can never be that easy.'

Kassia's hands were clenched into fists and the words, when she signed, seemed to burst out of her fingers. 'I should have told you, Jed. About our grandad. But it doesn't change anything. Seeing all this doesn't change what happened.'

'But if this is a test,' groaned Jed, 'how do I pass or fail?'

Dante picked up the glass pen and slipped it back into the box. 'You don't,' he said. 'Not yet.'

Jed sank to the ground again and he leant his back against the bricked up gate of hell, blew out a breath and then grasped at his chest.

Kassia knelt in front of him. 'You've got one bottle of ink left,' she said quietly, 'and then maybe the pieces of the puzzle will begin to slot together.'

He didn't look at her. Beside his feet, the feathers of the dead bird ruffled in the breeze. And the crumpled paper with the drawing of the swan lifted on the air and blew away.

August 15th 1951

The Topkapı Dagger

The handle and the case of the dagger ... of gold. The handle is ornamented with ... emerald stones and topped by a watch ... London. The emerald lid of the watch ... diamonds. The dagger was sent by Sultan Mahmud I (1730-1754) to the Persian ruler Nader Shah as a gift. Upon Nader Shah's death, the Ottoman mission brought the dagger and other gifts back to the palace.

...ntruder. Drawn from life by M...

LAMP
GIFTS
MORI

GRAND BAZAAR
ISTANBUL

DAY 251

5th November

'What is *with* you, mate?' Cole Carter leant back on his chair and folded his arms across his chest. 'Seriously, Viccy boy. You've been off programme for weeks now. Where's your focus, Hot Shot? These people keep us fed, pay our bills, put a roof over our head. And a pretty famous, swanky roof at that. What *is* your problem?'

Victor twisted his own chair from side to side. 'Have you ever wondered if we should actually be doing this?'

Cole lurched forward and thumped his hands on the desk. 'Not the worry about the girl in the water again, surely, Viccy boy. You need to let that go! I've told you, the girl ain't dead.'

'I'm not talking about the girl in the water,' Victor said defensively. In his head, she was no longer the girl in the water. She was the girl with the flowers. The girl from the cathedral. But it wasn't her he was thinking about. 'I'm talking about all this.' He waved his hand around the room in Department Nine, cluttered with papers and printouts, newspaper and reports.

'You've done all this before!' groaned Cole. 'Your doubting and your questioning. And I thought Montgomery talked you round. You wear the mark, after all.'

Victor rubbed compulsively at his shoulder. 'But there's this guy and I was talking to him and he just made me think, that's all.'

'Think what?'

Victor was embarrassed. 'He just said some stuff about the unicorn. And how there was a reason it got left off the ark.'

Cole shook his head theatrically. 'Stop with your book talk, Viccy boy. We're not here to talk myths and legends.'

'I know that, but . . .'

'Seriously, mate.' Cole's eyes were cold as steel. 'This is what your dad did before you. And I suggest you just shut up with your arks and your legends and instead you focus on what got us here at the crack of dawn this morning.' He pushed a newspaper cutting across the table. 'Here. Look.'

The article was in a language Victor didn't recognise. 'I can't read that,' he mumbled.

'Yeah, well, thank god for Google Translate then,' said Cole.

'You trust that system?'

'Seriously, Viccy boy. You've got to chill out and learn to trust someone.'

Victor smoothed the edge of the photo in his pocket with the heel of his thumb. The corner was so worn now it was fraying, the fibres of the paper splitting free. He was scared that the image would disintegrate in his hand. 'So what's it say?' he pressed reluctantly.

'Only that some kid in Turkey saved a man from becoming a human fireball after a car crashed into a kebab stand.'

'So?'

'Keep up, Viccy! It's obvious, isn't it? Our mate Fulcanelli just couldn't help himself and has gone out there showing the world who he is. We don't need no flight information any more from Interpol. Our boy's in Turkey and so the chances of bringing him in have finally improved.'

DAY 252

6th November

'I decided to use the conventional entrance,' said Kassia, hanging on to the door handle and leaning into Jed and Dante's bedroom. 'You OK with that?'

Jed smiled. At least Kassia's reference to his late night balcony visit a couple of nights ago wasn't lost on him.

'You heard of knocking?' he laughed.

'It's my brother's room. I've kind of got used to him not being very responsive to that.'

'Yeah, well, your brother is down at the car park putting oil in the jeep.'

'Nice. We're aiming to make the next stage of the journey without breaking down then?' she grinned.

Jed stuffed a couple of crumpled T-shirts into his rucksack. 'That's the plan. It'll make a change.'

Kassia winced at his lack of folding. 'My mum

would have a fit,' she said, letting the door swing closed behind her, and grabbing the T-shirt from him, shaking it out and then untucking the sleeves.

Jed laughed and sank down on the end of the bed, watching as Kassia smoothed folds in the shirt and slid it into the bag. 'Do you think about your mum lots?' he said quietly.

Kassia nibbled at her lip. 'I try not to. It makes me too sad.'

Jed ran his hand across his knee in a blatant attempt to fill the silence and Kassia shook another T-shirt from the bag to refold. A piece of paper fluttered free. A chart of sorts; it looked like sections of a calendar. Dates covered both sides of the paper. Some had been scored through with thick black lines.

Jed made a grab for the paper and went to stuff it in his bag on top of the T-shirts.

'What is that?' Kassia quizzed.

'Nothing. It's not important.'

Kassia made another grab for Jed's hand and this time she was too quick for him.

'Kassia, please. Give me that. It . . .' His voice tailed away.

Kassia tried to hold the paper still. But it shook between her fingers. 'A countdown chart?' she said. And her voice was flat.

Jed reached out and pulled it from her, folding it in half and scoring the crease with his thumb.

'You have a record sheet to show you how close we are to the year being up?'

He stuffed the paper into the top of the bag and pressed down on the T-shirts. Then he pulled the bag closed and hoisted it on to his shoulder. 'Come on,' he said, all lightness from his voice squeezed out like air from his bag. 'Dante will be waiting for us.'

'Do you think about it all the time?' she said.

His lips twitched, but they failed to hold a smile. 'I try not to,' he said. 'It makes me too sad.'

DAY 269

23rd November

It had taken a while to get to Cappadocia but at least the jeep didn't break down on the way. It was incredibly cold now, though, since the weather had turned, so Kassia insisted they stopped to buy blankets to wrap round them as they travelled. Giseppi's funds were diminishing, but Kassia told her brother, in no uncertain terms that did not look particularly attractive as she signed the words, that *she* was pretty close to diminishing if they couldn't find a way to keep warm.

'Seriously,' said Kassia, buttoning up the front of her fleece jacket and pulling the blanket tighter over her legs. 'It would have been cheaper to buy a car with actual doors and a lid on it.'

Dante couldn't really see her as she signed from the back of the jeep but it made her feel better to moan.

They'd thought that when they'd visited the

mineral pools of Pamukkale, that the place looked otherworldly, but nothing could quite prepare them for the landscape of Cappadocia.

The roads they'd travelled had taken them high above sea level and that helped explain the drop in temperature. But the land around them was arid like a desert. There were mountains ringing the area and, spread all around them, like some weird moonscape, were what looked like sculptures made of layered and weathered volcanic rock. Kassia soon learnt that locals called these towers of stone fairy chimneys, and it did look like the sort of place fantasy beings would come to hide. The tall, thin spires of rocks stuck out of the earth as if they had been placed there by someone having a joke. Giant pins sticking out of a pin cushion made of land. Some of the spires had what looked like stone hats on them where parts of the structure had worn away, making them bigger at the top than lower down. Kassia couldn't take her eyes off them. In some lights, they looked like totem poles. In others, like skinny pyramids chiselled from the stone. What they didn't look like was anything that should really exist on earth.

They followed signs to the town of Gerome, as this was where the ticket for the hot air balloon ride was stamped for, and here the geology got even weirder.

Ruffles of stones spread across the town. This looked to Kassia like a giant sea that had been frozen suddenly, the waves stopped in their tracks for ever. Houses had been built to fit in between the folds. But, even stranger, in places homes had been made out of the rock itself. Tiny, arched holes for windows peered out of the hillside. Stairs climbed the rock, leading to hidden rooms. Kassia learnt these houses were called pigeon homes. And they did look like the sort of dovecotes that birds might fly into when it was time to roost. They were miles from London. And in many ways it felt like they were in another world.

'So,' said Dante, pulling the jeep over at the side of the road, jumping out and admiring the view. 'We're really going to do this thing?'

They hadn't talked much about the balloon ride. Kassia wasn't completely sure it would be her thing. She wasn't totally keen to travel above the jagged rock in something that, just like the jeep, did not have doors or a roof. But Jed had the ticket from the envelope, and questioning the need to fly seemed a little ridiculous. If they weren't going to take the ride, then it made no sense to have come so far.

They checked the ticket and then made for the kiosk in town where the flights could be booked. It was easy to find. There was a miniature hot air balloon tethered to a sign outside.

They stood in line and the attendant at the desk eventually showed them a calendar of available slots which they could use their ticket for.

The flight was booked for early next morning. Flights at dawn were supposed to be the highlight of any trip to Cappadocia. Kassia just hoped they were a way of releasing memories. That, after all, was the reason they were here.

'Finally,' groaned Cole, taking a screen shot of the image on his computer and pressing the print icon with just as much speed.

Victor looked up from his own PC monitor.

'You got a sighting?' said Victor, rolling his chair across the polished wooden flooring so he could see the screen that had pleased Cole so much. 'Ooh, nice. I can be there when you tell Montgomery, right?'

Cole grabbed the document from the printer tray. 'So you're interested *now*, then?'

'I've always been interested. I'm just interested in other stuff too.'

'Yeah, well, finally now we have some live information and not just stuff for the archives.'

'Archives?' said Victor, trying to make his voice sound like he didn't really care at all if Cole did or didn't flesh out his comment.

'Floor forty-three,' said Cole, scanning the page from the printer and grinning broadly so that the lump of chewing gum which sat on his tongue was clearly visible.

'Department Nine archives?' pressed Victor, again doing all he could to keep his voice light and breezy.

'Yep. Where most of this paperwork ends up. Top secret to you, though, mate,' said Cole. 'Only Montgomery has a key.'

'Oh.'

'But this ain't something for the archives,' said Cole. 'This is hot off the press, Viccy boy, and Montgomery's gonna love it.'

Victor got up and followed Cole as he made his way down the corridor, the tails of his leather coat fanning out behind him.

Montgomery was sitting in a wing-back chair. The walking cane was resting by the arm and he was fiddling with the silver-topped end. 'This better be good,' he said, looking up as Victor and Cole entered.

Victor noticed how old he looked suddenly.

Cole grinned widely. 'So,' he said, flapping the paper in front of his boss. 'We had a face recognition programme running on as many programmes in

Turkey as possible.'

'Shame we didn't have the same system running when the kid left Paris and ended up there nearly two months ago,' moaned Montgomery.

'Point taken,' said Cole, who was obviously determined not to let the older man's mood dampen the excitement of his find. 'But we have it in place now. And it's worked.'

Montgomery grabbed the paper from Cole's hand.

'Somewhere in Cappadocia.'

'Where's that?' growled Montgomery.

'Some nice place in the middle of Turkey.' He shook his head, obviously slightly irritated at being asked for a geography lesson. 'Point is, there's this place where you can take balloon rides.'

'Balloon rides?' There were more groans of disbelief and Victor wondered if Cole would ever be able to actually finish what he'd come into the room to say.

'Yeah, over the countryside. It's really quite beautiful. Anyway,' he was trying to get the conversation back on track, 'this company agreed to use our face recognition package. And we've had a hit. The kid and his friends have booked a flight.'

Montgomery's fingers were so tightly gripped round the paper that the page was creasing and buckling in his hand.

'We're using every resource we've got to try and track down a boy who's going to live for ever and he's in the middle of a holiday, planning a sightseeing tour!'

Cole shrugged and the chewing gum snapped in his mouth as his clamped his teeth together. 'So you want me to stop the flight, sir? Get people on the ground?'

Montgomery considered his answer. 'Have we got time?'

Cole checked his watch and did some mental calculations. Then his face fell. 'Nearest team are in Istanbul, sir. I'm not sure they'd make it to Cappadocia before the balloon is scheduled to take off.'

Montgomery put the paper down, grabbed his walking cane and stood up. 'So we let him take the flight, but we customise it, understand?'

Victor didn't, but it wasn't Victor that Montgomery was talking to.

'Let him take his flight,' Montgomery growled. 'Just make sure the landing is not included in the price.'

Victor couldn't get his head round what Montgomery was saying. 'But he's not alone, is he?' Victor blurted. 'The deaf boy and the girl are with him!'

'You and that girl from the river,' said Cole, blowing a bubble with his gum. 'You seriously need to forget about her.'

Victor felt his jaw lock tight. She wasn't the girl from the river. She was the girl with the flowers. But the way Montgomery was scanning the print-out again and then reaching for his phone suggested that it didn't really matter who she was. NOAH had made up their mind.

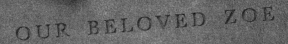

DAY 270

24th November

Jed checked the time on his pocket watch, and then swung his bag on to his shoulder. He'd packed the glass pen and the bottle of red ink, but he'd got absolutely no idea how exactly he'd be able to fit in the chance to draw something to unlock a memory when they were flying high in a hot air balloon. He knew better now though than to second guess the plan that they were following. He'd also got used to always having the pen with him.

Dante was already up and pacing in the hotel lobby and when Kassia arrived to meet them, it looked like she'd probably spent most of the night pacing her hotel room too. Her eyes were puffy and her forehead lined.

'You OK?' he whispered.

'Not that good with the idea of hanging around

inside a picnic basket in the air,' she replied.

There didn't really seem to be much he could say in answer to this, so he squeezed her hand.

Dante followed the instructions that the balloon company had given them and pulled the jeep off the road on to a flat and desolate field. It wasn't deserted though. Across the grass lay huge puddles of coloured silk, each attached to wicker baskets that were lying on their sides. People stood huddled round the various deflated balloons, chattering nervously. The chatting was regularly drowned out by bursts of sound from huge fire-breathing burners.

Dante led the way towards the sign for the company they'd booked with the afternoon before and Jed kept hold of Kassia's hand. He reasoned that if she didn't want to hold on, then she could easily let her hand slip free, but as far as he could tell, she had no intention of letting go anytime soon.

There was a fair amount of paper checking with the guide. Jed noticed that he seemed to be scrutinising the form they'd signed yesterday with much more care than he had done when they'd handed over their cash and reluctantly had their photos taken for the keepsakes on offer. The photos were company policy, apparently. He was far less chatty too and Jed wished he'd lighten up a bit. His nerves were clearly becoming obvious to

Kassia, which made Jed fear for the bones in his fingers if she gripped on any tighter. He wondered how long his fingers would take to heal if they broke. Hours, days, even weeks?

Eventually, the other balloons around the field began to inflate. People clambered into the attached baskets and waved enthusiastically as balloons plumped fully and then began to skirt the ground and rise. Jed silently hoped they wouldn't be the last to leave. The sooner they got this thing over with the better. 'It's just like the O2,' he said quietly in a desperate attempt to make Kassia smile. 'You coped with that brilliantly, and that was high.'

'Are you actually trying to make me feel better?' Kassia hissed.

Jed had to agree she had a point. The O2 hadn't been his finest hour, but surely all you had to do on a balloon ride was stand still and look at the view. How hard could it be?

Dante shuffled closer. There were now only three balloons lying lifeless on the ground. He was obviously keen too that they weren't left till last. But they were. The field was empty except for them, their flaccid balloon and their rather anxious looking pilot, and two support workers who looked even less happy than him to be there.

The pilot waved them closer and then, as his assistants tipped the basket upright, he jumped inside and triggered the release on the burner, doing something to the outlet which meant the roaring sound was loud and constant. Plumes of fire belched upwards and the balloon filled. 'Jump in,' the pilot said, pointing to the footholds made by gaps in the weave of the basket. Dante climbed in first and helped Kassia clamber in afterwards. By the time Jed had climbed in, the balloon was fully inflated and the tiny size of the basket below the vast expanse of scarlet silk became clear. 'Cramped' was putting it mildly. There was just enough room to turn and look at the view, which at the moment was only the empty field.

Jed put his bag down at his feet beside some sort of fire extinguisher and a first aid kit and this didn't do much to make him feel better. He looked at Kassia and tried to smile reassuringly.

And it was as Kassia smiled back that the pilot suddenly swung his legs out of the basket and jumped back down to the ground. 'A situation with the safety line,' he explained.

The burner was still directing flames and hot air upwards and it was obvious the balloon was at maximum capacity now, the coloured silk fully stretched like skin on the ripest of nectarines.

The pilot started fiddling with the drop line. He was saying something quite loudly to his assistants and they didn't seem very happy.

The basket skidded a little on the ground, bouncing slightly as it skirted the grass. Jed looked across at the pilot, then up at the engorged balloon. The burner roared. Jed imagined a very angry dragon would sound just like this as it breathed.

'What is he doing?' Kassia said at last, and she only used her voice as her hands were gripping tightly to the edge of the basket.

'Just checking something I guess,' said Jed. 'I'm sure it's fine.'

But in the next thirty seconds it became totally clear that the one thing it most certainly wasn't was fine.

The disagreement between the pilot and his assistants had escalated. One of them was shouting passionately and Jed had no idea what he was saying. But the punch he swung at the pilot showed that he was very far from happy. The pilot stumbled, reeling from the blow, and clutched at his puckered lip. Then he stumbled again and grabbed at the drop rope, kicking with his foot at some sort of enormous metal staple that was keeping the rope staked to the ground. The rope worked free. The assistant lunged at the man again and made his own grab for the rope, but the momentum of the inflated balloon was too strong.

The basket skidded again along the grass, bouncing so that Jed listed awkwardly to the side. But instead of hitting the ground again, the basket stayed airborne. At first it was by only a metre or so above the grass, but the balloon, as if finally aware it was now free, hauled the basket upwards so that in a matter of seconds the ground was at least a bus's height below. Then the height of a two-storey house. Then more.

'What is he doing?' yelled Kassia, throwing her words towards the pilot who was running along the ground, still holding the end of the rope.

None of the answers Jed had in his head seemed to fit with what was happening. Because *surely* the pilot was doing all he could to drag the balloon back to the ground. *Surely* he was wrestling to keep hold of the only thing that would keep them safe. But he was doing *none* of these things. As the assistants beside him scrabbled to grab the rope for themselves, he kicked out at them as he had done the metal staple. And then, glancing upwards, he let go of the rope and let the balloon float away.

Jed felt all the air escape his lungs.

Fire and gas still pummelled into the inflated canopy of the balloon as it ascended higher and higher.

Kassia began to scream Jed's name. Jed had no idea what to do. Dante was looking up at the burner as if somehow, just by looking, he'd be able to stop the thing. As if there was some sort of brake you could activate with a stare. But the burner was jammed to release fire. And the gas was pumping and the balloon was lifting higher and higher so that the three men left on the ground became tiny flecks.

'What d'we do?' howled Kassia. 'Turn it off! Make it stop!'

'I can't!' yelled Jed, scrabbling at the controls. The lever wouldn't budge.

Kassia clutched at his arms. Grabbed at Dante too. But her brother didn't need to use any signs to confirm that the situation was hopeless.

It seemed odd to Jed that a runaway balloon could float so majestically and gracefully above the ground below. No one watching would have had any idea what had happened. Sightseers in Gerome might even be taking photos, marvelling at the beauty of the balloon drifting above them, not having a clue that those on board might be in danger. Jed could not get his head round the fact that disaster would be disguised.

And he was just processing this idea when it became obvious that, even from the ground, the disaster that was about to happen would actually become clear to everyone.

The fairy chimneys of Cappadocia stuck like needles out of the ground. Sharp, ragged points of ancient volcanic rock like spines on a porcupine. And the balloon was drifting right towards them.

'Steer it,' Kassia sobbed. 'How d'we steer it?'

'You can't!' said Jed.

'But we're going to crash!'

'It's OK. It's OK.' But it wasn't OK. Kassia was right. The balloon was drifting straight for the spike of rocks.

Suddenly, instead of wishing that the balloon would sink down again, Jed began to pray that it would keep rising. If it lifted higher then there was the tiniest chance that it would skim over the spikes. But if they did, then what? Would they keep rising and rising as the flames chugged out of the burner?

Dante grabbed the fire extinguisher and gestured at Jed. His question was obvious.

But Jed didn't know the answer. If they used the extinguisher to put out the fire, would that work? With no flames from the burner, would they just be pumping helium out. Would that be safe? And if they did anything to make the balloon deflate, would that make them plummet down on to the rocks?

'Jed! Please! What do we do?'

The rocks were getting nearer. The balloon getting higher.

Suddenly, the basket jolted. It tipped to the side. Jed felt his stomach turn to water. He gripped to the edge. It lurched again, leaning further this time.

Jed peered over the side.

And then the reason that the basket was listing became starkly clear to him.

The rope that dangled from the bottom of the basket had got caught. It was trapped somehow, maybe on the branch of a tree below.

Jed jammed his feet against the edge to try and brace himself against the tilt. But it wasn't working. The rope was caught fast. The basket was leaning further. It was going to tip completely any minute, Jed was sure.

'I'm climbing down the rope,' Jed yelled.

'You can't leave!' Kassia yelled back.

The basket made a groaning noise. It was straining against the hold of the rope. Jed's mind was in overdrive. What if the rope snapped, and the basket ricocheted the other way?

'We have to, Kass!'

He waved wildly at Dante and tried to make his intentions obvious. Dante was braced against the lip of the basket as it tilted even more.

Jed swung his leg over the top. Kassia clung to his arm. 'Jed! Please!'

'I have to go first, Kass! To steady this thing from below. Then you can follow. You have to trust me!'

He had no idea if this would work. But the basket was creaking even more. And now, because he'd shifted to the outside, it was even lighter and so the lean to the side had increased.

But he twisted his legs round the rope and wrapped his arms round too and prayed and prayed that this would work and that he wouldn't start to shake so that it became impossible to cling on.

It was cold in the shadow of the basket. Wind chilled his hands and as he moved his legs, they cramped with nerves. The side of the fairy chimney was so far below, he wasn't sure he could keep climbing, but as he looked up he could see the basket was tilting further.

Hand over hand, he said in his head, as if only ordering himself what to do would prevent him from letting go and falling. And the weirdest sensation was that he knew in some crazy way this wouldn't matter. He wouldn't die. But he had to get Kassia and Dante to safety. That was the only thing that counted.

His muscles were straining. The cramp was shooting

through his calves. *Hand over hand*, he repeated. *Hand over hand.*

Finally, he'd climbed far enough down to see what the rope was caught around. A tiny outcrop of rock where the weathering of the stone had made a catch. Jed manoeuvred himself towards the shelf of rock. And then he swung his legs free of the rope and pressed his feet to the ground.

It should have felt so wonderful. But the reality was that he was perched halfway up a fairy chimney, while high above him Kassia and Dante were clinging on for dear life.

He yanked the rope to the side, anxious not to free its catch but maybe to right the basket somehow. But he didn't have the strength. His tugs on the rope were futile and he could see that, if anything, the basket was leaning even further over now.

Suddenly, he was aware of legs swinging free of the basket. Dante was clambering out too. Kassia was alone in the basket and the thought made him feel sick. Maybe she should have climbed down first. But supposing she'd fallen, slipped from the rope? He looked beyond the shelf at the pleats and folds in the rock below him and the thought of Kassia tumbling down replayed again and again in his mind.

Suddenly, he wasn't alone on the rock. Dante had

reached him and without words they tugged together on the rope as if they could somehow reel the basket in and drag the balloon down with it. But the balloon was still fully inflated. There was no way they would be able to wrestle the thing to the ground.

'I've told her to climb,' signed Dante. His signs were ragged and broken. 'Told her if we couldn't right the basket, then she was to get out too. She's got to get down!' Dante's eyes were wet with tears and Jed could barely choke back his own as they stared up the rope.

Kassia was swinging her legs over the basket. She was clinging on to the rope. Dante was doing all he could to keep the rope steady.

'Keep going!' Jed yelled. 'That's right. You have to keep going!' His heart hammered in his chest.

With the basket now empty and Kassia on the rope, the basket had lurched fully to the side. And this had forced the swollen silk balloon to veer sideways too, but in the opposite direction, as if to compensate for the change in weight. All the focus on the basket meant that Jed hadn't noticed the balloon was moving nearer to the ragged spikes of rock.

'No!' yelled Jed. With every metre Kassia moved further from the basket, the balloon was pushing closer to the jagged rock face.

He had no idea if Dante saw what he saw. And

no time to explain. Jed leapt upwards and began to re-climb the rope.

The basket tipped. The balloon strained. Jed climbed and Kassia hung on.

And then, as if the situation had reached a tipping point from which there was no return, the basket listed over completely. The balloon propelled itself in the other direction to compensate for the final change of weight. It ricocheted against the rock. Spears of ancient volcanic stone ripped at its silken canopy like the blade of a serrated knife. And as Jed wrapped his arms around Kassia, the balloon tore open and exploded, spewing fire and gas into the sky in a deafening blast.

Victor stood beside Montgomery's desk and waited. He couldn't blame them for getting cross with him. He hadn't exactly shown much enthusiasm for their latest plan and he supposed his history with Riverboy *was* a little patchy. Still, it annoyed him that he'd been made to wait like some naughty schoolboy in the headteacher's office, as if the senior management team were meeting with his social worker somewhere and coming up with an intervention plan.

He rubbed his shoulder. It itched.

Outside the windows of The Shard, London carried on with her life as normal. From so far above the city, he felt detached; distanced from the grime and dirt and urgency of life as it had been when he'd lived in Etkin House. Then, he'd had only himself and his wits to rely on. It was him against the world. There had been no one else. And so maybe that's why the fear had been less then. He'd had nothing to lose?

He rubbed his shoulder again, and looked down at Montgomery's desk. The pile of emails and cuttings was like a paper river. It was almost as if this man and all the others he worked with were drowning. Everything was about the chase for the unicorn. Everything.

Victor sighed, pushed his hands into his pocket and smoothed the photograph with his hand. But, somehow, even this didn't reassure him as it usually did.

Victor looked down again at the desk and for the first time he was aware of a small wooden dish set aside from the sea of notes and cuttings. And lying in the dish was a tiny silver model of an elephant. Victor looked more carefully. On the side of the elephant, a number had been worked into the metal. The number 43.

Victor picked up the elephant and as he did so he realised it wasn't just a model, but a keyring.

And hanging on the end of the keyring was a single, silver key.

Jed opened one eye. For the moment it was all he dared move. He blinked against the sun. Then he peeled open the other eye.

Working through his body, millimetre by millimetre, he tried to see if anything was broken. If everything was still attached. He flexed his fingers, one by one, then his toes. Then he bit his lip hard and tried to sit up.

He couldn't.

Perhaps his spine was snapped? Maybe he was paralysed? Would his toes still work if this had happened?

He was aware of a pressure grinding down on him. A dead weight.

He strained upwards and an arm fell by his side. But it was not his own arm.

Kassia!

Suddenly, he understood what had happened. Somehow in the fall, she had landed on top of him. And apart from her arm lolling to the side, she was unmoving.

He bit his lip again and strained to wriggle free from below her, stuttering and stammering her name as he rested her body on the ground and knelt beside her. He clutched at her wrist, searching desperately for a pulse. Her heart was beating, but only faintly. Her eyes were closed.

Someone was beside him. Dante kneeling too. He lifted his sister's shoulders, as if desperately trying to shake her awake from a very deep sleep.

'Kassia, please!' Jed stuttered. This could not be happening! Not again!

Suddenly Kassia's eyes flickered open, and she let out a groan.

'Kassia!'

She squinted her eyes against the sun and then raised her shoulders from the ground.

'Kassia. Oh my god. Are you OK?'

She rubbed her face, winced and then sank back on to the ground again as if the effort of lifting her shoulders had been far too much.

Jed's heart was careering in his chest. 'Kassia. Please. Say something.'

She opened her eyes and then her lips twitched into an awkward smile. 'Well, I won't be travelling in a hot air balloon again,' she said.

Jed blew out a breath of relief and sat down on the ground beside her.

Dante shook his shoulders, desperate for an explanation.

'She's OK,' Jed signed and then because he didn't know what else to do, he laughed. 'Seriously. We're all OK.'

It took Kassia a while to be brave enough to attempt to stand. Jed's body had acted like an airbag but they had still fallen a good distance. And the ground where they had landed was rough and uneven, a wilderness of bare and ruffled rock.

Dante and Jed linked arms either side of her and helped steer Kassia down to a less jagged terrain. It was here that the burnt remains of the balloon and basket had been scattered, flung there after the explosion. The scarlet canopy, shrivelled and twisted by the fire, was spread like roiled blood and the strands of wicker had been dropped like pieces of a giant pick-up sticks game. Amongst the devastation, Jed found the first aid kit. Dante found a bag too, and this one must have belonged to the pilot. They tipped the contents out. A few bars of chocolate and some matches, which Dante stuffed in his pocket. And copies of the paperwork agreeing to the flight. It was almost funny seeing the signed insurance form. Jed wondered if the insurance was still valid if the pilot hadn't taken the trip.

Less funny was the sheet of paper stuffed at the bottom of the bag, undamaged by the explosion.

It was in Turkish so impossible for them to read. But the stamp in the corner told them all they needed. NOAH.

'How?' said Kassia, leaning heavily on Jed. 'How did they know we were here?'

'How do they know anything?' said Jed. 'They've got eyes everywhere.'

They walked in silence for a while. It was clear they were miles from the nearest town and it was also clear that the sun was beginning to slip in the sky. 'We need to find somewhere to rest,' signed Dante, obviously keen to take charge before things got dark.

Jed and Kassia agreed and they moved on without talking, leaning together following a path through the rock and the wilderness in the desperate hope that they'd find somewhere they could shelter. And it was just as they reached what looked like the opening to a cave that Jed found another bag on the ground. His own bag, flung free in the explosion.

'The glass pen?' said Kassia as he scrabbled inside. 'Is the pen broken? What about the ink?'

Jed stared at her and knew his confusion was clearly obvious on his face. 'You're worried about that after everything that happened?'

Kassia pulled herself up straighter. 'Of course I am.'

'But surely if NOAH are after us, then we've just

got to focus on getting away. We haven't got time for this memory stuff any more!'

Something like anger flashed in Kassia's eyes. 'You have got to be kidding me. What are you on about? I didn't fall miles from the sky so we could give up on this now.' Her face was creased into a defiant pout. 'It's more important now than ever, don't you think?'

Her clothes were ripped, her hair was matted, she was covered in dirt from the desert. But Jed had to admit she looked quite beautiful when she was angry.

He reached into the bag again and then he smiled. By some miracle, the glass pen and the bottle of ink that had fallen from the sky were still unbroken. Back in Paris, he had longed for a miracle. Now at last, he finally had one.

The cave was damp and cold. Jed helped Kassia down to the ground so she could sit. 'Where does it hurt?' he asked.

'Where *doesn't* it hurt would be a better question.'

'I'm so sorry.'

Kassia smiled reassuringly. 'Hey, what are you sorry about? You don't have to feel bad. Without you as my landing mat I would have been a gonner.' She wriggled slightly, easing her back against the wall.

'I don't think we can really say none of this is my

fault,' said Jed awkwardly.

Kassia scowled at him. 'No one made me do this, Jed. And you can't be responsible for what NOAH do. Or the physics behind hot air balloon crashes.'

He sat down beside her and even though he didn't say anything more, he hoped that she would know how grateful he was.

Dante came in suddenly from the cold. His arms were laden with branches and twigs and he set about building a fire. Soon the cave felt warmer and even though it was dark outside, the flames meant they could see. 'We going to try the next memory?' Dante signed, and the shapes from his hands disfigured in the light.

'Really?' said Jed. He knew he was putting it off. He wasn't sure his heart was up to more turmoil yet. But then if NOAH were on to them here in Turkey, maybe Kassia was right and it was more important than ever to deal with the task Bergier had set them.

Jed took the glass pen from the case, and the final bottle from its velvet container. The red ink danced in the glow of the fire. Then he took the paper.

Kassia smiled encouragingly. 'You can do this,' she said.

The pen felt heavier in his hand. The ink spiralled up the nib and blotted as he rested the tip on the paper. Somehow the ink flowed more readily this time, his hand moving quickly so that the image that formed was clear and distinct. And Jed realised that he'd known what the image would be before he started. The third stage of alchemy. A swan had followed the raven and it was obvious then that a bird of fire would follow in the final stage. Jed put the paper down and looked at the phoenix he had drawn and the paper rippled in the breeze, making it look for a second as if the bird would lift and rise like the scarlet balloon and fly away.

Before this could happen, Jed took the watch from his pocket. He opened the case. And in the cold of the cave the hands began to turn, careering backwards through time. As they moved, they churned the air as if inviting in the dragon that swirled and twisted, circling the memory of the elixir day and dragging all of them towards it.

Jed looked up. 'Ready?' he whispered.

And the others nodded, joined hands and allowed themselves to fall.

The Fulcanelli that appears inside the circle scored by the dragon is wearing tatty clothes. Something suggests that the time of the memory is not too far away. But the location of the memory is very old. And very beautiful.

A fabulous garden. A park of trees, stretching out of sight. And in the centre, a beautiful palace. There are walkways and fountains, neatly clipped hedges and a grand canal. And there are orange bushes and sculpted figures that peer through the shrubberies, frozen in time.

But something is wrong. Very wrong.

A wind is blowing and it is whipping through the branches of the trees and tugging at the greenery as if the air is enraged.

Fulcanelli is bending into the wind. His arms are outstretched as if pinned back on a cross. And it's clear that this is not from choice but from necessity. Without his arms outstretched, he would be swept up with the leaves and the branches and the debris that is swirling around him. And the edge of the memory and the body of the dragon become one, swirling and spinning, battling against the wind.

Finally, it becomes clear that Fulcanelli is not alone. There is another man struggling beside him. 'We need to get to the palace,' the man calls, and his voice is strangled by the gale. 'Versailles is going to be destroyed!'

And Fulcanelli tries to answer but his words are ripped unspoken from his throat.

The man makes a grab for Fulcanelli's coat. A moment to steady himself against the wind, perhaps. But dark, black eyes make it clear that this man doesn't want

Fulcanelli to help him in his struggle. This man wants something else.

'The elixir!' the man yells into the wind. 'You have the elixir. I know you do!'

Fulcanelli stands his ground, arms still outstretched in the wind.

'I have hunted you across nations and across years,' the man shouts. 'You will not escape me!' He plunges forward and makes another grab for Fulcanelli's arm but Fulcanelli pulls away, whips his hand through the air, punching to be free.

The second man recoils. He staggers, his arms flung wide to stop himself falling.

But the energy of the air is stronger than the might of the men and it pushes them both back, unrelenting and vicious.

Suddenly, there is a searing sound. A wrenching noise, and a tree which has cowered in the storm with its branches over them is torn from the ground, its roots ripped from the earth, its trunk felled as if struck by an axe.

The tree falls gracefully. Its branches are so far flung that there is no escape for Fulcanelli beneath its shadow. The trunk of the tree, wide and ancient, presses him into the ground, crushing him against the dirt.

The wind howls around them. Branches snap and

splinter. The sky is as dark as oil.

But Fulcanelli struggles free. He pulls himself out from under the toppled tree and staggers upright. His hands are raw. Blood seeps from his fingernails.

Beside the tree, the other man has fallen too. Blood drips from a wound in his side, gashed open by a fallen branch. But the man lurches forward. 'You!' he yells and his voice tangles in the wind.

Fulcanelli races through the decimated gardens, clambering over fallen branches. He reaches the building, and tries every door. But all of them are bolted.

Finally, a door yields to his push and flies open. The man from the garden is behind him.

The room they have entered is long and lit. A hall of mirrors, stretching on and on. And in the light of the mirrors the hunter looks at the hunted. 'Who are you really?' the man pleads. 'Some sort of angel or some sort of devil?' Then he slumps to his knees, hands pressed tight on the wound in his side.

Fulcanelli lurches back from the injured man. He reaches into his pocket and he pulls out a tiny bottle. It is the fifth such bottle from the laboratory in Paris. And it is newly empty.

The man on the floor looks up. Blood drips from his side. The shine from the mirrors bathes him in light.

Fulcanelli turns. A line of reflections replicated like

those in a kaleidoscope. And he throws the empty bottle against the glass of the mirror so that both shatter on impact, his reflection twisting and expanding, distorted and changed again and again.

And Fulcanelli realises he doesn't know the answer to the question that the injured man had asked him.

The fire in the cave guttered and swelled and the flames leapt as Jed grabbed for the watch on the paper. The smoke dragon splintered into a thousand pieces, scattering like the debris from the exploded balloon.

'It's enough,' gasped Jed, crumpling the piece of paper and tossing it on to the fire. 'I can't watch any more.'

But as the paper crackled in the flames and the phoenix turned to ash, Kassia asked a final question. 'Who was the other man in the memory?'

'His name was Orin Sinclair,' mumbled Jed. 'And he worked for NOAH.'

rite --- to tell the tale
e doubly weak:
at can idle words avail,
the heart could speak?
By day or night, in weal or woe,
That heart, no longer free,
Must bear the love it cannot show,
And silent ache for thee.

DAY 271

25th November

Victor slipped the key into the lock and turned. Last time he'd used a key in this place, things had not gone down well with those in charge. But this time he wasn't opening a cage to let someone out. This time he was opening a door to let himself in.

The elephant keyring swung backwards and forwards against the door as he pushed it open and stepped inside.

Simply walking over the threshold made the lights click on. With each step, another click of the light, the sensors ensuring that his whole walkway was illuminated. This was good as there was no natural light spilling in from any windows. He might be on the forty-third floor of The Shard but it felt more like he was in some dusty basement. The air smelt stale.

Down each side of the long room he'd entered were

filing cabinets. Side by side, they created a wall, the space in between only wide enough to squeeze down. Good job he'd come alone, he laughed to himself. This was kind of cosy.

The filing cabinets were labelled, a sticker on each drawer, breaking the alphabet into segments. He walked deeper into the room, until he found the letter 'S'. Then he pulled open the middle drawer of the cabinet.

The inside of the drawer was segmented too. Rows of files kept separate from each other by tiny green tags. He flicked the dividers towards him, manila folders bouncing forward as he worked. Finally, his hand slowed, even though he was pretty sure that his heart had sped up. The name he was looking for was typed across the label. 'Sinclair – Orin'.

He pulled the files from behind the divider. And then, because waiting to get back to his room to look inside seemed like an eternity away, he knelt down on the floor and put the folder on the carpet. He hesitated for just a second before he flipped the cover open. 'OK, Dad,' he whispered, and his voice echoed off the metal cabinets. 'It's about time I got to know the full story.'

Jed's back was against the wall. The fire had long since burnt down. Only ash remained.

Dante had got up earlier and left the cave to see if there was any sign of civilisation nearby. The night before, they'd focused on simply getting out of the cold and resting after the trauma of falling from the sky. Now the reality of morning meant they were stuck in a desert with only two bars of chocolate for food, no means of communication and probably very little chance of getting help.

Jed choked back his panic and reached out his hand. Kassia had fallen asleep leaning against him. He smoothed his palm gently over her hair. She'd been sleeping for hours and he'd been watching, too afraid to move in case he woke her. She flexed a little, moving her head towards his hand and then her eyes flickered open.

'Hey,' he said gently.

'Hey.' She didn't move and he didn't pull his hand away.

'Are you sore?' he said at last, moving his fingers tentatively towards her shoulder.

She nodded and winced as if even this little movement hurt her. Then she pulled herself up so that she was sitting beside him, their shoulders touching.

'Where's Dante?' she said at last.

He let his hand fall on to his outstretched leg, suddenly grateful for the need not to sign. 'Gone to see if there's any human life nearby.'

'And if there isn't?'

He had nothing sensible he could offer in answer. 'Kassia, I just . . .'

She put her hand on his leg. 'Don't, Jed. No apologies. No blaming yourself. Not now. Please.'

He moved his hand on to hers. And neither of them said any more.

DAY 273

27th November

It was clear they needed to head off to find some sort of town. Getting hold of proper food had to be a priority. They managed to eke out the chocolate they'd taken from the pilot's bag for nearly forty-eight hours. They allowed themselves a square every three hours. Kassia wasn't sure if the rush of sugar was a good idea or if it actually made the hunger worse. But, somehow, having some sort of routine and system for sharing kept her from going mad. She began to wonder about her mother's charts and timetables back home. Is this why she made them? So that life did not slip completely out of control?

For a while, the pain of the bruised ribs caused by crashing out of a hot air balloon basket was what troubled her the most. But as the second night passed, hunger pangs definitely became the sharpest pain.

Her stomach twisted and cramped and, however hard she tried not to think about it, all she could focus on was food.

'Burgers,' she blurted. 'With cheese, mayonnaise and fresh lettuce. And maybe sweet potato chips.'

'Would they *have* to be sweet potato?' laughed Dante. 'You telling me that if I offered you a plate full of fish and chip shop chips soaked in vinegar and crisped with salt, you wouldn't grab my hand off.'

Kassia groaned and folded forward, trying to stifle the grumbling in her stomach with her arms.

Jed smiled at her, looked at his pocket watch and unwrapped the last, solitary square of chocolate and held it out to her.

She went to nibble the end but Jed looked across at her brother. 'I think she should have it all, don't you? We need to do all we can to stop her hallucinating pictures of crispy lettuce.'

Dante nodded. 'Go for it, sis. Enjoy.'

Kassia let the chocolate dissolve on her tongue and coat her teeth. It was ages before she spoke again, as if doing this would mean the food was really gone. Her stomach grumbled and did the talking for her.

They did at least have access to water regularly. Cutting through the rocks were tiny streams, and they knelt and cupped the water in their hands. It was icy cold and Kassia felt the burn as she drank. They had no way of collecting the water in containers, which meant that to conserve energy they needed to walk as close to the stream as they could for as long as possible. There were no proper paths and in places the stream forded what space there was. Initially, they'd tried to avoid walking through the water. But eventually, without any discussion, it was clear there was no other way.

Conversation then was hard. Walking one behind the other, sign language was more or less impossible. But Kassia was almost glad. She didn't have to move her hands, or focus on how to make the signs she needed as every thought she tried to form seemed to wring out all her remaining energy. And speaking would just diminish the taste of chocolate in her mouth. And as the taste faded, so did the hope that they'd ever get out of the desert and back to civilisation.

So she wasn't really sure how long they had been walking when she heard it.

She held her hands up. 'Shhh. Hear that?'

Dante pulled a face.

'Seriously. Do you hear that?' She glared at Jed as if just wanting him to hear the noise too would be enough to make it happen.

Dante tugged her arm. 'What is it?'

She strained to hear. It sounded human. 'Not sure. I think it's someone calling.'

'Calling what?' urged Dante.

She looked again at Jed. His face was puckered in concentration and he was turning in the direction of the sound.

Dante grabbed her arm again. 'So! What is it?'

She shook her head and stumbled after Jed who had turned and was scrambling away from them, clambering up the rocks that penned them in beside the stream.

'I hear it!' he yelled back. 'I hear it!'

Kassia and Dante followed him, loose pebbles and stones skittering free and splashing down into the water.

The noise was getting louder. It was definitely a human voice, lifting and swelling, amplified somehow so that it sounded tinny and unreal.

And then the realisation of what it was hit Kassia hard, like a weight swinging between the eyes. 'It's the call to prayer!' she fumbled eagerly with her hands. 'It's coming from a mosque. We must be near a town!'

And the thought was more delicious than the final square of chocolate.

Until just ahead of them the ground opened up and swallowed Jed whole.

One minute Jed was there. The next he wasn't.

He made no sound as he disappeared.

Kassia felt as if all the air had been sucked out of her body. She sank to her knees, crawling along, clutching frantically at the grass. 'Jed! Jed!'

There was no answer. No reply. Only the wailing noise of the call to prayer, which had seemed so positive only moments before, repeating now, again and again like some weird soundtrack to a disaster film.

'How? Where?' Kassia's signs were fumbled and incoherent. And Dante wasn't watching them anyway. He was crawling beside her, hands pressed into the grass, trying to make sense of what had happened.

And then, as the call for prayer rose to a crescendo, the earth cracked open again and sucked Kassia and Dante under too.

Falling from a great height twice in less than three days was not good for the ribs. And this time Kassia landed, not on Jed, but on bare and solid stone. Pain spiked through her back. And her eyes, for a while, could not focus as she stared at the chink of light seeping down towards her from the opening in the ground.

'You OK?' Jed's voice broke the silence.

'Define OK,' she laughed, using his own joke against him, although it seemed far from funny.

Beside her, Dante was groaning and clutching at his leg.

Kassia tried to pull herself up to sitting and she wasn't sure if the light-headedness she felt was due to concussion, internal bleeding or lack of food. Either way she didn't like it and sank back down again.

As she blinked and turned her head to the side, it became clear that they'd fallen into some sort of underground chamber. The space was quite large. A room-sized space, and, as her eyes got used to the lack of light, she could see that there was some sort of fire pit in the corner, and openings in the walls that led out of the space as if connecting it to other rooms. 'What is this place?' she groaned.

Suddenly, a shadow fell across her, blotting out the light from the hole above. And a voice she didn't recognise made a noise that sounded a little like a sneeze. 'Ozkonak,' the voice said, and then a hand reached out and helped Kassia sit up.

DAY 277

1st December

The next few days passed in a foggy blur of sleep and food.

The underground chamber they'd fallen into was, on occasion, filled with people. Then there were times when Kassia was sure the three of them were all alone.

She wasn't sure how much of what she saw or felt was due to delirium. And she wasn't sure, either, how long it took for her to be able to lift her head without pain and actually focus on what was happening around her. Hours? Days? Time had no pattern here, just like in the underground tunnels of Paris.

Eventually, one of the women explained to her what had happened.

The woman was about the same age as Kassia's mother. She wore her hair loose and was dressed in a

298

long flowing robe that made her look to Kassia like some sort of visiting angel. And her voice was soft and lilting. She wasn't Turkish, that was certain, and Kassia was pretty sure that her accent marked her out as Scottish, but she had no idea why a Scottish woman was living in an underground room in the middle of Cappadocia.

The woman's name was Flora and her first point of explanation was that they weren't just in a room underground, but that Ozkonak was in fact an enormous underground city capable of housing sixty thousand people. The networks of tunnels and storerooms meant it was possible for this vast number of people to live here on gathered supplies for nearly three months and have no need to leave the safety of the city.

Kassia felt a jolt at the mention of three months and she shot a look in Jed's direction. His eyes shadowed at the mention too, but he said nothing.

Flora went on to explain that they'd fallen into the city through ventilation shafts that were covered with grass to make entrances and exits as hard to find as possible. Only four levels of the city were in use now, but there were at least six more floors below these, making the city like a sprawling high rise tower block hidden underground.

'So why the need for such a massive space?' said Kassia.

'It was mainly used as somewhere for Christians to hide,' Flora said. 'There were times of persecution and Ozkonak and other underground cities in the region were safe havens in times of trouble.' There was a knowing glint in her eye, as if she was referring to more than just the past.

Suddenly, this truth became crystal clear.

Flora reached for a thin golden chain around her neck and pulled a medallion from behind the folds of her tunic. It was the mark of the Brothers of Heliopolis.

Kassia looked at Jed and Dante. She had no idea what they should say. Acknowledge the medallion or simply smile and look away.

Impulsively, she reached for her own medallion. But the chain wasn't there.

Flora smiled. 'Your medallion is safe,' she said, reaching into her pocket and taking out a second metal disc. 'The chain broke when you fell, but it's safe. Just as you are now.'

Kassia grabbed for the charm from her necklace and closed her hands around it. 'I don't understand,' she said. 'Are you . . . ?' It seemed odd to ask the woman if she was a Brother of Heliopolis.

Flora rocked back her head and laughed and the underground chamber echoed with the sound. 'You think being a Brother is a man-only thing?' She grinned. 'Och, sweetie. We're in the twenty-first century now, you know.'

The statement seemed particularly odd as they were seated in what amounted to little more than a sunken cave with absolutely no mod cons as far as Kassia could see.

'We've been expecting you,' Flora added. 'Metin said he had set things in place to send you on your way, although I have to acknowledge your arrival was more spectacular than we'd hoped. It seems the Brothers weren't the only ones tracking your moves.'

The thought of NOAH made Kassia shiver.

The woman took back Kassia's medallion and threaded it on to a long leather cord. 'Here,' she said. 'To repair it for now.'

Kassia mumbled her thanks and slipped the cord around her neck. The medallion was cold on her skin.

'So you know about the Brothers?' Kassia said nervously.

'About the Brothers and about Fulcanelli,' Flora said, smiling in Jed's direction. 'And about your tests to find the Emerald Tablet.'

'So you know where it is then?' Jed blurted.

And then the woman did something very odd. She nodded.

'Seriously,' said Kassia, shocked by Flora's calm and positive response. 'You know where the Tablet is. Well, you have to tell us!' She jumbled her words into sign for Dante and shock quickly wrote itself across his face too.

'Oh, we will,' said Flora, fingering her own medallion. 'But I thought you understood there would be testing involved in order for you to see the Tablet.'

This woman was funny. Hysterical, even. If she had *any* idea of the trials they'd completed to get here, she'd surely realise that they'd had enough tests to last them each a lifetime. And then, because the idea of lifetimes was no longer funny, Kassia allowed herself to frown. 'We've been tested enough,' she said.

Flora took a deep breath. 'You began the tests, it's true,' she said. 'And you are close now. The Emerald Tablet is indeed within your reach. And it will be possible, if you do well, for one of you to see it. But . . .'

'What do we have to do?' pressed Jed.

Flora took off her own necklace and put the medallion on the floor. She traced each shape engraved there with her finger. 'Three tests more,' she said quietly. 'For each stage of the Philosopher's Stone.'

And as the others watched, her finger moved over first the square and then the triangle before twisting again and again around the circle on the sign.

December 26th 1999

DAY 280

3rd December

The next morning, Flora led the three of them down a narrow corridor through the stone. It was clear the underground city was a labyrinth of rooms. In places, stairs had been cut into the rock to make travel possible from level to level, but, elsewhere, open voids gaped downwards. 'Watch where you step,' said Flora, gesturing at a particularly vicious opening in the floor to her left.

They walked for ages. Dante had to duck because of the height of the tunnels. Kassia put her hand on the walls to steady herself. They were smooth, as if millions of hands before her had done this and worn away the surface. She was so nervous that the air didn't fully reach her lungs. It fluttered around her chest like butterfly wings.

Flora finally stopped when they reached another

room like the very first one they'd been in. Kassia felt a little peeved that they'd walked so far to reach a room so similar to the one they'd left, but then she noticed one major difference between this room and the other.

In the centre of this room, instead of a solid floor, there was an enormous, gaping hole. Flora held her hand up to ensure that no one walked too close. And then, as if second-guessing the question that was bound to come, she peered over the edge. 'I think you'll remember,' she said, wiping her hands together, 'that the city runs to ten levels.'

Kassia tried not to think about how far away that would make the bottom of the fall.

Steering them away from the edge of the enormous hole, Flora led them to a small rickety table. Behind it, a long velvet curtain had been tacked in place at the top so that it hung unevenly right the way to the ground. Kassia had no idea what was behind the curtain but she was guessing somehow that it wasn't a window.

Flora took off her medallion and put it on the table. 'So, the testing room,' she said. 'There will be three tests taken here.'

'And if we pass, then you'll show us the Emerald Tablet?' said Kassia.

'If you pass all three, then yes, one of you will get to see it.'

'So, go on,' said Jed impatiently. 'What do these tests involve?'

'Stepping on to the void, crossing the void and facing the void,' Flora said, with a sense of occasion.

Kassia didn't like the sound of this.

'I've been chosen,' Flora went on, 'to ask you to take an enormous step towards knowing the information you need. You see, the Brothers have been guarding the information for decades and we have to be totally sure we are dealing with those who really understand the true value of what we have to show them, before we allow them to see the Emerald Tablet.'

Kassia could feel her stomach tightening. This woman had certainly made it clear that what they were going to do was important, but the way Flora kept bigging up the idea of the tests and what lay ahead was beginning to scare her.

Flora traced the design on the medallion again, her finger moving backwards and forwards along the line of the triangle. 'Test one is a test of harmony,' she said. 'Of balance.' Her eyes narrowed. 'It's a test to show us just how much you really want this. But more than that, how much you are prepared to risk.'

Kassia had started to shiver. Their whole journey had been about risk, but so much of what they had faced had come about as a result of accident. As part of a race against time. This woman was talking about something she wanted them to willingly step towards.

'What kind of risk?' Kassia whispered.

'How much are you prepared to lose?' Flora said, and there was a softness now about her face, as if just for a second she was letting go of her sense of obligation to do what the Brothers wanted her to.

Kassia didn't use words. She said her answer inside her head. She was prepared to do anything, surely. Wasn't that why she was here?

The older woman watched her and the tiniest smile of understanding twitched across her lips. 'Behind you lies the opening to the depths of Ozkonak,' Flora said. 'And all we ask is that the three of you stand together, totally steady, for a mere ten seconds above the drop.'

Kassia spun around to face the gaping hole in the floor. How on earth were they expected to do that? But behind her, the answer was becoming clear.

There was a tiny outcrop of rock that jutted out over the hole. The ground fell away beyond it and to either side. Kassia supposed it looked a bit like a very short diving-board platform hanging out over a very deep pool.

As she looked more carefully at the outcrop of rock, she saw two men pushing a long wooden plank out on to it. They weren't arranging it like an extension of a diving board stretching outwards though. Instead, they had put it in place, running across the hole, to make it look like a see-saw. A wooden box they'd positioned on the outcrop of rock lifted the plank at the middle so both ends strained sideways, unsupported over the void.

Surely they weren't expected to stand on the plank? It hadn't been fixed in place, just rested there, and, as the men moved back to stand beside Flora, the plank rocked slightly up and down at either end.

'You don't have to do this,' Flora whispered. 'It will be perfectly OK to say the risk is too great.'

'And if we do that you'll still let one of us see the Emerald Tablet?' blurted Jed.

Flora shook her head but it was obvious the action made her feel uncomfortable. 'Seeing the Tablet is dependent on completing the tests. You can walk away. But if you do, then the Tablet remains out of reach.'

Kassia wanted to laugh. A great, stomach-wrenching laugh. What were the alternatives? Risking their lives, or walking away as failures? How could this be a fair choice? 'You expect us to stand on that thing?' she said.

Flora nodded. 'Just for ten seconds.'

Kassia confirmed the suggestion to Dante and he made a noise like a car backfiring.

Flora acknowledged the laughter. 'I don't make the rules,' she said. 'But I work to protect the original inspiration for the recipe for eternal life. You must know now that alchemy was a series of tests and trials, determined by time and sometimes luck. There is a secret to this test. Harmony, as I have mentioned. A degree of working together. That is all the help I can offer you.'

Kassia blew out a breath, and then looked at her brother. 'It needs us all to risk everything,' she said in slow and stuttering sign.

'You're not doing it!' interrupted Jed. 'It's too much. Your lives risked for mine. Where's the sense in that?'

'But we've come all this way and the answer is so close.'

'It's madness!' said Jed. 'I can't let you do it.'

Dante held his hands up as if asking for silence. 'Do you want to do this, Kass?' he signed slowly.

She nodded, even though the tension through her body made it hard to move.

311

'So all for one and one for all then,' said Dante. 'Like in the best stories. We do this together. Agreed?'

Jed paced backwards and forwards for a moment, until Dante stilled him with his hand.

'Let us do this,' Dante said again, 'before we change our minds.'

Flora smiled and stepped away from them. 'My job is to watch you and not to intervene,' she said. 'But remember, you can *actually* change your mind at any time.'

Kassia shivered. The reality was, there was no way back now. The decision, she knew, had been made.

They spent ages looking at the plank and examining the hole. Every now and then, the ends of the plank lifted slightly, moved only by the air shifting in the hole below. Kassia crept closer to the edge. She got a sense of how deep the drop was because of the rush of cold that drifted upwards.

Finally, Dante clapped his hands to make them look at him. 'I should get on first,' he signed.

Kassia wasn't sure. If Dante stood on the plank, could he risk talking to them from there? Would the movement of his arms needed if he was to sign, unbalance the plank and make it wobble? But if he waited and one of them went first, would they be able to sign back to him?

312

'I'm going first,' he said defiantly, and he stepped closer to the lip of the hole.

Kassia and Jed stood either side of him, their shoulders almost touching. Dante looked down, not at the void but the plank. Then, as if he had decided that just like when ripping off a plaster, speed would lead to the least pain, he stepped out on to the centre of the plank, planting his feet solidly and squarely apart. The plank wobbled. It rocked to the right and Dante compensated by straining his body to the left, leaning as far as he could so the plank righted itself.

The plank stabilised. But Dante had his back to them. How could they possibly communicate about what should happen next? And with Dante not able to see their signs, how could they get him to turn?

'We should have talked this through!' spluttered Kassia.

'It's OK,' said Jed, although his voice made it clear he agreed with her. 'He'll work it out.'

But Dante stood with his back to them, his feet grounded and the plank rocking gently on its box.

Kassia felt something like rage begin to surge inside her. How could this be fair if Dante couldn't hear? And in that moment she felt something else. A sense of overwhelming shame that she could even think for a moment that she wanted Dante to be different.

But before she had time to shake away the thought that so repulsed her, Dante began to move. He was bending his knees, lowering his hands down towards the plank.

'What's he doing?' Kassia yelped.

'It's good. It's good!' urged Jed. 'Centre of gravity and all that!'

'What?' Kassia could hardly bear to watch. Dante's knees were near to the plank now. His hands touching so that he was crouched.

'If he gets his centre of gravity as low as he can to the plank,' said Jed, 'then everything will be more stable.'

Dante was kneeling now, and swivelling slightly to the side. He was going to lie down on the strip of wood.

But the plank was starting to tip! The top half of Dante's body was heavier than the bottom! The plank was lifting from the box. Its end was pressing down over the hole. It would surely reach a point when tipping over was inevitable. And Dante was pressed now like a torpedo being angled and ready to fire into the gaping chasm below.

Kassia wanted to shout. To fling her arms in sign. But there was nothing to say. No way she could help.

Kassia could see Dante's hands gripping tightly to

the edges of the wood. He was sliding his body backwards. His weight was shifting. The plank was realigning itself now. Finally beginning to steady.

Kassia held her breath.

And Dante turned his head a fraction to the side so he could see her. And with his eyes, he told her it was their turn to climb on board.

'How can we do this?' stuttered Kassia. There was barely any room on the plank. How could they possibly step next to him?

'We have to get on at the same time,' said Jed.

'But how?' The stepping space near the fulcrum was tiny. Only room for one pair of feet at a time. If they mis-timed it at all, then the weight of one of them would send the plank plunging free of the fulcrum and into the hole, carrying them with it.

And then there was the whole issue of weight. Jed was heavier than Kassia. How far away from the central fulcrum should each of them be to make sure the weight was evenly spread?

It was impossible. And all the while they thought this, Dante was clinging to the edge of the plank as it hovered above the hole.

Jed paced alongside the lip of the chasm.

'We have to hurry,' Kassia pleaded. She could see her brother's knuckles whitening. He was begging her with his eyes to be quick.

Jed stopped pacing. 'Do you trust me?' he blurted.

Kassia's stomach was knotted. Her legs felt like water. 'I'm scared, Jed.'

'I know.' He wiped his face with the back of his hand and she could see that it was trembling. He asked her again. 'Do you trust me, Kassia?'

'Always.'

'Then we have to step on together,' Jed said. 'And I don't mean side by side.'

Kassia didn't know what he meant.

'You have to get on to my back first,' said Jed. 'And then we'll step on as one.'

Kassia's knees were shaking.

'It means we can react together to keep the plank steady.'

'And you're sure it's the only way?'

Jed took both her hands and squeezed them. 'Together,' he said.

Kassia nodded. She let go of Jed's hands and wiped her sweaty palms down her trousers.

Jed turned his back on her and then crouched slightly. 'Ready?' he said.

She wasn't *nearly* ready. They were so close to the hole she could feel the air rushing upwards, cold and damp. And clinging on to Jed would put the decision making in his hands. All she could do would be to respond to his movement and to let him lead.

But they had to do this as one. The test was of harmony. And acting separately would make them fail. It was together. Or not at all.

Kassia jumped on to Jed's back and she gripped her arms around his shoulders, straining upwards so that her weight was as evenly spread as possible.

'Hang on,' he breathed gently.

And she knew if she didn't then it would be over. She would fall and probably drag Jed with her.

Jed manoeuvred himself towards the part of the plank which rested on the box.

There was just enough space beside Dante's prone body for two feet to stand.

'I'm going to step on with my right,' Jed said. 'So you need to lean to the left.'

Kassia didn't answer. She clung on as tightly as she could and angled her weight to the left.

'OK,' said Jed. 'Ready?'

How could she ever be ready? They had no idea how much the plank would give. No idea how much of a lean to the left would be needed. But as Jed lifted his foot, they stepped together over the point of no return.

The air was cold all around them.

The plank creaked under the extra weight.

It tipped to the left. Kassia lurched slightly to the right, attempting to correct the lean. Dante slid to the right too, thrust forward to compensate the lift. But the adjustment was too much. The plank dipped to the right now.

Dante was groaning. Kassia could see his hands, gripped to the edge of the plank. She could feel Jed bending his knees, trying to spread the weight.

'Centre! Centre!' he shouted, and Kassia pulled herself up straight, trying to fight against the rock of the plank.

Time stretched endlessly. Cold air surged up at them.

'Just ten seconds,' Kassia shouted. 'That's all we need. Are we there? Are we there?'

She had no idea how long they'd been balanced. Her whole body was shaking. Her arms straining. Her back buckling.

'I'm going to jump,' Jed shouted.

'Where? How?' Kassia yelped.

But there was no time for explanation. Jed's knees softened and he lurched forward, flinging himself and Kassia over the gaping hole to the other side. They fell as they had jumped, as one, the ground rushing up to meet them. Jed turned his body to the side so Kassia fell against him, his arms twisting and wrapping round her. And she tugged herself free as Dante scrambled up from the plank and flung himself over the void too.

And as he left the plank, it upended. It hovered for a moment, suspended on air. And then it rocked back into position, wobbled and stilled.

There were seconds of silence.

Kassia grabbed for her brother's hand. And she rocked back into Jed's hold. Together they looked over the void at Flora.

And she smiled. Then nodded her head. 'Well done,' she said. 'Precisely eleven seconds. That is part one of your testing successfully completed.'

DAY 281
4th December

Kassia's spoon dangled over the bowl of breakfast. She hadn't moved it to her mouth once. The food was cold now.

'We can do this,' Jed whispered.

She tried to whisper back but her voice got lost somewhere.

'Whatever the second test is, we can face it together.'

This time she nodded.

'Unless . . .' Jed's voice tailed away. 'Unless you want to tell them we can't go on.'

Kassia let the spoon fall from her fingers. It clanged against the edge of the bowl. 'I don't think so,' she said, her voice suddenly full of strength. 'In this together, we said. And nothing's changed.'

Jed smiled. 'Well, quite a lot has really,' he said gently. 'Hot air balloon crash, wandering starving in the desert, falling into an underground city where tests have been arranged for us.'

Kassia pushed the bowl of uneaten food away from her and smiled back at him. 'Nothing's changed,' she said, and she let her hand rest on his knee.

A couple of hours later, Flora led them again to the room of testing. Dante stooped his head as he walked through the twisting corridors and Kassia ran her hand along the stone, but it did little to reassure her. They walked without talking, through the underground city, to the room where they'd balanced together across a void, and the thought of how that could have ended so badly didn't cheer her much either.

This time, there was no plank stretched across the opening in the floor. Instead, a huge stone slab was standing, propped on the edge of the hole. It was as tall as a door and even wider. Kassia couldn't even begin to imagine what the Brothers of Heliopolis had in store for them today.

Flora stood, as she had done last time, at the side of the room. She took the medallion from her neck and placed it on the table in front of them. 'Your second test,' she said brightly, tracing the square on the medallion with her finger this time. 'A test of strength.' Her fingers stopped. 'And all you must do this time round is lower the slab across the void to make a bridge which you then cross.'

Kassia squinted and looked across at the humongous stone. It was certainly huge, but maybe if they worked like yesterday as a team and shoulder-barged the thing together, then it would topple over and span the void. They'd have to be careful that they didn't allow the momentum of the shove to carry them forward over the lip of the hole though. But it didn't look impossible. Surely this test was easier. Something they would manage. She felt the muscles in her face relax. Her heart stopped thumping at the base of her throat. This couldn't be too hard.

Then Flora took something from her pocket. A small rectangular slab that looked as if it was made of polished, white bone. 'There is a catch, of course,' she said, putting the tiny slab on the table. 'To fell the stone, you have to use this.'

Kassia felt her heart press again at the base of her throat. 'You're joking, right?' She picked the tiny slab up. It sat in the palm of her hand. 'We have to use *this* to knock *that* over,' she said, waving across at the door shaped stone that stood poised on the edge of the hole.

Flora grinned. A tiny part of her was obviously enjoying this. 'I warned you. The Emerald Tablet is not something we allow access to lightly.'

Kassia fingered the tiny sheet of bone in her palm.

The use of the word 'lightly' seemed ironic. This thing was tiny. There was no way it could be used to knock over the giant slab.

'You must ensure that at the moment of manoeuvre, your hand touches only that piece of the puzzle,' added Flora.

'But you're going to tell us how to do this, aren't you?' urged Kassia.

Flora grinned. 'It's a test, dear. There can be no assistance.' She smiled again. 'But there is a time limit, of course. You see, the huge stone slab has been rigged with a detonator. And the fuse allows a burn of precisely ten minutes.'

'And what exactly happens when the fuse burns down?' asked Jed.

'The stone will explode,' Flora said matter of factly.

Kassia curled her fingers over the tiny slab.

'It's ridiculous,' signed Jed, walking towards the giant door-like structure. 'You want us to knock this thing over with something smaller than a playing card and, by the way, we've got ten minutes or else the whole thing will blow up.' He gave a long anguished sigh. 'It's impossible.'

Kassia put the slab down on the table so she could sign. 'Like making an elixir of life was impossible,' she said.

'Yeah. But then I must have known what I was doing,' groaned Jed. 'I'd been working on it for years. You've seen that. It wasn't something that happened in ten minutes!'

Flora smiled at them and then she made her way towards the towering stone slab. She took a small timer, like the kind you might use in a kitchen, and set the hands to ten minutes. Then she bent down and lit the fuse that had been taped to its edge.

Kassia watched the spark of flame gutter but all she felt was a creeping cold that tightened round her.

Dante had started to pace along the line of the drop in the floor. They threw around ideas but two minutes passed and they'd got absolutely nowhere. 'Let's focus on the stages,' Dante signed, thoughtfully. 'Connections to be made. That's been important in all the tests we've tackled up till now.' He stopped and peered closely at the huge stone slab that towered above him. 'Maybe there's an opening? Something on the stone we're missing?'

'You can't go near the thing,' yelped Kassia, her eyes latched firmly on the ever reducing fuse.

'But maybe there's a keyhole? Some slot we place the smaller slab inside?'

'We're not allowed to touch it, though,' said Kassia, as if the fact that the stone was taped with dynamite wasn't enough of a reason to keep away.

There were seven minutes left. But from where they stood, there was nothing to see on the huge stone doorway. No mark, no grooves, no keyholes. Nothing. Except the dynamite. And it didn't matter how hard they stared, it was totally obvious that there was no way at all that the tiny bone slab could be used to topple the giant stone one.

Kassia slumped down to the floor as all her energy drained away. Having no breakfast suddenly seemed like a really bad idea. The first test had been so scary. But it had seemed clear from the start that the key to that test was working together. What was the key to this task? Strength? How could something so small possibly be strong enough to fell something so big? And they had only six minutes left to sort it out.

She curled her toes inside her shoes and pressed her feet down hard on the ground. The pain in her toes hurt, but somehow this was a relief. Pain that made sense. And dulled out the deafening sound of the ticking clock inside her head.

Jed sat down too, and pressed his hands flat against the stone paving. How could they sit when time was racing? But they needed to think. Needed to work out a plan.

Kassia said nothing as she saw a drop of blood stain

the stone as Jed moved his hand.

Jed saw her looking and wiped his hand nervously across his jeans. Then he scratched at the surface of the paving stone as if he could make the mark of blood disappear.

Suddenly, his hand froze. He looked across at Kassia, his eyes sparking.

'Supposing it's another test of putting things together?' he blurted. 'Puzzle pieces, Flora said!' He scrabbled at the edge of the paving stone as he spoke. 'Supposing we have to use other stones?'

'But we were told that tiny slab on the table was the thing we had to use,' signed Dante, and Kassia could see the desperation in his hands. They had less than five minutes to go until the stone was destined to explode.

'To start the thing,' said Jed, lifting the edge of the stone he'd been sitting on and pulling it free of the dusty soil that embedded it in place. 'But there are stages in between just like there were memories between then and now that I had to face.'

Jed wasn't making much sense. But what he *was* doing was dragging the stone he'd lifted out of the ground towards the edge of the hole. Then he knelt down and began to ease another stone free of its bedding.

'Stages,' he blurted. 'Like dominoes.'

Surely now he had completely lost his mind.

'We need a collection of slabs and if we stand them up together then we can make a line.'

'And how will a line work?' signed Dante, after he'd helped Jed lift another stone from the dust, obviously without any real idea of why he was doing it.

'Dominoes,' Jed blurted again. 'We've got three minutes left! We need a topple line.'

Kassia still wasn't sure exactly how this plan would work but Jed seemed adamant and so she did exactly as he directed. They eased stones from the soil bedding and dragged them towards the edge of the chasm. Once they'd raised ten stones, they lined them up in order of their size with Jed shouting and signing instructions. Eventually, spreading out from in front of the giant slab standing on the edge of the hole, was a line of slabs diminishing in size, until the final stone was hardly bigger than the one Flora had given them. They had one minute left.

'Are you sure this will work?' said Kassia.

Jed shook his head.

'Seriously. You're *really* not sure?' she said.

Jed took the tiny initial slab from the table. Kassia could see his fingers were curled tightly around it and when he opened his palm there was a splash of blood on the surface of the stone.

'We have less than a minute,' he mumbled. 'I don't think we have time to be sure!'

Jed knelt at the end of the line of stones. Kassia and Dante crouched beside him. If this worked, the slab would fall into the void and explode. They'd pass the test. If it failed, they might be injured in the blast. And the chance to see the Emerald Tablet would be gone.

Jed stood the initial slab at the end of the line. The other slabs radiated out from it, a line of ever-increasing barriers spreading towards the chasm in the floor.

Ten seconds left. It was this. Or it was over.

Jed knocked the initial slab with his finger. It wobbled and then it rocked. And as it fell forward, it leant against the stone in front. The second stone wobbled too. That leant forward and it fell. And one by one, along the line, the stones toppled, leaning forward, their weight pressed against the bigger stone in front.

Incredibly, as the final seconds on the time limit sounded, the penultimate stone rocked forward. It pressed down on the giant stone that guarded the entrance to the hole. And it began to fall. Elegantly and smoothly, the enormous stone rocked, then toppled over. It crashed down, fording the gap across the void.

'Hurry!' yelled Jed, grabbing Kassia's hand. 'We have to cross it!'

The fuse was fizzing. There were seconds left.

Kassia thundered after Jed as he scrambled across the stone bridge they had created that spanned the hole. Dante followed.

And then, as the fuse wire fizzed and spluttered, and the timer began to sound its alarm, the dynamite exploded, the slab cracked and buckled across the centre, splintering into tiny fragments that plummeted downwards. Smoke and dust billowed upwards as Kassia, Jed and Dante flung themselves to the ground on the opposite side of the hole.

And from behind them, Kassia heard the sound of clapping. 'Well done,' came Flora's voice, cutting through the smoke and dust. 'You have completed the test of strength. And that means that one single challenge remains between you and the secrets of the Emerald Tablet.'

SÉE DES ÉGOUTS DE PARIS.
LE DE NETTOYAGE

DAY 282
5th December

Kassia sat in the corner of the room and twisted a thin leather cord around her fingers. They'd been given breakfast, but her stomach was so unsettled that once again she'd pushed it away.

Jed sat down beside her. 'You should eat something,' he said softly. 'You might need your strength.'

She tried to smile but failed.

He reached over and took the medallion from her fingers, allowing it to swing for a second on the leather cord. 'Test three,' he said, stilling the medallion and tracing the raised circle on the design, just as Flora had done with the triangle and the square. 'Want to make any guesses about what that will involve?'

Kassia didn't. Flora had explained that each test focused on the void. But balancing above it on a plank and then racing across it before the bridge exploded

332

under them seemed like enough challenges to do with gaping holes in the floor. 'You?' she said.

'Well, the circle represents resilience,' Jed offered. 'So I guess it's to do with that somehow.'

'Resilience? How will that work?' She was pretty sure that everything they'd faced over the last few months had shown that they were more than a little capable of coping with bad stuff.

'No idea,' said Jed.

'As long as we can do the test together like the other two,' said Kassia. 'Strength in numbers and all that.'

Jed agreed. But it was soon clear, once they reached the testing room, that Flora had no intention of allowing them to face their final test together.

And something else was also very clear.

A group of workers stood around the edge of the hole and were pulling some sort of stretchy thick material up from the base.

'What is that?' asked Kassia.

'Trampoline fabric,' said Flora.

'What! That stuff was down there all the time, stretched across the bottom of the hole?'

'Of course,' said Flora gently. 'Invisible protection. It was there to catch you and keep you safe in both the tests.'

'But . . .'

'We're not here to harm you,' Flora interrupted. 'Did you really think I could let you face such overwhelming danger and stand back and do nothing?'

Kassia was confused. She wasn't sure if she should feel angry for being tricked or grateful that the risk hadn't been as bad as she'd thought.

'We are here to guard something precious,' went on Flora, 'and to be sure we keep the secrets for those who are worthy. You believed you were at great risk. But you were prepared to take the test anyway. And there is a lesson there, perhaps. That what we fear most might not actually be as bad or as final as we think.'

Kassia didn't really follow her argument. But there was no time to dwell on this. As the protective material was dragged up from the bottom of the pit, Kassia could see that a rope was being lowered. An abseil harness had been attached. What sort of game had the Brothers got in store for them now?

'You can't seriously expect us to go down there?' Kassia blurted.

'Well, you don't have to,' said Flora.

Kassia felt relief flooding every part of her body.

'If you don't want to pass the final test,' Flora added.

The relief bottle-necked somewhere around Kassia's oesophagus, making it very difficult to breathe.

'But there's only one rope,' said Jed.

'As this test must be taken separately,' said Flora.

'So just one of us needs to take it?'

'No. All of you must be tested. But on your own, this time.'

Kassia was pretty sure she was going to be sick. 'So what's down there?' she said, waving at the rope as it hung over the opening.

Flora looked thoughtful. 'It will be different for each of you. Having spent time with you over the last few days, we have personalised the test.'

The explanation wasn't making much sense.

'You will take it in turns,' Flora went on, 'to climb down into the void. Each of you will have a key and you will use that key to unlock a cabinet that is stored in the lower floor of the city.'

'*And*?' pressed Kassia, as her translation for Dante floundered.

'And that is it,' said Flora.

'So we just climb down, unlock a cabinet, and then climb back up?' said Jed.

'Exactly,' said Flora.

She led them to the far corner of the room and pulled aside the green curtaining that was draped across the wall. Three nondescript keys were hanging there, each slightly different.

Flora took each one in turn and handed them over.

'And who goes first?' said Kassia shakily.

'I will,' volunteered Dante. 'You're not going down there until I've sussed it out.'

Kassia hugged her brother and watched as Flora helped clip him to the abseil rope. She translated all the instructions to him about how he should move his hands and how he should lean back to allow his legs to stretch so they were perpendicular to the wall. And as he disappeared over the edge of the hole, she held her breath.

'Have you ever done this before?' she asked Jed nervously.

'What, abseiled into a pit in order to unlock a door when I've got no idea what's on the other side?' Jed laughed. 'I'm not sure. I don't remember. You?'

'Never,' snapped Kassia. 'Do you think my mum would have allowed anything as dangerous or as time wasting as this?' And the mention of her mum brought the tightness back across her throat. She wasn't sure she could do this. If the test needed them all to pass, then what would happen if she failed? If she, out of the three of them, couldn't do it?

'It will be OK,' Jed said, staring with her into the hole as they watched for signs of Dante in the darkness.

Kassia wasn't sure how she should treat such an obvious lie.

It was about half an hour before Kassia heard heavy breathing from the edge of the hole. A hand flung upwards and gripped tight to the lip of the chasm.

Kassia stumbled forward and she and Jed helped ease Dante out of the hole. He was shaking, his face slick with sweat and the pupils of his eyes were massively dilated where he'd struggled to draw in any glimmers of light. He stumbled as Flora helped unattach him from the rope, slumping down to the ground which was still dusty from where the paving slabs had been raised the day before.

Kassia fought to get Dante to focus, but he wouldn't look at her. His eyes were wide, flicking away.

'What was down there?' she stuttered with her fingers, repeating the sentence over and over until he finally watched her hands.

He grabbed for her arm.

'Dante, please! What was down there?'

When he moved his hands in answer it was as if every word was painful to form. 'A cabinet. And inside there was a straitjacket and . . .'

He couldn't finish. 'I don't understand,' Kassia mumbled. Why would this freak Dante out so much?

Why did he look so terrified?

'You must hurry,' said Flora, who was holding out the carabiner and harness ready to attach it to the next climber. 'Which of you is next?'

'Me,' Kassia heard herself saying. The sooner this was over the better.

'Are you sure?' blurted Jed. 'Don't you want me to go next?'

Kassia shook her head and watched as Flora talked her through the feeding of the rope. 'If I don't go now, I never will,' she said.

Flora helped her clamber over the edge of the hole. The air was cold and, as Kassia kicked against the lining of the shaft, a stone skittered free but she did not hear it fall to the bottom. The hole was dark. With every part of the descent, it grew blacker still, as if the darkness was choking out the light from above. Kassia did as she'd been shown, but she was trembling so much that instead of her legs being pressed straight out from the wall, they buckled and she crumpled forward, banging her knees and her arms against the surface of the stone as she was lowered further and further.

Finally, when the air was so cold she was shivering, and it was so dark she could barely see her hand in front of her face, she felt her feet scuff along the ground. She collapsed downwards and pressed her hands on the floor for a while, as if hoping the earth would send strength through her and allow her to stand. And when she did, she saw a candle burning on the top of a cabinet propped against the wall. The cabinet had three doors and Kassia fumbled for the key.

The first door she tried didn't open. But the second door allowed the key to enter the hole. But the key didn't turn. With shaking fingers, she slid the key into the final lock and the door swung silently open.

Dante had said his cabinet had contained a straitjacket, but behind this door, Kassia saw a pile of books and diaries and photograph albums. She fumbled to take them out, flicking them open so the pages swam in the light of the candle. But there was nothing in them. No writing. No photographs. No images at all.

Sticky corners marked sections in pages where photos should have been. Dates marked the top of pages in the diaries. Blank pages stretched on and on. But there was nothing else. Nothing had been recorded to be remembered.

Kassia shoved the books back inside the cabinet, slammed the door and locked it shut.

And now she understood.

These cabinets held the things that she and Dante feared the most. For him, the fear that because his deafness distorted his ability to speak, others would see him as mad. And this terror would be overwhelming if his hands were strapped down by a straitjacket so that he couldn't speak at all. Hearing silence, being silent; Dante's greatest fear.

But for Kassia, what she feared most was a life that was empty. No stories; no friends; nothing worth recording. An emptiness that needed no words, even if they could be said and heard.

She choked back the tears that fought behind her eyes and looked up towards the top of the hole. And as she stumbled and faltered to clamber to the surface, she began to cry.

The tears were partly for herself and partly for her brother. But some tears fell because she was pretty sure she knew what would be inside Jed's cabinet when he opened it.

And the thought of him alone and staring death in the face broke her heart.

'We have to talk about it, Jed.'

'Why?' Jed was pacing backwards and forwards, and no matter how many times Kassia begged him to, he wouldn't stop and face her.

'I've told you what I saw!' she pleaded. 'Dante told us both about the straitjacket! Why won't you tell us?'

'Because it's not important.'

Kassia didn't really see how that could be true, otherwise what was the purpose of the challenge? But the fact was, that according to Flora, they'd passed the test. All the trials and escapes and the accidents and the tears were over now. And the Brothers had deemed it possible for Jed to see the Emerald Tablet. But for some reason Kassia couldn't understand, the fact that Jed wouldn't tell her what he'd seen inside the cabinet at the bottom of the void irritated her. It played at the edges of her mind like a mosquito bite. Tiny and insignificant but so itchy that she couldn't possibly ignore it. 'Was it death you saw?' she blurted suddenly.

Jed looked at her and his eyes were so sad that she regretted her words as soon as she'd said them. 'Yes.' It was his final answer.

She looked down at the ground. 'I'm sorry. I just . . .' The problem was that she couldn't explain it. But that wasn't true either. She knew exactly why she felt like she did. It was, after all, exactly what she'd seen in the cabinet. A life that wasn't shared. A silence. An emptiness.

When she looked up, Dante was standing in the doorway. He was beaming. His own cabinet of horrors forgotten by the time Kassia had clambered up from the hole and hung on to him as if her life depended upon it. 'It's time,' he said with his hands. 'The Brothers are ready.'

Flora had explained that now the tests were passed, they were to leave the city of Ozkonak. A tall man with bright green eyes, called Tomas, and a younger man with a laughing smile, called Mazood, would take them to see the Tablet. Flora waved them off as they left the city, and this time they walked through a door rather than falling through a hidden ventilation shaft.

There were horses waiting to carry them. They formed a line that snaked through the desert, past fairy chimneys and abandoned caves. There was something reassuring about being carried to their destination. Something very comforting about the steady clopping of the hooves through the dust. Kassia tried to put Jed's silence behind her, like the void they'd balanced on, and crossed and entered. All the tests had been about this moment. The chance to see the Emerald Tablet. The ultimate story stone, far better than any of the images or pictures they had tried to piece together for meaning in Prague. The Emerald Tablet was the very first record of the elixir of life. The very first recording of the possibility of living for ever. After everything they'd been through, they were seconds away from answers and she was determined not to let anything spoil it.

And her excitement only intensified when the horses stopped and Tomas explained they'd reached their destination.

In front of them, beyond the expanse of grass, was a high cliff formed of white stone. As they got closer, they could see windows straining out of the cliffside, and archways carved around them. 'This is Karanlik

Kilise,' said Tomas, dismounting from his horse and gesturing for them to do the same. 'It is called the Dark Church because very little light penetrates the tiny windows.' He tied the horses to a tree and began to lead the way towards the cliff. 'But inside you will find all the light and all the answers you have been looking for.'

And Kassia knew she believed him when they stepped into the church and looked up at the pictures painted on the wall.

The biggest picture stretched above them, the colours rich and vibrant, unfaded and undiminished by damage from the sun. The picture showed a man stepping out of a discarded shroud.

'Who is that?' asked Kassia, pointing upwards.

'It's Lazarus,' Tomas said. 'A man who was raised from the dead. Here we call him the Phoenix Man.'

And Kassia felt her heart race.

Everything that Bergier had told them had been part of an interconnected puzzle that had led them here.

Even back at Ozkonak, Flora had made it clear that only one of them could see the Emerald Tablet, but Jed wished Kassia and Dante could be with him.

Tomas had led them through the Karanlik Kilise to

a small room set away from the main chamber of the church. Here, a single hole had been drilled in the rock ceiling and the only light in the room spilled through this opening. Jed felt it was like a search-light beaming directly in his face.

'Here is what you have been seeking,' Tomas said slowly, and he pointed towards a small bundle wrapped in cloth and lying on a stone shelf set away from the beam of light.

Jed nodded awkwardly.

So this was it. The answers they'd spent months searching for. And the answers that must have led to Fulcanelli being able to make the elixir in the first place. Jed could hardly breathe.

He reached down and with sweaty fingers he pulled back the cloth covering. Underneath was a solid green tablet about the size of a hardback book. It was shiny, almost like a mirror. Jed squinted against the light. Etched on the surface were lines of texts. He squeezed his eyes and concentrated. 'But how do I . . .'

Tomas stepped beside him. 'You want to read the Tablet?'

'Of course.'

Tomas smiled. 'The stone was not always hidden,' he said quietly. 'In the past, alchemists and magicians have studied the text to try and unlock its secrets.' He

345

took a small sheet of paper and held it out. 'This is Isaac Newton's translation,' he said. 'You may find it helpful.'

Jed suddenly felt a wave of confusion. 'The text of the Tablet has been available all this time?' he stammered. 'All the tests and the trials to get here and I could have read someone else's translation after all.'

Tomas smiled again. 'Others have tried to read the ultimate story stone,' he said gently. 'But you will find the words have infinitely more power if you make sense of them yourself.'

'How do I do that?' urged Jed, taking the translation Tomas offered and then looking down at the polished green stone.

Tomas gestured forwards and so, almost on instinct, Jed pressed his hand against the Tablet. There was a surge of power. A blinding light filled the room. Pain raked through Jed's chest and he folded forward, clutching at his ribs as the skin there burnt and singed.

But instead of staggering backwards and struggling against the pain, Jed held his ground and energy pulsed inside of him.

'You know what it says now?' Tomas asked.

Jed nodded. And he did. He knew what would be needed to make the elixir of eternal life. '*That which is below is like that which is above,*' he said.

PL. LVII

August 20th 2003

'I'm not waiting any longer!' Victor was standing at the information desk at St Paul's Cathedral. He was leaning so heavily on the desk that the guide seated behind it was recoiling. She'd been fiddling for a while with the walkie-talkie but the answer she was getting from the tinny voice it conveyed to her was not doing much to appease her visitor.

'I'm so sorry, sir,' the guide mumbled, fiddling again with one of the dials. 'I have explained to you that Reverend Cockren is not in the cathedral today.'

'And you said the same yesterday. And the day before,' Victor snarled. 'I've been coming every day for a week now.'

'And I have explained every time that the Reverend is a very busy man and he has parishioners to see and people to attend to.'

'*I* need attending to!' Victor shouted, waving the dossier he held in his hand.

'Please, sir.' The guide was looking around. 'You are troubling other visitors. I would ask you to . . .'

There was a sweep of black clothing from behind. 'It's OK, Nancy. I can take things from here.'

Victor spun round. 'I knew it,' he yelped, flapping the dossier in Reverend Cockren's face. 'They told me you weren't available, but I knew you were here!'

The Reverend gripped tightly to Victor's elbow and steered him towards a doorway to the side of the east door. It led to a stairwell: a curling, twisting flight of steps that stuck out from the wall as if suspended by their own weight. Reverend Cockren drove Victor down to the bottom of the stairs.

'You needed to see me,' he said, turning Victor to face him.

Victor flapped the dossier again with his hand. 'It's all here,' he said.

'What's here?' asked the Reverend.

Victor thrust the pages at him so they crumpled and spilled against his chest. 'NOAH. Elixirs. Churches. Death.'

Reverend Cockren fumbled for the pages but Victor was ploughing on, striding backwards and forwards in the footwell of the stairs.

'You warned about the unicorn. You said there was a reason it got left behind. But I had no idea how much you knew until I saw this and then everything made sense to me!'

'I don't know what you're talking about, son!'

Victor bristled with anger, spinning round to face him. 'Don't you ever call me that!' he shouted, and his voice echoed up the stairs, bouncing in the space that bordered the church.

Reverend Cockren fumbled with the papers, scanned the first page and then, as if he had been struck hard across the face, he froze.

Victor grabbed the pages back from him. 'You better get explaining, man of God,' he shouted, 'how it was that you were there on the day my father died.'

DAY 287

10th December

Jed sat hunched in the corner of the room. He pressed his back against the cold stone, but his shoulders arched forward, his face turned to the ground. Beads of sweat prickled on his forehead.

Tomas had led him to this room, after he'd held the Emerald Tablet. This room made sense of why the church in the cliff was called the Dark Church. There was hardly any light here at all. There was a hole in the ceiling, but the sun had slipped in the sky and the only light that filtered through now was fleeting and feeble. It gave no warmth at all.

Jed sat in the semi-darkness and he fought to make sense of all that had happened. His mind stretched backwards and forwards, dragging through all they had seen, both in truth and in memory. His stomach flipped inside him. And that was because he'd made the final link, the ultimate connection.

He rubbed his hand across his chest. It hurt so much. Both inside and out. It was almost funny. '*That which is below is like that which is above*,' the Tablet had said. And so Jed understood now what this meant. And what it *would* mean.

Suddenly, he was aware of footsteps. He lifted his head. He was no longer alone.

Kassia stood in the doorway. In one hand, she held a glass jar which swung from a metal holder. Inside the jar was a lit candle. The flame fought against the dying light from the sun, making the space glow. Kassia herself was ringed with light. Jed bit his lip and tried to look away but Kassia held his gaze and stepped in closer, dropping his bag that she carried with her, gently to the floor and then sinking to her knees so her face was close to his.

'Tomas said it was all right if one of us came to see you. Dante is waiting outside.'

Jed was glad that Kassia had chosen to be the one who came.

'Well?' she whispered. 'You saw it? The Emerald Tablet? So you have the answers now? You know what to do?'

His eyes flickered and he gripped his hands so tightly together that his fingernails dug into his skin.

'Jed?' She reached out, and put her hand on his. 'What is it?'

Jed took a deep breath. 'I lied to you,' he said.

'What?'

'About the final test.'

'I don't understand.'

'You asked me if I saw death. And I said I did.'

'But . . .'

'You guessed it was my greatest fear.' He hesitated and took another breath. 'But it wasn't. It *isn't*.'

She leant in closer. 'So, in the cabinet? Down in the void? What did you see?'

He made a noise that he knew sounded like a laugh, but nothing had ever felt less funny. 'I saw a mirror.'

Kassia's face was wrinkled in confusion, distorted but somehow made more beautiful by the flickering of the candle light.

'In the void, where we faced our deepest fears, I saw *myself*, Kassia.'

'I don't understand.'

He shrugged and pressed his back harder against the wall as if the strength of the ancient structure would give him strength in return. 'Neither did I, until I saw the Emerald Tablet. At least, I wasn't sure until then. But now I am.'

She waited for him to say more and he sensed she

was scared that, if she interrupted, the story would never be shared.

'This journey has been so full of tests and I thought at first that they were unrelated. Just a mess of things we had to do. A waste of time even, all that stuff in Prague. And then I realised that everything has been linked. All of it meant. All of it necessary.'

'So what did the Emerald Tablet say?' she asked a second time.

'It was another part of the test,' Jed said. 'The final part, but bound up with all the others.'

'What did you have to do?'

'I haven't done it yet.'

'Oh.'

'I couldn't, until you were here.'

'Oh.'

'You see the message of the Emerald Tablet is, *That which is below is like that which is above.*'

'So how does that involve me? And you seeing a mirror?'

'It means,' said Jed, in barely more than a whisper, 'that I have to face who I am – who I *really* am. And that I have to show you.'

'Show me what?'

Jed took another breath and then he stood and held out his hand to help her up so that they were facing each other, the light from the candle making patterns on her face. Very slowly, Jed began to unbutton his shirt to reveal his chest.

Her revulsion was obvious. Kassia clapped her hand across her mouth. 'How did that happen? Does it hurt?'

Jed let go of the edge of his shirt. 'A section was formed after every memory we looked at,' he said quietly.

'But you never said anything. You never . . .' She reached out her hand, her fingertips hovering over the puckers and disfigurements scored on to his skin. 'The pain when you saw the memories, I just thought it was all too much for you. I didn't know this was happening. Why didn't you stop? Why didn't you give up?'

'Because the scars are part of the memories,' said Jed. 'And I know I have to keep going.'

'What do you mean, you have to *keep* going?' Kassia blurted.

Jed stood up tall and he looked down at the mark of the dragon burnt and scarred like a scorch tattoo across his skin. 'Because it isn't finished, is it?' he said.

And he knew that Kassia saw that a section of the circling dragon was missing. The part where the dragon closed its mouth around its tail. The completion of the circle.

357

'Every memory we saw burnt a part of the ouroboros on to my chest and if I am going to find the elixir and make the change in me permanent, then I have to complete the final part. *That which is below is like that which is above*, the Tablet said.'

'But we looked at every memory,' pleaded Kassia.

Jed shook his head. 'We looked at four. You know there is a fifth. One more to see.' He reached into his bag and took out the box which held the glass pen.

'There's no more ink,' Kassia blurted. 'The three stages of alchemy. Red, black and white. We did all that. We used up every bottle Metin gave us.'

'But I've explained,' he said gently. 'All the parts of the tests are connected. Even the bits we thought were wasting time.'

Her face showed thorough confusion.

'The liquid you collected in Prague. That's the final ink we need.'

And he lifted his other hand where the life-line was gaping and bleeding and he rubbed his palm along the sweat from his brow. Blood and sweat.

'But what about the mirror? And you seeing yourself?' Kassia blurted. 'How does that fit in with this?'

And these were the very words he needed. A single

tear splashed into his open palm. Blood and sweat and tears. Then he took the pen and he twisted the nib in the folds of his palm so that the fluid travelled up the shaft of glass. He took the translation page for the Emerald Tablet that Tomas had handed him, and knelt down again. He put the paper on the floor and rested the tip of the glass pen on the page. Then he looked up.

'Are you ready?' he said.

'I don't know. Are you sure?' Kassia mumbled as she knelt down beside him. 'Are you certain you want to do this?'

'I have to,' Jed said, and then as he pressed the nib harder to the page and as the liquid began to flow, he mumbled three more words. 'I'm so sorry.'

The liquid seeped into the page. It flowed freely with no stops or starts or hesitations. And the image on the paper was one they'd seen a hundred times before. The tail-eating dragon. The symbol that had begun the adventure in the first place. In the beginning, it had been in segments, slotted together like pieces of a puzzle. But this dragon, like the swirling dragon they'd seen in front of each memory, was whole.

Jed put the pen down on the ground and it wobbled in the dust.

Then he took the silver watch from his pocket,

clicked open the case and put it down on the paper too.

Finally, he reached forward and took hold of Kassia's hands. And then, as she lifted her face to look at him, he stuttered the same three words again. 'I'm so sorry.'

'Why do you keep saying that?' she said.

The hands on the watch began to spin backwards and a smoke dragon flickered in the light of the candle. 'You'll see,' he said.

In the memory the air is stifling. The heat pressing in so tight it is difficult to breathe. Fulcanelli looks as he did in the hall of mirrors in Versailles. But this time the air is not whipped with the rage of a hurricane. It is calm, unmoving, hot.

Fulcanelli is running. Sweat makes his shirt cling to his back and form rings under his arms. His hair is wet.

He is running towards a church. Not an enormous, ornate cathedral but a tiny village church. The signage shows the church is in France.

Fulcanelli pushes open the door and steps inside. The coldness of the air hits like a buffer and Fulcanelli staggers slightly and looks around.

At first it seems the church is empty and he is all alone. But then it is possible to see that a lone figure stands at the front of the church. His hair is long and black. He is dressed casually, his shirt open at the neck, where a medallion glints against his skin. This man is no business man or vicar. And when he turns, Kassia tries to drag free of the memory. But Jed grips tightly to her hands and holds her inside the image. And her dad smiles. Not at her, because she is watching the memory, she is not in it, but at Jed, because he is both these things. Participant and observer.

And as Kassia fights to get free, Jed holds on even tighter because he knows she must see everything.

Kassia's father, Tristan Devaux, smiles and his eyes sparkle in recognition. He knows Jed. He has been waiting for him. Something else sparkles. The golden medallion glinting at the base of his throat. A circle, within a square, within a triangle. The mark of the Brothers of Heliopolis.

Tristan nods and it is clear now that he is holding something in his hand. A stack of books.

Fulcanelli walks up to Tristan Devaux. 'So you are the keeper of the elixir,' he says.

Tristan nods. 'A job passed down to me. A family tradition. And you,' he says quietly, 'are the unicorn.'

Fulcanelli nods. 'What are those?' he says, gesturing to the books the other man is holding.

'Another answer, perhaps. Another way.'

'There is no other way,' says Fulcanelli.

Tristan's shoulders slump and he puts down the books on the end of the pew. Then he turns and leads Fulcanelli across to the side of the church, bends down and loosens a stone that slots into the pillar. The stone slides free and reveals a cavity. Fulcanelli nods and slips his hand inside, taking out a small glass bottle.

'The penultimate one,' says Tristan.

Fulcanelli's eyes widen greedily.

But Tristan's eyes are narrowed in fear. 'Are you sure?' he says quietly. 'After all we have told you. Will you not reconsider?' He points to the books on the end of the pew.

Fulcanelli rocks the glass bottle in his hand, but before he can answer, the door of the church flings open.

A man from a memory stands in the doorway. The man from Versailles. The man Fulcanelli had been trying to escape. The hunter. Orin Sinclair.

Fulcanelli looks angry.

'It's OK,' says Tristan, holding up his hand. 'Orin and I have an understanding now.'

'But NOAH?' Fulcanelli pleads.

Orin stumbles deeper into the church. His footsteps ring out on the cold stone flagstones. 'They are on their way,' he shouts. 'I came to warn you!'

'You come to warn,' blurts Fulcanelli. 'After all these years of chasing. Can someone really change their side?'

Orin looks up at the stained glass window of the

church. His face runs with sweat. 'We make a choice every day about which side we are on,' he says.

Suddenly a third man runs into the church. And Kassia knows this man too, but not from NOAH or memories Jed has shared. She has seen him at St Paul's.

And so the four men face each other, four sides of a square. And beside the pillar in the Eastern wall, Fulcanelli stands twisting the bottle of elixir in his hands.

'NOAH are coming, son,' the Reverend shouts, and the words echo off the stone walls.

But Fulcanelli makes no effort to escape. Instead, he uncorks the bottle, raises it to his lips, and drinks.

An explosion of light fills the church. Fulcanelli collapses to the floor. And when he looks up, the space is filled with strangers. But he is transformed. A mirror image now of Jed. The memory and the man, totally indistinguishable.

Men from NOAH race towards him but he crashes towards a doorway in the western wall.

Orin darts forward and tries to block the path. But the men from NOAH barrel into him, sending him lurching to the side.

There is a lectern at the end of the aisle. A golden eagle, wings outstretched, and Orin clatters into it, felling it like a tree as he falls too. The golden wing of the eagle catches on his side. It slices at a ragged wound that has taken

363

years to heal. And as Orin crumples from the blow of the wing, he grabs for the pew and the books tumble free. The Reverend falters beside him, sinking to his knees and scooping the injured man into the protection of his arms. But the gaping wound in his side suggests that all the Reverend can do now is hold him. Blood splashes on to the books that lie beside him.

Fulcanelli stumbles from the church. He dashes between the gravestones, and careers towards the graveyard wall, vaulting it with a surge of strength. He lands in the road, turns left and starts to run. There is a car behind him. Lights blazing. A horn sounding. He turns. He sees a golden medallion glinting at the base of the driver's throat.

The car is closer now. There is a bend in the road. The driver flings open the passenger door. 'Get in!' Tristan shouts. 'Get in!'

But Fulcanelli hesitates.

A second of indecision.

Men surge across the graveyard.

A single shot is fired.

Fulcanelli flings himself to the ground. Missed.

But the bullet finds a target.

And something like surprise registers in Tristan Devaux's face as he creases forward against the steering wheel.

And the car careers out of control and crashes into the graveyard wall, crinkling like a tin can.

This time Jed could no longer hold Kassia inside the memory. She reared free, pulled her hands out of his and staggered to her feet. Her face was stretched and shadowed in the light of the candle, but rage and confusion had worked with the flickering flames to distort her features. 'It's your fault!' she spat.

'Kassia, please.' Jed lurched up from the ground and grabbed for her arm, but she pulled away, plunging her fingers deep into her hair, as if she could not bear for him to touch her.

'You were with my dad! And he was trying to help you! Protect you!'

'Kassia, please!' He reached out again, but this time she turned her back on him as if she didn't even have the strength to look at him.

'My dad died in your place!' she yelled, and every word was forced through clenched teeth.

'I'm sorry! I'm so sorry!'

She spun round to face him. 'SORRY!' she screamed, flinging her hands wide. 'I knew our families were connected. I should have worked out that the medallion Dad wore made him a Brother of Heliopolis like my grandad. I should have connected it all. But I didn't want to see it. Didn't want to make any connection that might have meant . . .' she searched for the right word, 'this!' Her hands slid down until they covered her face. 'How long ago did you remember?' she said.

'Just when I saw the mirror,' said Jed. 'When I was on my own in the darkness, and I saw myself, I remembered things I'd tried to hide from the other memories.'

'What d'you mean?'

He tried to steer her towards him so he could face her as he spoke, but she pulled away again and shook her head. 'Just tell me!' she blurted.

'OK. OK.' He took a deep breath. 'Each time we saw a memory from the days of the elixir, I knew you saw the sort of person you hoped that I would be.'

She shook her head again, confused.

'We saw the same memory each time, but I knew afterwards, from watching you, that you hadn't seen what really happened.'

'So tell me then!' she shouted.

He fumbled his hands together as if signing would be easier somehow. But Dante wasn't here. Spoken words would be enough, if he could find the ones he needed. 'In the first memory,' he said, 'you thought I made the elixir because I loved my sister.'

'Didn't you?'

'I loved her, Kass,' he spluttered. 'But there was anger there too. That she'd been taken. It wasn't love that made me make the elixir.' He hung his head. 'It was rage.'

'And the second memory? The day of the train crash? You ran away because you needed to keep what you'd done a secret?'

'I ran away,' he said quietly, 'because I was scared of all the death and I didn't want to look.'

'But not publishing the manuscript? That was to keep people safe, wasn't it?' Her voice was cracking.

'Was it?' He doubled over, breath catching in his throat. 'Or was it just to protect myself?'

'In the asylum? What had you done then?'

'I tricked a girl into breaking all the rules just to help me. If she had paid more attention to the bread she'd given out, then there's a chance she might have noticed it was contaminated. But all she was worried about was my gold. And I wanted her help.'

'But . . .'

'You only focused on seeing your grandfather there. You didn't think about the girl. About the bread.'

'And in Versailles?'

'I could have helped that man when we reached the hall of mirrors.'

'He was hunting you!'

'But I left him there.'

Kassia clenched her arms around herself as if she needed to do this to stop herself from falling. 'I saw your memories, Jed! Why are you changing things?'

'I'm not changing anything. I'm just asking you to look. To really look!'

'But I did!'

'And you saw them all how you wanted to. You saw a version of me that made sense of the memories. And you always saw that person as good.' His words were faltering. 'But there was another version of me, hiding just like the man in the mosaic we saw back in Istanbul. A Phoenix Man.'

'But how could I have been wrong?' she sobbed.

The next sentence burnt as he spoke it. '*Because you believed in me.*'

She stood totally still. 'And that final memory. What didn't I see then?'

'Nothing,' he said. 'You saw everything.' He could barely speak. 'I was the reason that your father died.'

Kassia's legs wobbled beneath her and she sank down to the floor and held her head in her hands.

'All this time,' he said slowly, 'you hoped I was a man worth saving.' He pulled back his shirt again and the scars of the dragon burnt red and raw on his chest.

'But now I've seen the Emerald Tablet I know that I can't hide from who I was any more.'

'So what does this mean?' Her lips were trembling, her eyes tearing.

'I don't know,' he stuttered and his throat was clogged so that his voice sounded torn. 'But you've seen everything now. The whole truth. There are no more secrets.'

She turned slowly, her face rigid now, like stone. 'What about Jacob?' she said sharply. 'Did I see the truth the first time round when I wasn't sure what happened on the tower at Notre Dame?'

'No!' Jed's reply was urgent. 'No! He fell, Kassia. I didn't push him.'

'But everything you've said means you were no better than him after all. You wanted power too.'

Jed clutched for her hands. 'I know. I know. Please, Kassia. Everything was muddled then and everything is clearer now.'

The flame on the candle flickered and swelled.

'The Brothers said I had to decide who I *am* and who I *was*, but also who I *want to be*. And I *can* be different, I promise. I *can* be the man you thought I was. Make all that you've done for me and all you've given up for me worthwhile. I can make the right decisions. I can.' His voice choked in his throat.

She stared at him, her face in shadow.

'If you will help me, I can deal with these scars, I promise.' He clutched at her hands, begging her with his eyes. 'Will you help me? We could find the final elixir together, now we know I have to face all that I was before. We still have three months. I know we can do this, if we do it together.'

Kassia waited for just a moment, and then she pulled her hands out of his hold and stood up. 'No, Fulcanelli,' she said. 'I can't.'

And with that, she turned and made her way out of the church built into the rock.

And as Jed watched her go, the flame on the candle guttered in the breeze, flickered and finally went out.

It was night. The darkness was complete.

DAY 288

11th December

The morning sun filtered through the opening in the rocks, spilling narrow shafts of light on to the ground.

Jed pulled himself up to stand and the light dappled his skin, tracing across his scars.

Kassia was gone.

Jed had never felt more alone.

And yet, somehow, even though for hours he'd believed it to be impossible, the darkness had gone and the sun had risen.

He took a breath and tried to focus. To make sense of what had happened.

During the night, rage had surged inside him. Anger that Kassia had left. The same rage that had driven him to make the elixir in the first place. A need to change what was into something new.

And then, just as before, fear had flooded in. Panic

that tightened his chest and made it almost impossible to breathe.

But as the sun strained to throw light into the dark corners of the church within the rock, Jed began to feel something else. There was no logic for the feeling. No guarantees. But the feeling was real. As real as the scars on his chest, and the dusty ground beneath his feet.

Hope.

Hope, that if he had time, he could persuade Kassia to believe in him again. Hope, that even though all the signs around him suggested it was over, that it wasn't. That there was still a chance, as intangible but as bright as the flickering light of the morning sun, that he could change things again.

Because *changing things* was what he did.

Jed knew one thing for certain.

This was not how things would end.

Until the year was fully over, he would keep fighting. And he would keep hoping.

And if Kassia had left, then he would follow.

And he suddenly knew now, with more certainty than he knew anything else, that he would make her see that he *could* be the person she had hoped he was.

That, stepping out of the darkness, he could really be a man worth saving.